CHARISMA

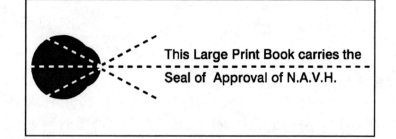

This Large Print Book carries the
Seal of Approval of N.A.V.H.

CHARISMA

BALLER'S WIFE

NIKKI TURNER

THORNDIKE PRESS
A part of Gale, a Cengage Company

Farmington Hills, Mich • San Francisco • New York • Waterville, Maine
Meriden, Conn • Mason, Ohio • Chicago

LIBRARY OF CONGRESS CIP DATA ON FILE.
CATALOGUING IN PUBLICATION FOR THIS BOOK
IS AVAILABLE FROM THE LIBRARY OF CONGRESS

ISBN-13: 978-1-4328-4563-6 (hardcover)
ISBN-10: 1-4328-4563-2 (hardcover)

Published in 2018 by arrangement with Urban Books, LLC and Kensington Publishing Corporation

CHARISMA

CHAPTER 1
NOTHING WILL GO WRONG

Baltimore, December 29 . . .

"If you don't care whether you live or die, then just g'on ahead and shoot yourself, already. Just g'on ahead and get it over with." She shrugged her shoulders just to add insult to her rebuke of Uncle Vess's bluff.

Charisma didn't mean to speak so harshly to her uncle, but the man just wouldn't listen to any kind of reasoning. He'd been her legal guardian since she was eight years old, eighteen birthdays ago. Hands down, he was the strongest man she knew, and by far, he was also the most stubborn.

Uncle Vess was smack-dab in the middle of a knockdown, drag-out bout with the flu and was confined to his bed. If the battle were a prizefight, the flu would have raised the belt about three or four rounds ago. He was barking louder than a dog and looked a hot mess. His pecan complexion was looking kind of green, and something slimy kept coming from his nose. And he couldn't get a good sentence out, because a couple of sneezes always beat him to it.

The last time Charisma checked Uncle Vess's temperature, the digital thermometer had read 101 degrees. Their family doctor had made Charisma promise that if her uncle's temperature rose more than another two or three degrees, she would get him to the emergency room immediately, whether he wanted to go or not.

Good luck with that, she thought. She'd have a better chance at success if she tried to get a Sunni Muslim to chow down on a honey-glazed ham sandwich. Uncle Vess hated hospitals, and he didn't trust doctors. So the likelihood of getting him to an emergency room was slim to none. And Slim was out for lunch.

"Don't be so dramatic. . . . I'm fine," he croaked.

His voice was so hoarse, it sounded like his vocal cords were made of worn leather. And sweat oozed from his pores like beer from a leaky tap, although Uncle Vess hadn't touched as much as a drop of alcohol in more than twenty years.

"Sure you're fine, Uncle. That's why your skin is such a healthy shade of green and as

8

clammy as a bowl of Boston chowder," she said.

"Fine or not, there's no way —" More coughing. It sounded like at any moment he might spit up a lung. "In hell I'm going to let a little cold . . ." Cough! Cough! "Stop me from taking care of my business." After catching his breath, he went on. "If I don't get this shipment of liquor from my dude, we may not be able to keep the doors of Legacies open much longer."

Legacies Bar & Grill — a trendy bar and eatery in downtown Baltimore — was Uncle Vess's life. The establishment had been opened in 1923 by his great-grandfather Latimar, but it hadn't become legal until ten years later — post-Prohibition. Latimar was one of the first black men in the city of Baltimore to own a legit tavern. At one time or another, hustlers from up and down I-95 had paid homage to Legacies back in the day. Big Latimar had lived to be seventy-three. And before he passed, he'd gifted Legacies to his eldest grandson, Lewis. And before Lewis passed, he'd gifted the family business to his oldest boy, Sylvester.

Three generations in all.

But recently, Legacies had fallen on really hard times. The trouble had first surfaced when Uncle Vess's wife, Sandra, woke up one morning feeling *funny*. Sluggish and depleted of energy. Aunt Sandra was diagnosed with breast cancer after one visit with a specialist. Uncle Vess did everything in his power to keep her alive. When the hospital bills ballooned and got out of control, he took a second mortgage out on the bar to help foot the tab. And with the help of a team of the best doctors and medications money could buy, Aunt Sandra fought the ugly disease for seven years, before dying in her sleep. That was four summers ago.

The loss devastated Uncle Vess. And he never fully recuperated from either the loss of his wife or the financial quicksand he'd fallen into.

"I booked Fabiola . . . Chaka Khan, and a top band to perform on New Year's Eve," he said, then broke into a fit of coughing. Then, as suddenly as it began, the coughing stopped.

"I know, Uncle Vess." Charisma had spoken to both of the artists' managers and had booked hotel suites that were of their liking.

"Then you know we just don't have the money to pay retail for all the liquor we need." He shook his head in shame. "And, sadly, if we don't have the alcohol to sell, we won't make enough money to even keep

10

the lights on. And the light bill will be the least of our problems, baby girl . . . because if the mortgage isn't made, the bank is going to padlock the door. Permanently!" Uncle Vess tried to push up from the bed. When he got to his feet, his legs shook, then went limp like two wet noodles just before he collapsed back onto the mattress. "Shit!"

Charisma tried to console him. "Maybe you'll feel better tomorrow. The party isn't for another two days."

Uncle Vess scowled. Charisma wasn't sure if the expression was from the pain he felt or from what she'd just said.

She went on. "I know it's cutting it close, but still —"

"If the deal doesn't go down tonight . . ." Cough! "It's a wrap. The connect will sell the liquor to someone else. I talked him down from thirty thousand to twenty thousand for a hundred thousand worth of top-shelf booze. He'd be a fool to sit on it for an hour longer than he needs to, let alone another whole day." Cough, cough, sneeze, sneeze. "I'm fucked."

Charisma had never heard her uncle sound so defeated, and it was making her sad. If she was feeling awful about hearing it, she could only imagine how he was feeling, given that he had actually given voice

11

to what was truly a reality. She had to do something.

Charisma got a bright idea. "I'll do the transaction," she said.

She'd worked at the bar since she was fourteen. Even when she'd gone off to college, she'd come home and worked the bar during the summers and on holidays. She'd met her uncle's bootleg connect on many occasions as he came into the bar all the time. He was a tall older fella with a clean-shaven head. Her uncle and a few regulars at the bar called him Shampoo. Charisma thought back. Hadn't her uncle once told her that back in the day he and Shampoo went to Lake Clifton High School together?

"It's not going to happen," Uncle Vess said firmly between coughs as he picked up an open bottle of Tylenol cold medicine from his night table. "If it was a legal transaction," he said after downing what was left of the bottle, "that'd be one thing. But I'm not about to send my favorite niece, or any niece of mine, for that matter, to do not a damn thing illegal."

Charisma tried to reason with him. "It's either that or we lose the bar. You said it yourself. What's the alternative? And who else can we get to do this?"

Cough! Cough! "No!" Cough. Cough.

Cough. "Hell no."

"Look, we can't just quit and lose the one major family heirloom we have. Grandpa Latimer worked his tail off for this and entrusted it to us. Sometimes a girl gotta do what a girl's gotta do."

She could tell that he was thinking deeply about the solution she'd offered, so she made it easier for him to agree. "I can get Chucky to ride with me," she said. "He's been calling me to come pick up my Christmas gift, anyway. And he has a Denali truck."

"If anything were to go wrong, I would never be able to forgive myself."

"Nothing will go wrong."

"Do you have the money?"

Charisma didn't recognize the voice on the other end of the line, but she was sure that it didn't belong to Shampoo.

"Whom am I speaking to?" At that moment she hated herself for talking so proper. The man would probably think that she was a square.

"You police?"

But she didn't think he would accuse her of being Five-O.

"No." She sucked her teeth. "I'm not the police. Why would you even ask that?" she

13

said to the stranger on the phone, starting to feel majorly uncomfortable. She was sitting in the front passenger seat of Chucky's truck, which was parked behind an old warehouse on the west side of Baltimore. Twenty thousand dollars neatly stacked inside two bank envelopes rested on her lap. Maybe this wasn't the best of ideas, she thought.

"Because I don't know you," said the guy on the other end. "That's why. I was supposed to be meeting with the ole head nigga, Vess, and some chick calls my phone, talking all proper and shit. What da fuck!"

He was just as nervous as she was.

"Well," she calmly explained, "I'm not the police. We can be clear on that." She paused for a moment. "And," she reminded him, "I don't know you, either. I was supposed to be calling Shampoo's phone to take care of some business for my uncle Vess, who is at home, sick with pneumonia. And you answered. So it seems we both are somewhat blind."

"Blind people bump into things."

Click!

Chucky asked Charisma, "What's wrong?" He could tell by her expression that something wasn't kosher.

"The booze connect" — she stared at her

phone — "like, just hung up on me."

"Maybe we should bounce," Chucky suggested.

"Nah, we can't. I have to make this happen for my family, or we are going to lose everything."

Charisma redialed the number she'd got from her uncle. She had no intentions of quitting because of a little hiccup. She'd convinced her uncle to let her handle the business, and that was what she was going to do. Handle the business. Besides, the life of the bar was on the line. What choice did she have other than exhausting all her options before she even considered giving up?

He picked up. "Listen," the man said, "I'm hanging up. And don't call back."

"Wait!" Charisma shouted before he disconnected again. "I'm not the police. If you ask Shampoo, he'll tell you I'm good people."

A couple of beats went by. It felt like an hour.

"Are you alone?" he asked.

"Except for the driver of the truck I'm in," Charisma said quickly.

"Do you have the money?"

"Yes."

"How much?"

"The amount my uncle and Shampoo

15

agreed upon."

"That's not what I asked you, is it? What's the agreed-upon number?"

Charisma told him, "Twenty."

He must've been cool with what he heard, because he said, "Get your driver to back into the loading dock that is farthest to the left. He stays in the truck. Got it? You get out and walk up to the gray door. Come inside. Once you're inside, I'll count the money and you can inventory the boxes, if you like. Then I'll have the boxes loaded onto the back of your truck. Can you handle that?"

She said that she could. The call ended.

"Back the truck in over there," Charisma told Chucky as she pointed to the spot where the man on the phone had told her to park.

Chucky wheeled into the loading dock with one hand and without looking over his shoulder, using the rearview mirror to navigate instead. He slipped the Denali into park once he was satisfied with his handiwork. "Are you sure you're good? Who's going to pack the boxes in the truck?" he asked.

"The man on the phone said that he would have someone load them for me. He said that it wasn't a problem."

16

She was about to get out of the truck when Chucky stopped her. He looked around. Most of the buildings in the neighborhood had been abandoned or were in need of renovation. But that was the case for a third of the city. "I don't care about what's a problem for dude," Chucky said. "My concern is with you. How do *you* feel?"

"I feel fine. But if it makes you feel better, call my uncle if I'm not back in ten minutes."

This time she got out of the truck.

"Hey, Charisma?"

She shut the door, leaned into the open window. "What's up?"

Chucky smiled and said, "You're beautiful. Just wanted to say that. That's all."

"Boy, you crazy."

Charisma and Chucky had been friends for a while. But lately, the brother-and-sister feelings they had for one another had started to feel different.

"Fo' sho'," Chucky said. "Crazy about you."

Charisma walked away from the truck without responding. The two envelopes of money were in her purse. She headed to the gray door and was about to knock when she remembered that the man had said to come in. So she tried the knob. When the knob

17

turned, she pushed the door open and stepped inside. She was surprised by what she saw. The warehouse was brightly lit and relatively clean. For some reason, she had expected it to be dim and dirty. She had no idea why she'd imagined it to be that way, but she had.

In one of the corners, crates of liquor were stacked atop other crates. Each tower of booze was at least fifteen feet high. Hennessy, Patrón, Cîroc, 1800. And a forklift. Deeper into the warehouse was a tiny office. The door to the office was open. Inside, a guy sat behind a desk, talking on the phone. The guy behind the desk was slim and wore dark blue jeans and a pair of tan Timberlands. Once he noticed her, he waved her over.

The office was a little less than a city block from where she stood. And by the time she covered the distance, the guy had ended his call. The first thing he said when she entered was, "Where's the money?" No small talk at all, just straight to business.

Charisma fished the two bank envelopes from her Coach purse, laid them on the old wooden desk. Dude scooped up one of the bank envelopes from the desk, opened the flap, and thumbed through the crisp new bills. He seemed pleased.

"By the way," he said, "my name is Joe."

Then Joe went into the desk. And pulled out a gun.

"Now, sit your ass on the floor while I think about what I'm going to do with you."

As she sank to the floor, Charisma remembered how her conversation with Uncle Vess had ended.

If anything were to go wrong, I would never be able to forgive myself.

Nothing will go wrong.

"Shampoo and my uncle went to school together. Lake Clifton. They're friends, like, really good old-time friends," Charisma said.

Joe shoved the money into his jeans pocket. "I wouldn't give a fuck if they'd went to Sunday school together, bitch. Twenty K is twenty fucking K. If it had been your uncle, he'd be dead already. You . . . Well, I haven't decided yet. It's a coin flip." Joe spoke as cavalierly as a man trying to decide which fast-food joint he would choose for lunch.

Charisma almost pissed herself, but she tried not to show that she was scared fucking shitless. "What about my friend?" she said. "Just let us go, and you can keep the money."

"Well," Joe said, "thanks for the generosity." He looked at his watch. "But your friend is already dead." He'd sent his partner out the side door to smoke the driver of the truck. He was on the phone with the shooter when the hammer dropped. "And the money is mine, either way."

Right then, Charisma's heart dropped. She had got Chucky killed and had lost the bar on a bad play. She might as well be dead herself.

As if he could read her mind, Joe pointed the silver revolver at her head.

"I'll give you a choice," he said. "Because you're a pretty bitch. I can give you one last fuck before I kill you — who knows how long it may last? — or I can just pull the trigger now. It's your choice."

The choice was easy. "I'd rather die than watch you put your stinking dick inside of me," she said.

"Like I said, it's your choice."

Boom!

He dropped the hammer.

The damage from the hollow-point .357 was catastrophic. Shattered bone and brain matter splattered all over the wall, creating a chilling portrait of violence. Death was instantaneous.

"Are you okay?" said a male voice.

Charisma was confused, until Chucky

helped her up from the floor.

"I — I thought you were dead," she said, in shock.

Chucky looked her over, making sure that she wasn't hurt. "I thought the same about you," he admitted before giving Charisma another inspection. "Are you sure that you're good?"

"As good as one can be after coming within a millisecond of death's door. But the guy, Joe — if that's even his real name — said that you were dead."

"I'm from South Baltimore. We don't go without a fight. I didn't feel right from the jump. So I got my strap from the glove box as soon as you went inside."

"Where did you get a gun?"

"That's not important. It's a good thing that I had it. Dude thought that he'd caught me slipping. I played like I didn't see him creeping. He was talking to someone through a Bluetooth. That may have distracted him. I don't know. But when he got to the side of the truck and tried to swing in my direction, the surprise was on him. I dumped on him."

Charisma thought that she was going to be sick. "You killed him?"

"It was either him or me," Chucky told her. "Under the circumstances, it was an easy decision."

"I guess you're right." The boy she'd gone to school with had killed two people in one night and had saved her life in the process. "Thank you," she said.

"That's what friends are for," he said. Then he asked, "Where's the money?"

"He put it in his pocket."

Chucky walked over to the dead man, bent down, and took the envelopes out of the man's pocket. "Think I seen a forklift back there. I'm going to load some of this here booze for your uncle. It'll only take a minute. The buildings on either side of this warehouse aren't occupied, so no one would've heard the shots. I don't think, anyway."

CHAPTER 2
LIFE IS GOOD

Life is good, Manny mused before silently reprimanding himself.

Who was he trying to fool? If a man couldn't be honest with himself, well, he wasn't worth the nut sack on a roasted pig.

Manny's life was absolutely fucking amazing. And that was the unadulterated truth.

And why wouldn't it be? He was young, good looking, and motherfucking *rich*! And if those weren't reasons enough to tip his hat to God, being able to see the rotation on a baseball thrown upwards of ninety-five miles per hour by the best arms in Major League Baseball — and put wood on it — surely was. That was a skill that had earned him a base salary of twenty-five million dollars a year, not including the multimillion-dollar endorsement deals. He had enough money to take care of his mother and himself for the rest of their natural lives, and whomever else he decided to spread love to "the Brooklyn way." He couldn't front; it was more money than he'd ever dreamed of making. If that wasn't blessed, the Virgin Mary was a two-bit whore.

Coming from a single-parent household, one in which his mother had done everything but sell her soul and butt to make ends meet, mad Manny respected a dollar. Regardless of how great his mother was, Manny had learned early on that no one was coming to rescue them. Not his daddy, not the pastor, not the mailman. There would be no superheroe sin their future. He had promised himself back then, at age eight, that he'd be his mother's Superman.

And being able to hit a baseball had helped him fulfill that promise.

Now his mother had everything her heart desired, plus things she could never have imagined before.

Tonight Manny had the night off. With his legs crossed at the ankles, he relaxed on a California king four-poster bed, wearing nothing but a pair of his Lucky Brand boxers, his trademarked boyish grin, and a Dodgers-blue do-rag, which covered a perfect pattern of freshly cut waves. The high-thread-count sheets and the TEMPUR-Cloud mattress threatened to seduce him into sleep. But he wasn't ready for slumber, not yet, anyway. He needed more than the hot shower he'd taken; he needed a little excitement in his life.

Sexual excitement.

Contemplating which lucky female he'd call, Manny flipped through his phone's contact list, then started searching through endless pictures of some of the sexiest and prettiest, naked and best-dressed women in the world. But for some hideous reason, his mind kept going back to his ex-girlfriend.

Bing.

Mama used to say that everything that glittered wasn't gold. And that maxim perfectly described his two-year relationship with Bing.

When he first met Bing, she was everything that he'd ever wanted. At least, that was what he'd thought. She was hot to death. Smart. Witty. Well traveled. And she spoke three different languages. When things were good between them, Bing would always be the center of attention whenever they went out. Men loved to be around her, and women hated being near her. Bing was the ultimate trophy piece for Manny, or any man, for that matter. On the surface, most men would sell their soul to have a woman like Bing on their team . . . arm . . . and bed. But having Bing as a first-string star player had come at a very hefty cost.

In the beginning Manny hadn't minded paying the price to be the boss. What was the use of having money if he didn't enjoy it?

But Bing had had to have everything she saw on television or on social media. Every fucking thing!

The girl had acted as if she didn't know that the designer gowns and jewels her favorite actresses wore on the red carpet were loaners. Or that most of the people flaunting their wealth on Instagram were flat-out lying.

Either she hadn't known or she simply hadn't given a fuck.

It was a given that Bing had to drive the fastest cars and carry the *most* expensive of the expensive purses. "Perception is everything," she would say whenever he would casually mention that the pocketbooks she carried cost more money than she could afford to put in them on her own.

She was right about perception being a serious thing, but so was reality. And the reality was that at the end of the day, he wouldn't be playing baseball forever. "In a few more years I'll be unemployed," Manny had said during one of their heated discussions about money. "And I'll still be in my thirties."

She'd responded by saying, "As long as you work out and eat right, you'll play for another fifteen years. So no time for slipping." And then she'd ended the conversation the same way she ended all their controversial conversations: with a monster blow job. Of course, when she was done, she'd asked for that crocodile Hermès Birkin bag to rock at the upcoming game against the Yankees.

It always went like that, but after one night too many of having that same conversation with her, Manny pumped the brakes. "Look, Bing," he said, "there's no need to spend that kind of bread on another stupid purse. That's a hundred grand we could use to invest in a town house and have some extra income coming in."

Bing laughed as hard as she'd ever laughed in her life. She couldn't stop. "Stop it, Manny. You're killing me."

"I'm serious, Bing."

Bing wasn't feeling what he was touching on. "What?" She looked at him like *he* was the crazy one. "Are you serious?"

"Are you?" was what Manny started to say, but at the time, he was still under the deep throat spell of that good head she'd put down on him. So he then tried to explain his position in such a way that she would understand where he was coming from. "Yes," he said. "As a matter of fact, I *am* serious. If we can find a place in foreclosure and get a good steal, who knows? Maybe we could double our investment."

But Bing laughed hysterically. Manny had no idea what Bing found so funny.

"You're so silly, Manny. The only steal you need to be worrying about is you stealing second base and hitting a baseball. None of that other stuff is important."

The girl was crazy. But Manny was just as patient as she was crazy.

"It's not all about playing baseball and spending money. I want you to get in the habit of making money. I know if you put your head to it, you can do it," he said. But he thought, *Or is your head only good for giving über blow jobs?*

Bing attempted to stop laughing, but she was finding it difficult. Finally, she said, "Let's say we do find a place for a hundred grand, we put a few more dollars into it, and then it doubles in value."

Now she is on the right page, he thought.

"At least that's what I was thinking," Manny said, happy that she was getting it.

Then she burst his bubble. "But, really, how much rent are we going to get for a two-hundred-thousand-dollar property? What? Like, fourteen to sixteen hundred a month?" Before he could answer and share his own calculations, she exclaimed, "That ain't shit for us! We piss that much money away after drinking a good bottle of wine for dinner. What difference would that little bit of money make to us? You have a twenty-five-million-dollar contract!"

And, just like that, they went at it again.

"You're missing the point, Bing."

"No. I caught the point, all right. And I'd rather catch the bag, because fifteen hundred dollars isn't going to do anything for me. I can barely buy a pair shoes for that short money."

That was the proverbial straw that broke the camel's back. At that moment — two years ago — Manny knew. Well, he'd known for a while. But that night it hit home.

There was no reason to continue a relationship with Bing . . . well, besides the sex. And he literally could get that anywhere.

Manny and Bing were from two different worlds. Bing's parents were upper-middle class and had always been financially secure: a big house with a three-car garage, 401(k)s, savings accounts, and health plans. And Manny was from the lowest income bracket there was. He had grown up so poor that there was no income bracket to define it. It was just poverty. And he'd vowed not only to himself but also to his mother that they'd never, ever go back there again.

Manny never wanted Bing, or anyone else, to make the mistake of thinking that he didn't want to enjoy the fruits of his labor. Because he really did. His lifestyle was filled with the best. Houses, clothes, parties, and a deep passion for expensive German engineering, which sometimes he overindulged in, but he was a long ways from being anybody's fool, including Bing's. His responsibility was to his mother and their future, and that was it, and that was all. There was no need for him to continue to build a nest egg for their legacies if Bing was going to spend it all up on fucking expensive, double-digit handbags that would be "out of style" or "out of season" by the next year.

Their two-year relationship had been serious, but after Bing's many acts of greed and selfishness, it was obvious that she was not the woman for him.

But Manny couldn't deny that he loved Bing's freaky ways. Bing's pussy was unlike any he'd ever indulged in, in his life, and he'd had more than his share of beautiful woman and incredible sex. He racked his brain, trying to come up with the name of another person in his ho-o-dex who could compare to Bing when it came to sex. The list was endless: models, singers, actresses, CEOs, doctors, nurses, lawyers, strippers, executives, video vixens, students, teachers, bimbos, bartenders, and regular old big-booty hoochies.

Damn!

Manny hated to admit it. But the truth was the truth. And the truth was, no one else came close to satisfying his sexual appetite the way Bing did.

Manny sucked in a deep breath, exhaled, then pulled Bing's number up on his call log. Hesitating, he thought twice about what he was potentially getting himself into. Did he really want to go backward? The answer came by way of the boner in his pants, which had shown up just from him *thinking* about how good Bing's sex game was.

She answered on the second ring.

She sang into the phone, "Hi, baby! You finally called me. I missed you sooo much." She sounded good.

He tried to keep it poppin'. "What's up with you, Bing?" As if he wasn't yearning for what she had to offer. "Where you at?"

"My parents' house. But I can be wherever you want me to be. Just tell me where you need me to be, Manny. . . ."

"Come to the Tabby . . . you know, the one I like. You still remember, right?"

"Of course I do, silly. I'll be there in two hours. What's the room number?"

"Forty-oh-one." It was the biggest suite the hotel had to offer. "Hurry up. I . . ." He paused. "I missed you too." Then he killed the call. *Already sounding like a herb,* he thought.

He sat his phone down on the bed, went over to the minibar, and grabbed two of the small bottles of Cîroc. He drained both mini bottles in two swallows and then tossed the empties in the trash. He could feel the vodka warming his insides as he walked back over to the bed and then made himself comfortable. The remote to the fifty-inch flat-screen was on the nightstand. He punched in 405. The music channel was playing Mary J. Blige's "Mr. Wrong." Her voice and the buzz from the alcohol relaxed his mind.

A little more than an hour later, someone knocked on the door. Bing was early. She'd burned that highway up to get there to him. Manny rose, walked through the living room, stepped up to the door, and looked through the peephole. Bing, unaware that he was watching, stood there, looking into a handheld purple rhinestone mirror. He shook his head before unlocking the door.

Bing wore a red Alexander McQueen cat-suit, the soft material hugging her like a jealous lover. Her feet were strapped into a pair of black Zanotti six-inch heels, which matched the sixty-five-thousand-dollar Hermès Birkin bag parked on the bend of her arm. The clear Russian diamonds he'd bought her when they were together sparkled on her neck, wrist, and ears. And her hair — cut and styled into long, curly, bouncing tresses — fit her exotic facial features to a tee. He had to admit, Bing was beautiful. And very high maintenance.

Bing beamed with excitement when he opened the door. She sashayed inside and tossed her Birkin bag on the sofa. "Hey, baby!"

The moment she opened her mouth, Manny began to regret ever making the phone call. What was he thinking? A strong dislike, bordering on hatred, settled in his gut.

But he was also infatuated with her.

Oblivious to Manny's ambivalence, Bing beamed a one-hundred-watt smile his way. And from a pair of voluptuous red-painted lips, she cooed, "You like what you see, don't you? I know you missed me. It's written all over your face. But don't worry, baby. All you have to do is ask me to move back in, and I'll come home in a heartbeat."

Why did she have to be so obnoxious and pushy?

She went on. "I know that while we were apart, you were fucking with this ho and that ho in every city you played in. But that was then, and this is now. And I know for a fact that there's not a bitch in this world that can make you feel like I make you feel."

Bing had a valid point, but Manny never tipped his hand.

"Even you," he said with a raised eyebrow, "aren't vain enough to think that, are you?"

"I don't *think* so. I *know* so," she said before softly kissing him on the neck. "I knew you'd miss me." Bing mistook Manny's silence for an endorsement, and that encouraged her to press on. "I knew that you would eventually come to your good senses, wise up, and call me."

"Is that right?"

"As right as the Audemars Piguet watch on your wrist. Boy, you wouldn't be able to function without me in your life. Without this good pussy. Please. Without these . . ." She licked her lips and playfully smacked herself on the backside. "Please."

It's a good thing the bitch do give good

monster face and has snapper between her legs, because her mack game is weaker than a light beer, he thought. He'd known before she got with him that she was accustomed to dealing with lames. So he gave her a pass for not knowing better. *Damn!*

Five minutes later Bing cupping his balls and blowing on his dick changed his thought process instantly. She put all eight inches of him inside her wet, warm mouth. Manny instantly knew that she had the upper hand. Not only did she have his balls in the palm of her hand, but she also had his heart.

Her mouth released his dick with a popping sound as she disengaged the suction from around the head. "I'm so glad we're back together," she said. "But we're going to have to make some changes in order to make this work."

"What type of changes?" asked Manny.

That hundred-watt smile of hers shone even brighter. "First and foremost," she said, "we need to get our wedding plans in order."

"Wedding?" Where had this come from?

"Uh-huh. A girl needs security in her life. And I need an allowance too. You got a lot of making up to do." Her ass bounced and swayed from side to side as she strolled toward the minibar. The material of the catsuit worked overtime to hold all that she was working with inside. At the minibar, she poured herself a drink. Patrón. "I want to be officially taken off the market. Or you can kiss this good-bye, forever."

Initially, Manny had just wanted some good drop. Now he wanted to teach her trick ass a lesson or two. To show her that she was not God's gift to the world, but just a semen bucket among many.

"Get the fuck over here!" he ordered. "And take all that high-priced shit off you that you're wearing." His tone caught her off guard, but she obeyed. "Let me be clear. Ain't no weddings jumping off. I called you to fuck. And I'm fixin' to change my mind." Manny turned and walked into the bedroom. Bing followed. He sat on the bed.

She slapped her hands on her hips. "Manny, you don't have to act like that. I thought you would be happy to see me, that's all."

He didn't even entertain that noise she was talking. "Why the fuck you still got your clothes on! Take that shit off, all of it!" He picked up the remote, turned the music up. Alicia Keys's "You Don't Know My Name" flowed through the speakers of the surround sound.

Bing kicked off her heels one at a time.

Next, she slowly peeled away the skintight catsuit she wore. Underneath it, she was completely nude. Nothing but her bare necessities. Her body was boss. Just the way he remembered it. Bing stared at Manny with a puzzled look on her face. As if she was trying to read his thoughts. She'd figured that when he called her, he wanted to make up, clean the slate and start their relationship anew. For the life of her, she could not read the man, so she decided that she would do everything in her power to win him over before she left the hotel. Like with any man, the best way to get to Manny was through his dick! And she would do anything that he wanted her to do to make him happy. All he had to do was say the word.

But Manny said nothing to her.

Deep down in his gut, Manny knew that Bing was his forbidden fruit, and that there would be a price to pay for partaking of its ripe flesh. A price he no longer desired to pay. That was why he'd parted ways with her the first time. His mind told him to tell her to put her clothes back on and leave his hotel suite, but his manhood took over the show.

Bing stared into Manny's ruggedly handsome face. Then her eyes darted to his muscular arms, stomach, legs before resting on the bulge underneath his towel.

I know this nigga missed this good pussy. I'm about to suck the shit out of my dick. Yeah, it is still mine and always will be, she thought as a sneaky smile snaked onto her lips. *Let me just go for what I know.* And just when she was about to put her move down on him, Manny beat her to the punch.

"Back up," he ordered. "I want to see you dance!"

Bing backed up and turned around, then slowly made her cheeks bounce up and down. The gap between her thighs was irresistible, and Manny's manhood jumped to attention when she bent over to touch her toes.

Her shit was tight.

"Play with your pussy," he said

She did as she was asked . . . or told. It didn't really matter who was in control. Her two brown basketball-like mounds of jelly parted, revealing a valley of pink flesh. Her flower was already soaking wet. Using both hands, she gripped her ass cheeks and spread them wider, then looked back at him through her legs. She ran the fingers of her right hand across her slit. Eased two of them inside as far as they would go. When she pulled the two fingers out, they were coated with her sweet nectar. She slowly sucked the juices off.

"Yeah, baby," she teased, remembering how he used to eat her pussy. "It still tastes good."

"Get over here and suck my dick, bitch!" The towel dropped to the floor.

For a second Bing was taken aback by Manny's blatant disrespect. She looked at him strangely; he had never talked to her in such a derogatory manner before. Even when they had been role-playing. Bing took the blow on the chin and kept it moving. If it was rough sex that he wanted, that was what he'd get.

She took two steps toward the bed and got on her knees. Grabbed his man candy and took him in her mouth, deep throating him hungrily. The slurping sounds her mouth made as his dick banging against her jaw aroused the demon inside of Manny.

Or maybe the demon had already been lying dormant there?

Manny grabbed two fists of her hair, pushed her down roughly on his swollen dick. She gagged but continued to put in that work, pleasing him. When she came up for air, he wrapped her hair around his fists to get a better grip, then rammed himself inside her mouth, acting as if he wanted to bust out of the back of her head or something. Initially, she had tried to enjoy every second of him and his beastly actions, but now he had got too carried away, and she couldn't handle it. She had no choice but to pull away.

She took a few steps back. "What are you trying to do? Choke the shit out of me?" she asked while trying to catch her breath. The perfect hairdo she'd come with was now a hot mess. Saliva ran down her chin.

"Bitch, I said to come suck this dick. I thought your freaky ass was into trying new shit. You gon' bitch, or you gon' freak me like I asked you to do?" He palmed his dick like a knight in medieval times wielding a sword.

Hesitantly, she walked back over to him. When she got close enough, Manny slapped her across the cheek with his sword. When she tried to lasso it with her mouth, he moved it away. She reached for it. He evaded her.

"No hands," he said.

Without touching it, she herded his dick into her mouth and sucked it like a starving whore. Manny humped her face, shouting vulgarities.

"Suck this dick, you nasty bitch! Yeah, like that, you fuckin' slut! Put this dick down your throat. More. Play with my balls." The more Bing obeyed his wishes, the more things Manny commanded her to do. Nothing was off-limits. "Slap 'em on your chin," he said. "Ahhh." He put his hands on top of her head, enjoying the bolts of electricity shooting through his body. Suddenly, he pushed her head back and pulled out of her mouth.

"Daddy?" she whined, looking up at him, dumbfounded. "What's wrong? I was enjoying myself. I know you were too. I could tell."

Her enjoyment was the least of his concerns. "Get on the bed and lie on your back!" he instructed.

Of course, she gave in to his wishes. Manny climbed on top of her. He was going to fuck her.

About time, she thought.

But then he crawled up toward her head, bypassing her pussy, and drilled her in her open mouth with jackhammer-like thrusts. Manny felt his nut building, reaching volcanic proportions. He jerked, then spit inside her mouth. It felt good. He wanted to moan, but he didn't allow himself to do so. Instead, he pulled out and squirted the rest of his cum on her pretty face and hair. This blatant act of degradation excited Bing.

41

Manny climbed off her chest, walked over to the minibar, and got another drink. "Take your ass in the bathroom and clean yourself up," he said to her. "Then bring that ass back out here, 'cause we ain't done yet!"

Bing said submissively, "Yes, Daddy. Your wish is my command." She still had his semen running down her forehead.

While she was in the bathroom, Manny lay back on the bed and smirked. He couldn't believe that she'd allowed him to carry her the way he had done. He should've done that shit a long time ago, he thought. While she cleaned herself up in the bathroom, he quickly started to come up with other ways to break her spirit.

CHAPTER 3
F*#K THAT

Bing turned the handle to make the water in the shower as hot as it would get. As she waited for the water to get hot, she looked in the mirror over the sink. Dry semen was splattered all over her face. She smiled.

It wasn't a happy smile.

It was an "I'll get the fuck even" smile.

A voice in her head said, *You just want to fuck, huh? This motherfucker is mad! Out of his mind, mad! If he thinks he can do this to me and send me on my merry way, he's got another thing coming.*

Another voice in her head said, *Do you really think that after you tried to spend his money quicker than he could make it — and after you stole sixty-five thousand dollars from him — that he was going to let you waltz back into his life, feed you bonbons, take you back in his arms, and tell you how much he loved you? Really?*

The first voice answered, *That's exactly*

what I thought. Pussy is power, especially mine.

The second voice retorted, *Think again. He only wants pussy, but you . . . you are done. Let's face it. You'll never get back into his good graces. He isn't as stupid as you think.* Her common sense gave it up raw. It was exactly what she needed to hear.

However, Bing wasn't giving up that easy.

And he's not getting rid of me, she thought. *Ever! That's on everything I love.*

Whose voice was that? she wondered. Her conscience or her common sense? Who was she kidding? It was her ego talking. She didn't have a conscience.

"Uh, Bing . . . ? Bing! Hurry up in there! We got shit to do."

We sure do, she thought.

Then she answered, "Yes, Daddy!"

She pulled herself together and got in the shower. There was unfinished business to be done, and he had better believe she was going to handle hers.

CHAPTER 4
RED FLAGS

Manny's dick awakened and stretched another inch or so when he heard the shower stop running. A few beats later the bathroom door opened. Bing stepped out, wearing nothing but a white Turkish towel wrapped around her raven hair, which hung loose and cascaded down her back.

Even in defeat the bitch was fine as vintage wine.

Manny shook his head. His description of Bing as fine was just an understatement, like describing Bill Gates as being worth a pretty penny. Bing — who was Chinese by birth and had a body that stopped and redirected traffic — was astrologically fine. Her beauty belonged among the stars.

All of Bing's physical attributes — breasts, lips, ass, hips, and eyes — were courtesy of the best plastic surgeon in Europe. If her doctor's skills and creativity could be compared to those of a famous artist, as some cosmetic magazines had done, then Bing would have to be considered an exquisite and priceless work of exotic living art.

Bing stood in front of the door, watching Manny watching her. A mixture of baby oil and water had beaded up on her skin, and the beads were coursing down the center of her toned back, toward her tapered waist, before finally disappearing between her ass cheeks, a pair of cheeks that exhibited the perfect amount of jiggle when she walked. As Bing trained her jade eyes on Manny, a seductive half smile and half pout was balanced purposely on her voluptuous lips. Lips that — when used correctly — could make a grown man beg, moan, and confess his sins.

"You see something you like?" Her eyes caressed Manny's body as thoroughly as his did hers.

What was there *not* to like?

She'd graduated from a top fashion college in Europe. She had the face of an angel, the body of God, but a mind like the devil himself.

The perfect seductress . . .

The scent of lavender, from the soap she'd used, found Manny's nostrils. She knew that lavender was one of his favorite fragrances. Manny had detected the scent of the floral soap even before she'd got out of the shower. He had always had an acute sense of smell.

"I see a lot that I like," he said honestly. "You are beautiful, as always."

So how come after two years of being in a relationship, he hadn't wifed Bing up yet, taking her off the market?

The answer was simple.

Before Manny could make a woman his wife, he had to be sure that he could trust her! And, besides to jerk off his money, Manny just was damn sure that he couldn't trust Bing.

The red flags had been few in number and cute at first. Then they had grown more conspicuous, like renegade weeds in a garden, impossible to miss.

Looking at Bing in front of him now, it was easy for him to be sucked back into her web of seduction, but his mind managed to take him back to that night those 180 days ago, when he decided all bets with Bing were off.

The night had begun at the Palazzo Hotel in Vegas. A poker night with the boys. Everyone attending the poker game had been a ballplayer — football, basketball, or baseball, but mostly baseball. With a couple of well-known hip-hop moguls sprinkled in.

Manny had a knack for reading cards and people. So a table filled with intoxicated, weed-smoking egos who had more money than they knew what to do with had been easy work for him. Within a couple of hours, Manny had snatched more than 350 thou off the group.

"I hate to take your bread and run . . . ," he lied while stacking the winnings evenly in his Louis Vuitton backpack, "but I have a pressing engagement that just came up."

The reason Manny had to bounce early was that Bing was continuously blowing up his cell phone. The constant distraction was making it difficult for him to concentrate on the cards. So he'd decided that he might as well quit while he was ahead.

Red flag.

But instead of going straight home to Bing, Manny decided to make her wait. He pushed his yellow Ferrari into the packed parking lot of Cheetahs. Cheetahs was one of the hottest strip clubs operating in Las Vegas. Maybe in the country. Manny had known the old owner, before the guy had got indicted by the feds. At the front door Manny grabbed his Louis backpack and handed his keys to the new Ferrari to the valet. Before he got inside the club, his phone buzzed. He didn't have to look at the screen. He already knew who it was. He had told Bing that he would meet her at the crib shortly. Before stepping into the club, he wondered, with a chuckle, if Bing was monitoring the GPS on his cell.

Another red flag.

He dismissed the paranoid thoughts and went inside. Figured that he would have a couple of drinks, maybe share some of his winnings with the hardworking girls, before going home. A complimentary bottle of Belaire reached his table at the same time he did. The waitress was cute, with a banging body. But she wasn't even in the same league as Bing. Very few were. Speaking of Bing, she had continued to TNT his phone.

Fuck it, Manny thought. *She wins. No need to fight it.*

He had wanted to make her wait for a while for interrupting him during the poker game, but Bing wasn't having it. And she was the type of chick who wanted what she wanted when she wanted it. And right now, Bing wanted to get fucked by her man. So he bounced just as quickly as he'd arrived, leaving the bottle of Belaire on the table, unopened. Manny didn't like to admit it, but he was pussy whipped. It was as simple as that. Bing had that good good. And she knew what to do with it.

Back outside, he ran into an ex-teammate he used to play with back on the East Coast. The two chopped it up while the valet scooted off to get the Ferrari. ESPN had been murdering his boy over a steroid-use scandal. He'd been suspended from Major League Baseball for fifty games. It wasn't worse than the A-Rod shit, but it was serious. Steroids and HGH were things Manny didn't get involved with. It wasn't getting caught that Manny feared. As far as he was concerned, any test could be beat, unless you got caught slipping. It was the side effects that he was afraid of. It had been well documented that one of the side effects of steroid use was penis shrinkage. And no amount of hits on a baseball was worth his family jewels being reduced to diamond chips.

Fuck that.

The valet showed up with his whip with the quickness. Manny gave the man a nice tip for his trouble. Then he dapped his boy and told him, "Catch you later." That nigga's money and dick were probably shorter because of that bullshit. *Damn, my dude.* And then Manny was out.

Miraculously, Bing didn't call or text him the entire trip home. Except for one text, which was some foreplay shit. In the text

50

she told him how she was going to fuck his brains out when he got to the crib. The text ended, I hope U ate UR Wheaties 2day. Six smiley faces followed.

Weird, Manny thought as the Ferrari hit a corner at a ridiculously unsafe speed, with ease. He had eaten his Wheaties today.

Manny's seven-million-dollar, West Coast–chic mansion was about an hour's drive away. It had been modified to his unique specifications. Fifty minutes later, he whipped the Ferrari around the circular driveway, grabbed his backpack, and hopped out. Bing met him at the French doors, wearing nothing but a coquettish smile. Her body was covered with baby oil, and the hair on her pussy had been shaved into the shape of a heart. The shit was crazy. She took his hand and pulled him inside. A soft glow from about twenty candles lit the foyer, and the candles' reflections flickered on Bing's oil-drenched skin.

Wasting no time, Bing began to undress Manny. "I thought I was going to have to start without you," she said. Her words came out breathy, sounding sexier than they should have. Manny dropped the backpack onto the marble floor and helped Bing with the chore of removing his fourteen-hundred-dollar Balmain jeans. Then Bing

51

placed her hands on his chest, as if she could read his mind by the beat of his heart. Satisfied with what the rhythm told her, she allowed her slender fingers to cruise slowly southward, down to his rock-hard stomach and then farther still, until she had a handful of what she'd been waiting for all night. Satisfied with her prize, she pushed her tongue inside his mouth, kissed him as if she were trying to steal his breath away.

Her tongue tasted and smelled like peppermint and eucalyptus.

After stealing his breath, Bing shifted gears. As delicate as a feather floating on a soft breeze, she descended to her knees and shared a kiss with his dick before swallowing it whole. She went at it hungrily, as if she'd been famished all night. And maybe she had been.

If there was a place past cloud nine where ecstasy was found in abundance, Manny was approaching it at a rapid pace. As his dick swelled to its utmost inside her warm mouth, unexpectedly, he began to feel a cool yet hot sensation. The sensation he was experiencing no doubt had something to do with the peppermint and eucalyptus he'd smelled and tasted on her tongue just a few moments ago. As his head ascended above cloud nine, he mused to himself, *The acro-*

batics this girl can perform with her mouth is amazing. And when it came down to sexual gratification, her talented mouth wasn't even Bing's best feature. Not even close.

The next morning Manny woke up next to Bing in the California king bed in his master bedroom, spent, satisfied, and in an all-around terrific mood. He took his time sliding out of bed in order not to wake her. She deserved all the extra rest she could get. Last night had been fuck-tastic.

Manny showered, dressed, and then drove to one of his favorite places, Exotic Machines. Manny — flush with the money he'd won in the poker game, money that was still in the Louis backpack — spoke business with the owner of the luxury car dealership. A heavyset cat named Felix. The car Manny was interested in was the Saleen S7, a beautiful turbocharged, 750 horsepower machine with a feisty attitude.

The perfect present for my boo, thought Manny. *An exotic ride for an exotic lady!* It would be a nice surprise.

Felix was asking $585K for the S7 and, in true salesman form, gave all the reasons why he was chasing top dollar.

"Now that you got that out of your system," Manny said, opening the Louis bag so that Felix could look inside, "let's talk about what it would cost in cash. Like, right now cash. Not when the bank opens up on Monday morning."

Looking at the bread, Felix swallowed hard and croaked out a new number. "Four hundred K."

Manny countered with three hundred, and the two men finally agreed at three-fifty, the exact amount of Manny's winnings from last night.

Once all the proper paperwork was done, Manny dumped the contents of the backpack onto Felix's desk. Together, the two counted the stacks of rubber-banded money. Twice.

When the numbers didn't add up either the first or the second time, they counted the dough again. Each time they counted it, they came up with the exact same number: $285,000. Sixty-five thousand dollars lighter than it had been when Manny got home last night. Manny was 100 percent certain of the amount of money he'd won at the poker game, and neither the Louis backpack nor the money had left his sight . . . until he got home.

Damn! he thought to himself.

Another red flag!

This one might be the deal breaker.

CHAPTER 5
BYE, BITCH

Cumberland, Maryland, ten months later . . .
"How many times are you going to apologize to me?"

"As many times as I have to. For the millionth time, I feel awful that you landed in this goddamned place." Charisma surveyed the depressing visitors' room. "It's just awful."

Western Correctional Institution, a two-hour drive outside of Baltimore, housed both minimum- and maximum-security inmates. Chucky's trial had lasted a couple of days, and it had turned out that it wasn't as bad as he had thought it was going to be. The cops had said that both guys whom Chucky had killed were on the Ten Most Wanted List for murder, drugs, assault, and grand larceny, not to mention a laundry list of other charges. The police hadn't connected Chucky to the bodies until a homeless man, who collected the reward money, gave the detectives on the case a license plate number of a truck that he'd seen leaving the building around the same time they believed the murders took place.

After hearing what had gone down, along with Charisma's heartfelt testimony at trial, in so many words, the judge said that Chucky had not only done the state a favor but had also secured justice by getting those two bozos off the street. They were just bad apples and had been for a long time. Since Chucky had never been in trouble with the law before, the judge dismissed the double homicide charges. However, he also concluded that as much as he hated to, he had to give Chucky the minimum mandatory sentence of five years for the stolen gun. He had no choice. And that was dished out only because Chucky had refused to rat out the person who had given him the weapon.

"At least we got the liquor, though," Chucky said to Charisma, trying to see the silver lining in the situation. "And your uncle got to hold on to Legacies."

"But five years is a really long time."

Chucky thought about that. "True." And then he tried hard to put a spin on it. "But the way I look at it, it's better to be tried by a dozen of your so-called peers than to be lowered into a hole by a half dozen friends and family members. Don't sweat it. I don't blame you one bit for my outcome. I hate to even think about how things would've gone down had I not been there. Or had I not been lucky enough to get the drop on dude."

Charisma swallowed. She didn't want to think about it, either. But that didn't stop her from feeling sorry for her friend, who had indeed saved her life and the future of her family's bar.

"You want something out of the vending machine?" she asked.

"Damn right. The food in the mess hall tastes like crap."

Chucky was allowed to go to the vending machines with Charisma, but he couldn't touch the money or the machines. He had to point to what he wanted. Charisma purchased two chicken sandwiches, three bags of sour cream chips, a Snickers bar, and an orange soda for him. She put the sandwiches in the microwave to heat them.

"I'm going to have to leave early, because I have to work the bar," she told him.

"Girl, all you do is work. What about your dream of becoming a best-selling author? That's all you used to talk about. That and one day leaving Baltimore."

"True," she sighed. "Don't remind me."

At college Charisma had minored in creative writing. But she couldn't run out on Uncle Vess. The fact was that none of his three biological children gave one solitary fuck about the bar, which had been in their family for generations. His son, Marcus, had wanted to play basketball, and since that hadn't worked, he now wanted to be a hustler. And the two girls, Vanessa and Wanda, both wanted to look cute and be taken care of by a man, and they acted as if they were allergic to real work. Her uncle Vess needed her. And Charisma never wanted to let Uncle Vess down.

When the tables were turned, when Charisma's mother was so sick and out of touch with reality that she didn't know how to take care of her daughter, it was Uncle Vess who had stepped up to the plate. No questions asked. He'd raised Charisma as one of his own. And there was no chance in hell that Charisma would turn her back on him when he needed her.

"Well, I hope that one day you do leave Baltimore, and you live the life you have secretly always wanted to live," Chucky told her.

Charisma chuckled a little bit. The boy knew her almost as well as she knew herself. As the timer on the microwave ticked down, she began to daydream about the life she secretly wanted to live. A loud voice brought her back to reality.

"Go to your seat," the guard ordered Chucky. He then threatened Chucky by saying that he had to go back to the table, or the visit would be terminated.

Chucky made his way back to the table, leaving Charisma to babysit the microwave.

Beep. Beep. Beep.

The sandwiches were done. She hoped she hadn't overcooked them. If they were scorched, she'd have to buy two more. She pulled open the door to the microwave and stuck her hand inside. When she touched the top of one of the sandwiches, the bread was soft and warm. The sandwiches were fine.

And so was Chucky.

Some chick was at his table. While Charisma had been getting his food together, he'd been entertaining company. And the chick was all up in his face. They acted as if they didn't notice Charisma when she walked back to the table.

Charisma placed the food on the table. "Ummm . . ."

Chucky looked up. "My bad." He introduced his friend. "Charisma, this is Donna. Donna, this is Charisma."

"How're you doing, Donn—"

"What the fuck? Motherfucking Charisma!" Donna shouted before Charisma could get the greeting out. "So this the bitch that got you locked the fuck up? And she got the nerve to be coming to see you?" Donna was stunned.

"Hold on, Donna," Chucky said, trying to defuse the situation.

"Hold the fucking Donna nothing, you black-ass nigga! You crazy?" Donna spat back. "Fuck that! And this bitch got the nerve to be ugly and country and homely looking too."

Homely? Charisma was well aware that she wasn't any beauty queen and had never really been anybody's glamour girl. She had never really tried to put any effort into being pretty. She had been taught that when beauty faded, smarts and heart would go a long way.

Donna had slipped into the visitors' room so quickly and unexpectedly, and her presence caught Charisma off guard more than her insults. Still, except for the occasional drunk patron at the bar, Charisma had never had to deal with someone being so confrontational and disrespectful. Her heart started to beat fast.

"Bitch, you being here, with that thin-ass,

ugly-ass ponytail in your head, is a straight disrespect, and both make me wanna whip your ass," Donna yelled.

"Hold on, Donna," Chucky said, trying to intervene.

The guard came closer to the table. "Miss, keep it down."

Donna shot him a look, then followed up by glaring at Charisma. The chick was blatantly disrespectful, and she looked nasty. Charisma looked over at Chucky, hoping that this would prod him to say something else and straighten out this tacky wench.

"Charisma's a good friend of mine," he finally said. "And I'm not going to have you talking reckless to any of my friends."

Donna rolled her eyes.

A good friend, Charisma thought. True, they weren't fucking or anything, but she had thought he would defend her honor a little better than that. And why hadn't he ever told her about Donna? They had talked about everything, she thought.

Feeling herself, Donna said, "Okay, bitch. Thank you for the chicken sandwiches and tater chips. You can go now. Your services are no longer needed up in this bitch."

Before Charisma knew it, she had smacked the disrespectful heifer in the face with a hot chicken sandwich. The extra mayo she'd put on the sandwich — Chucky loved extra mayo — came in handy. It clung to the corner of Donna's left eye, to her hair and her lips, creating the impression that someone had just jacked their meat off on her face. Which was kind of what had happened. Donna had the nerve to lick her lips.

"Whore, that shit probably makes you feel right at home, doesn't it?" Charisma shot.

From across, the room, the guard had watched the altercation, and now he was making his way over to their table.

Out of the corner of her eye, Charisma saw the guard heading their way and said as boldly as she knew how, "*Now* I can go, bitch!" Then she gazed into Chucky's eyes. "Enjoy your visit."

CHAPTER 6
NOT ON MY WATCH

What a freaking day! she thought to herself.

There'd been a massive five-car pileup on U.S. Route 40. The accident had turned what should have been a leisurely two-hour drive from the prison into a four-hour nightmare, making her late for work. And she'd been on her feet all day, and her dogs were killing her. Charisma made a promise to get herself a new pair of comfortable shoes to work in. The Skechers she was wearing just weren't holding up their end of the bargain, especially tonight.

And it wasn't just her sneakers that were worn out. This was the third double shift she'd had to pull this week. Mary, the kleptomaniac who used to work the second shift, had got canned for finger-fucking the cash register once too many times, and Uncle Vess insisted that everyone pitch in until he could find someone to take Mary's place. Only God knew when that would be.

Uncle Vess could be a cheapskate when he wanted to be. And he didn't trust people outside of family with his business. Though she didn't press the issue, Charisma hoped that he hired someone soon. Like yesterday.

After closing out her final ticket for tonight, she thanked God for giving her the strength to get through another day. But she was even more thankful that the shift was finally over. The bar was empty, except for her and one customer. A tall, dark, and handsome hunk of a guy perched on a stool. And he was plastered. Charisma had already called a taxi for the customer.

With his finger, the inebriated hunk motioned for Charisma to come over to him. "Ayo!" he called.

Charisma nodded her head, then made her way down the length of the counter to see what was what.

"You make one hell of a drink," he said once Charisma was within earshot, "but I'm sure you already know that." Then he pushed a tip into her hand. "This's for you." When she looked, there were five one-hundred-dollar bills. "I'll go outside to wait on my taxi."

"Thank you. I really appreciate you," she said, but she was unsure if she should take such a large tip. She didn't want to take advantage of any of her drunken customers.

Charisma allowed his eyes, which were glassy and crimson red from all the alcohol he'd consumed, to meet hers. "Are you sure you want to give me this? You do know how much money this is, don't you?" she asked, just to make sure, to show kindness.

"Why?" he slurred. "You don't want it?" He was smiling.

"I didn't say that," she replied, hoping she hadn't blown the fat tip.

"Cool then. You deserve it. I feel . . ." He smiled. "Good. Real . . ." He paused, as if he was searching for some profound word, then settled for a more mundane one, saying, "Nice. And you're the reason why."

Charisma blushed. She made the best drinks, hands down, of any bartender for twenty miles. At least that was what many of her customers had told her. Plus, she had a great listening ear, a tool that had proved more helpful than a heavy hand. By listening, she had learned the many reasons why people insisted on poisoning their liver into submission with spirits. She'd discovered that some customers drank to celebrate special events: graduations, promotions, childbirths, weddings, and even divorces. And, on the flip side, some wanted to wash away a bad memory or two, such as getting thrown out of school, losing a job, enduring a death in the family, or going through a divorce. It depended on the prospective. But most of the time *heavy* drinking had two causes: money or heartbreak. At the end of the day, it didn't matter why the customers knocked them back. Charisma's job was to pour the drinks, not to judge the people tossing them down, and she never did the latter.

After the last customer was out the door and she'd cleaned up, she took one last look around, making sure that everything was in order. Satisfied, she headed to the door and punched in the eight-digit code for the alarm. The alarm blinked green. The only thing on her mind as she walked out of the bar was a hot bubble bath and a soft be—

"Fuck *you!*" The words echoed through the night air, caught her off guard. "Fucking towel head!"

It was the hunk who had tipped her the five bills. He was standing in the middle of the parking lot, giving the cabdriver a hard time. It was late, and she didn't want the people who lived over the bar to complain. Out of concern *and* her obligation to the bar, she walked closer to the altercation, in case she needed to intervene.

Charisma was only a few feet away when

the cabbie barked, "No foock me!" His English was broken, and he had a Middle Eastern accent. "Foock you, nicca!"

Uh-oh. He went there.

The hunk's face got real serious, real quick. He looked as though he was going tosnatch the driver from the vehicle he was sitting in and put a whupping on that foreign butt for the racist slur, ignoring the fact that he'd just called the man a "towel head." But the driver must've seen the expression on the hunk's face, because the wheels on that cab got to spinning faster than an episode of *Scandal.*

"That's what I thought!" the hunk shouted at the vanishing taxi as the cabbie burned rubber. Then he stumbled over to his spanking brand-new black Lamborghini.

"Shit!" she cursed out loud.

Then she thought, *The last thing I need is for some good-looking man to kill himself, and possibly someone else, by driving a fucking Lambo — of all cars — while intoxicated from the liquor I served him.*

She could see it now, the lead story of the morning news, flashing in front of her, her picture in the upper right-hand corner of the TV screen. And they'd probably use that ninth-grade school photo she hated so much. The one in which she wore those old

Coke-bottle glasses, braces, and a hairdo that sat on top of her head like a bird's nest. Underneath the horrendous high-school photo would be a still shot of a twisted-up Lamborghini and its dead driver. She would be blamed for the accident, since she was the one who had served the customer all that alcohol. The bar would be fined an obscene amount of money, would maybe even be shut down.

And she'd go to jail.

Nope! Not on my watch.

The drunken hunk was about to open the door of his expensive sports car when Charisma intervened, putting her hand over his. "Can I be of assistance to you?" she asked.

The hunk gave her an odd look, as if he wasn't sure if he was getting propositioned by a hooker. Then it clicked. "You're da, um . . . b-bartender, right?"

Her outfit must have ruled out the hooker theory. She smiled. "Most days and nights. But my mother calls me Charisma."

A warm smile. "I'm Roc."

"Hi, Roc." Just her luck, it began to rain just then. And she didn't have an umbrella or a hat. How much worse could the night get? "Let me drive you to your destination!" she suggested, grabbing the car door and placing her body in front of the handle so that he couldn't get into the vehicle without moving her out of the way. Before Roc could reject her offer, she said, "My car's right over there." She pointed to the other side of the parking lot. "And I'm a really good driver."

"Shit. Anybody can be a good driver of a fucking Ford."

"Hey, hey. Be nice," she said in a firm but sassy kind of way. "Listen, I'm the best designated driver you are going to get at this time of night, or any other time."

As the rain continued to fall, Roc, rocking on his feet, seemed to contemplate the offer before finally conceding. "If your driving is as good as your drinks, then I guess I might be in good hands."

"Just like Allstate."

Together, they dashed over to Charisma's Ford Focus and got in.

Charisma had no idea that she was about to go on the ride of her life. . . .

CHAPTER 7
BE CAREFUL WHAT
YOU ASK FOR

Roc lived in a high-rise. The elevator was enormous and brightly lit. Drenched from the downpour that continued to inundate the city, Roc and Charisma both stood statue still as the elevator quietly ascended to the top floor. From somewhere inside the elevator — Charisma had no idea where — speakers played soft music. Jazz. Normally, jazz music would've soothed her wandering mind, but not tonight.

Their wet clothes clung to their bodies. And Charisma's sandy-blond weave, which was tied into a ponytail, was draped over her right shoulder. She wrung her hair out, and the water dripped onto the elevator floor. Then she mentally cursed herself for going against her better judgment. Why had she served Roc so many drinks? If she had cut him off, he would not be in this drunken state, and she would be home, in the comfort of her own warm bed, by now. After she'd worked for sixteen hours, the last thing she needed was to be someone's designated driver. But her conscience wouldn't allow her to abandon the man. He was well beyond the legal limit of alcohol consumption to drive. Hell, he was past the limit to walk properly.

Despite the fact that the elevator was twice as large as her car, Roc stood only inches away from her, staring at her. Despite her loose-fitting sweater and baggy pants, there was little doubt of her sex appeal. Underneath her work clothes, Charisma had a banging body. She ate right and worked out religiously to maintain it. Roc gazed into her hazel eyes. They commanded his attention.

"Those contacts?" he asked.

"Nope," she said proudly.

"They look good as shit."

His words were like music to her ears, and he knew it. A wry smile found his lips. Charisma reciprocated with a little bit of attitude. Just for fun.

"Damn, sexy. W-why you looking at me that way?" His speech was slurred.

"Because you're a mess," she told him. "And thanks to you" — she looked down at herself — "so am I. Look at my hair." Using the chrome interior of the elevator as a mirror, she tried to do something with it. But it was useless. Her ponytail was bloated with water and had unraveled at the end.

"You're beautiful. The wet look is sexy on you!"

Roc's comment surprised her. She was flattered. And he was cute, confident . . . and, apparently, rich. But that didn't mean that she would fall for his bullshit. "Whatever, Mr. Roc. You can save your game for the next chick, okay?"

He seemed to be sobering up. "I am serious." He wrapped both his hands around her wasp-thin waist, then spun her around. Now her back was to him. He had big hands and a firm grip. "Look at your reflection in the mirror," he said.

Instinctively, she tried to pull away. But Roc's grip was tight, encouraging her to do as he'd asked. She acquiesced to his request by taking a long look at herself. She'd long ago got past her low self-esteem days of high school, but she'd still never seen herself as anyone's beauty queen. Whereas most young women put a lot of energy into how they looked — fussing endlessly with makeup and clothes — Charisma let it do what it did. Her focus had always been on getting good grades and nurturing the family bar. Of course, she glammed it up on special occasions, but those were rare and —

"You are beautiful," Roc said, interrupting her thoughts. "But I'm sure that you already know this." This time he drew her in with his eyes. It felt as if he was appraising her. "I think you are perfect. Natural. Basic. Sexy." He continued to size her up in the reflective wall of the elevator.

"Stop looking at me that way." She felt like she was in a fishbowl.

Charisma had dated a few guys here and there, but none of them had been in Roc's league. His swagger and confidence were more than a little overwhelming to her, but she covertly enjoyed the attention. Still, she didn't know how to handle his attention or him.

"I told you already, you're a mess," she said.

"What'd you expect? Those strong-ass drinks you concocted . . ." He laughed. "How could I *not* be a little drunk? I think that it may've been your intention to get me messed up," he said in an accusatory tone. Charisma wasn't sure if he was playing or not. "But it's all cool," he added. "Maybe you could help me clean up." He shot a seductive look at her, undressing her with his eyes.

"Nope." He had the wrong girl for that.

"No one put a gun to your head and made you drink all that cognac. And I was the one who called you a cab, remember? Give me credit for that. And I am also making sure you get safely up to your swanky penthouse apartment, Mr. Big Shot!"

"I appreciate it. Your compassion and generosity show me that you're one of the few. . . ."

She asked, "Few what?"

"Caring people left in this uncaring world," he replied.

"Well, it's not like you're a complete stranger. I must've served you at least a hundred times before in the bar."

"How come you never asked me my name before?"

"How come you never offered?" she retorted.

Roc and his big-time friends — usually doctors, lawyers, accountants, and sometimes celebrities — always rented out the back room when they came into the bar en masse, and their bill was always an enormous one. She wasn't sure exactly what he did for a living, but whatever it was, she knew he made really good money doing it.

Roc chose not to answer her question, or maybe he didn't hear her. Instead, he drank in her countenance and her looks. He noted that her light brown skin was glowing in the elevator's LED lighting. Long, natural eyelashes fanned her hazel eyes. Out of habit, Charisma's tongue swiped across her naturally pouty upper lip, just below a beauty mole, which men seemed to find extremely sexy. Roc's curious facial expression caused her to smile, lighting up the elevator more than it already was.

Ding!

They were on his floor. The elevator door swooshed open, and they stepped out into a lavish sitting room.

"Won't you come in for a moment?" he asked.

Charisma was hesitant, but she was also curious. She'd never seen a place that was this spectacular. She stood there, admiring the beautiful floors, and that was when his landline phone rang. That was her cue.

"I think I should be going," she said.

"No, not at all. Stay and let me you show you the view." His eyes never left her as he reached for the phone and turned the ringer off.

She knew good and well that she should be getting her butt back on that elevator, with her only focus being the ground floor. But she didn't budge. Instead, she asked, "How come you keep staring at me? Do I have something on my face?" She was stalling. Why was she stalling? She'd done what she had set out to do. Roc was home safely, and her face wouldn't be on the morning news because he'd accidentally killed himself and someone else. Now it was time for her to take her ass home, get some rest. After all, she had to open up the bar in a few hours.

"Only your extremely good looks," he said in answer to her question. "Your eyes . . . are they real?" he asked.

"Would you be disappointed if I told you they weren't?" she said coyly.

"It wouldn't bother me if they both were made of glass."

She laughed. "Yes," she said, still smiling. "This is their natural color. No contacts."

After taking her hand, he guided her through the penthouse. In the living room, he stumbled, and his right arm brushed against her left breast as they both fell onto a white sofa. He purposely stumbled, Charisma thought as she tried to remove Roc's torso from her lap, but he was too heavy.

"Come on, Roc! Work with me here!"

He played like he was drunker than he was now, and he refused to shift his weight and remove himself from her lap. Somehow she managed to push him onto one of the

76

silk pillows that adorned the sofa. Then she stood up and looked down at him as he looked up at her. He was so sexy and fine that it gave her goose bumps.

"Roc, you need to get up and get out of those wet clothes. Before you get sick," she asserted. "I'm about to go."

"A'ight," he said, slurring, and then he removed his jacket, his button-down shirt, and his V-necked T-shirt. She hadn't expected him to disrobe immediately, allowing her to catch a glimpse of his body. She tried not to look, but she couldn't help herself. Roc's body looked as if it had been sculpted by a master carver. He was the ideal man, and he looked like he should be on a billboard somewhere.

Before she knew it, Charisma's breathing quickened. She was afraid that if it got any louder, Roc would hear it and think she was having a heart attack. She was momentarily caught in the straitjacket of lust. She'd never before reacted this way to a man's body. Her ex-boyfriend Sam had a potbelly, and it had never turned her on this way. And she and Chucky had never had sex before. She could never put her finger on why. Chucky had always had her back, and she had just figured that maybe one day something would happen. But Roc's body was perfection. His combination of sexiness and cockiness affected her in a way that she'd never experienced before. His muscles and his abs were definitely real masterpieces. . . .

What was she doing? She made up her mind. She was getting out of there. Then Roc stood up. And his six-pack seemed to force her eyes to venture below the belt. It would have been impossible not to notice the enormous print in his pants. *This man must have a weapon in his pant,* she thought. Then she quickly raised her eyes and focused them back upstairs.

Roc had caught her looking. He eased toward her. Came so close to her, she could feel his breath tickling her eyelashes. "I wanna thank you again for making sure I got home safely." His voice was thick and sweet, like dark molasses. "I owe you for that. You're a good woman. And beautiful." It felt as if he was putting a spell on her. "Can I tell you a secret?"

Her heart sped up. "Sure."

He smiled. But this time the smile encompassed his entire body. He had a wide tongue. It darted from his mouth, painted his lips in one quick swipe. Then he shared his secret. "I've had a crush on you ever since I started coming into your uncle's bar. That's why I go there so often."

He has a what on me? she thought, not certain she had heard right. This definitely came as a surprise. He seemed to be full of them. Or was he full of something else and just running game? It was hard to tell.

"Really? I thought you were just a good-looking alcoholic," she quipped, not knowing what else to say.

"But you thought I was good looking," he said, catching her off guard.

"I m-mean —" she stammered, but he cut her short.

"You can't take it back. Do you still think that?"

"Do I think that you're an alcoholic?" She played dumb.

"Jokes." He sat down on the sofa. "No. Do you still think that I'm *good looking?*"

"I guess." She paused. "In a playboy sort of way," she added.

"That's the way you see me? You think I'm a playboy?"

"Well, you do drive a Lamborghini, wear designer suits, and live in a penthouse, so . . ."

"If the shoe fits, huh?"

"You said it, not me."

The longer Charisma was around Roc, the more comfortable she felt in his company.

"You're always hiding behind those baggy

79

clothes. You need to let your hair down and live a little, Charisma." He reached over and gently caressed her arm. His touch was sensational.

"Wait." She pulled away. "What are you doing?" She knew damn well what he was doing. And she liked it. "I have to leave, Roc. You're drunk. What you need —"

"Tell me what I need."

"A shower and some sleep are what you need," she said. "And I need to get home to do the same. I have to be back at the bar in the morning."

"Or do you mean you need to . . ."

"You heard me." Charisma took a couple of strides in the direction of the elevator.

He stood, caught up with her, and grabbed her hand. "The things I would do to you," he said under his breath. "Charisma, listen to me." He made sure that he had her undivided attention before continuing, which wasn't difficult. "You work, work, work all the time. Just relax and enjoy the moment." He spread out his arms. "Enjoy this. . . ."

Charisma was unsure if he was talking about the penthouse or himself. Both were tempting.

Roc drew closer to her, eliminating what

little space remained between them. The top of her head reached the top of his pectoral muscles. She could feel the heat emanating from his body, could smell the alcohol — which she'd provided — as it was being released from his pores. She wondered if he could feel her heart beating.

Then, as if he could read her mind, and maybe he could, Roc said, "I can tell that you're feeling me. Live a little."

"How can you be so sure that I'm feeling you? Maybe you're feeling yourself a bit too much."

"That's not it. If it were, I would tell you. Tell me this. Since you've been working at your uncle's bar, how many people have you given a ride home?"

"I call cabs for people all the time," she said.

"But that wasn't my question," said Roc. "The question was, how many people have you actually *given* a ride home from the bar when they've had too much to drink?"

"I've worked at the bar for a long time. It's the family business." She was stalling. And she knew that he knew it.

"But how many?" he asked again.

"In total?" she asked, looking up and to the left, as if she was searching her brain for the answer.

"Yep." He was patient. "In total."

"You were the first," she finally said.

"My point exactly," said Roc.

"But I have to go."

"Let me kiss you."

Huh?

"Let you do *what* to me?" she said.

"You heard me. But just so that we're clear, I said, 'Let me kiss you.' All over your body."

Charisma imagined Roc's thick lips roaming her body, as if in search of lost treasure. Would she share her treasure with him if he found it? She wasn't sure. Her mind was saying no, but her body was singing an entirely different tune.

Roc did not wait for a verbal response. He leaned in and kissed her softly on the lips. Trapping her bottom lip between the two of his, he sucked on it. When she loosened up, he slipped his tongue into her mouth. It was warm and wet.

"Tastes like mints. I wonder what the rest of you tastes like," he mused.

Everything inside of Charisma screamed, *Pull back! Stop him!* But she could not. She'd been weakened by his touch, and his aggressiveness had lit a fire within her. She found herself reciprocating with kisses of her own, getting lost in the erotic slow dance of their tongues.

She felt his hands touch the sides of her face and then make their way down her neck, over her shoulders, down her arms, and over her hips, until finally reaching her backside. When he squeezed her there, a warm tingling sensation shot through her body.

Charisma knew that this was wrong. One-night stands went against everything she believed in. She had never slept with a man on the first night, nor had she ever desired to do so. She felt that nothing solid could ever come from two people who didn't know each other randomly hooking up. But at this moment who cared?

Wait, she told herself. *What are you doing? What are you thinking?* These were just a couple of questions asked by her conscience. A conscience that would normally hold her accountable for her actions. But she hit IGNORE. And for the first time in her life, she let go and did something on the edge, something out of the ordinary.

Besides, hadn't her ex-boyfriend Jack said he'd cheated on her because she was boring? Nothing was going to be "boring" about this night, she thought and smiled, both on the outside and the inside.

On that note, she wrapped her arms

around Roc's neck. Roc wasted no time lifting her off her feet. Immediately, she became lost in the passion of the connection. She felt her womanhood getting hot, which ignited a blaze throughout her body, awakening feelings that had lain dormant for a long time. Who was she kidding? She'd never felt this way before.

Ever.

Her love box thumped, tingled, screamed, and begged, *Let him inside, please. . . . Let him.*

Roc lifted the damp sweater over Charisma's head, tossed it onto a marble-and-glass table. Then ran his hands slowly across her flat stomach. Next, his touch found her breasts. Charisma closed her eyes, took a deep breath, and allowed an overwhelming feeling of lust to surge throughout her being. And before she knew it, her bra snap popped, and her black silk bra was removed from her body and tossed in the air. It landed on top of the sofa.

Charisma had second thoughts. "What are we doing? I — I — I . . ."

"Shhh . . ." Roc placed a finger to her lips. "Don't talk," he said. "Allow me to give you what your body has been craving."

There was something about the confidence in his voice and the compassion in his eyes that helped Charisma relinquish herself to him. Roc took control. Bent down and licked around her right nipple with the tip of his tongue, his left hand cupped around the other ever so gently. Charisma closed her eyes, savoring the moment. Roc caressed and sucked her breast with the skills of an advanced sex addict. Her nipples hardened beneath his touch, adding fuel to her already burning body. Roc didn't miss a beat. He moved to her neck. Then his lips found her earlobe. Sucked on it slowly. As if they had a mind of their own, Charisma's fingers probed Roc's muscular back.

Suddenly, her conscience returned, telling her all the things that she already knew. *Oh my God. I have to stop him! I have to stop myself! What the hell am I doing?* she thought as his hands slipped inside of her sweatpants. He slid them down. She stepped out of the legs, and the cotton fabric puddled at her feet.

Roc marveled at Charisma's mostly naked body. If his manhood was any indication, he was impressed with what he saw. Her peach poked out through a pair of black lace panties. Roc seemed temporarily confused, as if he had expected straitlaced lingerie. But he quickly regained his composure. He scooped her off her feet and placed her on the sofa before she could muster a protest. Not that she wanted to. Charisma loved every second of this.

He wedged open her thighs and buried his face in her essence. Charisma knew she wasn't at her freshest down there. But Roc didn't seem to care that she'd worked a double shift. His rhythm was perfect — not too fast or too slow. His tongue gave her clitoris the business. Never shortchanging or rushing her, Roc took his time as he lightly licked the peak of her peach with the tip of his tongue.

Charisma was in ecstasy. Unbridled moans escaped her lips. The sounds seemed to excite Roc, motivating him to give her more. Give her all he had. He folded his tongue around her clitoris and massaged it. Charisma left her last bit of inhibition at the door and came out of her proverbial shell.

"Oh my God, Roc! Make me come!" she cooed, her breasts bouncing freely as she dug her nails into his back and neck, drawing fresh blood.

Roc carried her over to a table, shoved everything on top of the table to the floor, then laid her on top. She could tell that her flexibility surprised him when she brought her legs up to her ears. She'd taken gymnastics from the age of four to the age of fifteen.

Roc pulled her closer to him. Looked into Charisma's hypnotic hazel eyes, then buried his face in every heterosexual man's weakness. He rubbed his nose up and down the length of her slit, and then, using only the tip of his nose, he pleased her for ten minutes without ceasing. It was amazing.

Then he used his fingers. Played with her buttons like a virtuoso pianist on a baby grand piano. Played for a captive audience. Aware that she had become weak at the knees, Roc took full advantage of the moment. Charisma was putty in his hands. She spoke in tongues, screaming words of pleasure.

Roc continued to take her slow. He thoroughly licked her peach, then up and down her thighs, finding every crevice and orifice in the process. He returned to her forbidden hole, used his tongue as a small shovel to break through the entrance. She nearly lost her mind when Roc kicked down her proverbial back door with his tongue. No one had ever pleasured her in such a way. The man had moves that would make a stripper blush.

If this was ecstasy, Charisma never wanted to return to Earth. When she came — the first, second, and third time — her entire body shook. And he hadn't yet unholstered that monster of a weapon he had tucked in his pants.

He took a break. He turned on the stereo. R & B music blared from speakers hidden somewhere in the walls, or maybe they were in the ceiling. She wasn't sure. Aptly, Usher's "U Got It Bad" filled the penthouse suite.

Roc walked back over to her. "You ready for round two?"

She was so ready. "There's more?" she said, pretending to be unmoved.

But Roc wasn't buying it. He took her by the ankles and pulled her toward him. Then he cradled her body, carried her back to the sofa, and placed her down on it. "You haven't seen anything yet."

He ain't never lied, she thought.

Roc flipped her onto her stomach, grabbed her by her ass, and spread her cheeks. Her peach stuck out, and juices still streamed down her thighs from all the oral she'd received.

"What are you trying to do to me?" she asked.

He didn't respond. Instead, he planted soft, wet kisses on the base of her back. Then on her shoulders. On her sides. And then dipped back down to her heart-shaped backside.

She heard the zipper release before he removed his pants. Roc stepped out of his boxers and jeans at the same time, freeing his caged animal. Charisma reached back and touched it. *Damn!* His anaconda was three levels beyond hard. Pre-cum glazed the head. He flipped her onto her back. When he climbed in between her thighs, she saw pure, unadulterated lust dancing in his eyes.

Charisma caught a glimpse of Roc's length. It was bigger than she'd imagined. And she was certain that it would stretch her peach out of shape, if it would even fit inside. Fear of him ripping her to pieces made her want to put on the brakes, but she'd come way too far for that. Besides, her womanly needs had completely overridden any rational thoughts she might have had.

Roc's rock-hard body felt orgasmic against hers. Their bodies melded together and became one. He didn't try to put his length inside of her, opting instead to take it easy at first. He was gentle as he rubbed his anaconda-like pleasure tool up and down her slit. The teasing was more difficult to handle than the real thing, she thought. So she took matters into her own hands.

Literally.

It took both hands to get a firm grip on the lifesaver that hung between his legs. She felt his heartbeat — *thump-thump, thump-thump, thump-thump* — pulsing through the shaft. She froze.

Sensing her hesitation, Roc asked, "Are you sure that you're ready for this?"

Of course she wasn't sure. But if she didn't do it now, when *would* she be ready? *No time like the present,* she thought. *Right?*

But when she tried to put it inside of her, Roc pulled back.

"Take it easy," he said. Then shooed her hand away, taking control again. With one hand on his lifesaver, he used the other to guide Charisma's left nipple into his mouth. Then rubbed the head of his lifesaver over her slit, barely inserting a portion of the head as he did so. Then an inch or two of the head breached the door.

When Charisma jumped, Roc asked, "Are you okay?"

She tried to assured him that she was. "You startled me, that's all."

"Take your mind off me penetrating you, and instead, concentrate on me sucking your breast. Okay?"

She nodded her head.

After a few minutes, he still hadn't entered her, and she begged him to put it in.

"Please," she said. "I want you to do it."

Her grandmother used to tell her to be careful about what she asked for in life. Charisma had never thought twice about what that really meant. Saying this had made no sense to her, because she would never ask for something unless she wanted it.

Now she understood.

Charisma wondered if her grandma had ever had a Greek god of a man sucking on one of her tits, with a giant anaconda swinging between his legs.

"Please," she begged. "Stick it inside of me." The foreplay had done its job, and now it was driving her stark raving mad.

Roc played around for a few more minutes before breaching the door again.

Be careful what you ask for. . . .

Charisma belted out a gut-wrenching scream. "Oh! My! God!"

The pain was immeasurable. On a scale of one to ten, ten being the highest level, the pain was a cool zillion. She couldn't remember if a zillion was a real number or not, but the pain certainly was throbbing. It stole her breath away; she literally couldn't breathe. And Roc had only a little more than the head inside of her.

Roc asked her, "Do you want me to keep

91

going, or what?"

She panted. "Y-yeah. Keep going."

Roc obliged. But Charisma could tell that he was still trying to be gentle. To Charisma, it felt as if the head of the anaconda had crawled into her stomach inch by inch by inch by inch . . . with no end in sight. Then everything went black.

All at once, she exhaled. "Ahhh!"

When she came to, she had no idea how long she'd been in that darkness or if she'd really passed out. The pain was still intense, but not like before.

Roc pulled out, to the head, then pushed it back in a couple of inches. Charisma's pain started to resemble some semblance of pleasure. He repeated the same motion thrice and then eased it in a little deeper on the fourth run. By now she could at least take it without blacking out. She gasped for more air, counted to ten before releasing it. Oxygen was her friend. Her walls tightened around his massive girth. Her eyes felt as if they were the size of golf balls. She bit down on her bottom lip and slowly started rocking her hips.

Roc had been using slow half strokes, getting her acclimated to his size. But when he felt her swaying her hips, he pushed farther inside. She dug her nails into his back as the pace of his strokes increased. The sound of flesh smacking flesh, her peach popping, and screams and moans blended with the music.

Beyoncé's "Drunk in Love" came on, and Roc sexed her in sync with the words and the beat of the song. The irony wasn't lost on Charisma that their night together had started because he had been ridiculously drunk and had been unable to drive home.

Roc put his back into it, digging deeper inside of her — so, so, so deep — until he ran flat into a wall. He'd literally run out of space to put his dick. He'd managed to travel the full length of her love tunnel, using only half of his monster. Charisma's muscles clenched up each time Roc slammed into her back wall. Her screams of womanly pleasure heightened with every thrust.

Roc gripped Charisma's waist. Charisma wrapped her legs around his back. He rode her like a porn star, giving her every inch of his dick, which her body could physically hold without screwing anything up. And she reciprocated his passion. Sweat dipped from Roc's brow onto her breasts as he gave her the most intense sex she'd ever had in her life. Their sweaty bodies were intertwined, making sweet music.

He pulled out of her warmth, turned her on her side, and entered her again. She screamed into the pillow. Roc placed his right hand on the small of her back, put his right leg on the sofa, then dropped down to the hilt.

"Ughhh," she panted. "Boy! You! Trying! To! Kill! Me!" She spit the words out in spasmodic jerks.

Roc rocked from side to side and in and out of her soaking wet peach.

She yelled out, "I'm comin', Roc." It was the fourth time tonight. Or was it the fifth? She'd lost count. In one night, she'd come more times — without self-stimulation — than she'd come in six months. "Fuck me!" she said.

Be careful what you ask for. . . .

Roc — more than happy to do exactly what he was told — temporarily eased out of her, then grabbed her by the waist and pulled her up to her knees. Her face was buried in the pillow; her cheeks were parted. He stood up on the sofa, squatted down, and then thrust his glazed neck home. His family jewels clapped against her backside in approval, but Charisma wasn't as accommodating. She wanted Roc in the worst way, but under her terms. She needed to control the entrance of his penis into her vessel.

She screamed for him to take it easy. "Roc, please don't put it all inside me like that! I can't take it! Wait!"

Her pleasurable cries fell on deaf ears. Roc was caught up in the moment. She had to push him in the stomach to get his attention.

"Okay, baby. No problem." Roc was driven by her pleas and moans of pleasure. But he yielded to her immediate wishes.

He went slowly. She rocked her hips, slowly pushing back onto him.

Perfect.

"Like that," she said. "Just like that." She gave a sigh. "You got my pussy speaking in tongues, Roc!"

They went at it that way for about an hour.

At the end of the round, they took a five-minute break.

Then Roc said, "Tell me you want it again."

"Oh, I do. But not tonight, honey."

CHAPTER 8
GOOD-BYE

6:00 a.m.
Ringgg!

The ringing phone roused her from sleep. Disoriented from the aftereffects of a deep sleep, she was uncertain of her whereabouts. The last thing she remembered was that she'd been dreaming.

The dream had been vivid and clear. And it had entailed this amazing night of incredible sex with a stranger. It had unraveled like some scenes taken straight from a sexy movie, one with two beautiful leading stars. And the funny thing, Charisma thought, was that the dream had been so graphic and lifelike, she still felt sore inside.

Then the vestiges of sleep evaporated, and Charisma's reality came into greater focus. The man she thought she'd been dreaming about — the hunk from the bar — was lying next to her, with his arm slung around her waist.

What had she gotten herself into? Why was she lying in the arms of a man whom she knew nothing about? And where in God's name was she?

Ringgg. Ringgg. Ringgg.

She felt around the bed for her phone, trying not to wake up what's his name. But she had no luck finding her phone. Then she realized this ringing couldn't be coming from her phone, because the sound didn't match her ringtone. What she was hearing came from a landline somewhere inside this penthouse. She somehow managed to unwrap herself from the comfort of Roc's muscular arms. Once she escaped, she tiptoed around barefoot in search of a bathroom. She had to pee like it was nobody's business. Which was a funny thought, because what she did in the bathroom wasn't anyone's business. The floors were made of marble, but they weren't cold. In fact, the floors were heated. And the lavishness of the penthouse apartment only started there.

A girl could get used to something like this real quick, she thought. *Mind-blowing sex with a sex god in a multimillion-dollar condo, where no expense has been spared in making it the most comfortable living space in Baltimore.*

97

Ringgg. Ringgg. Ringgg.

After searching for five minutes, she finally discovered the location of the master bathroom. She stepped inside, quietly shut the door, and made her way in the dark over to the toilet. She found her way owing to the built-in blue light in the toilet, which illuminated the water. And the moment she sat down on the toilet seat, another dim light lit up. This setup afforded enough light to take care of the business, but not enough to jar a person awake in the middle of the night.

"Ahhh." She always felt better after relieving herself in the morning. A magazine rack sat by the lighted toilet. Charisma helped herself to a *Robb Report* magazine, then paged through it, though she could barely read a word in the dim light, as she allowed herself time to drip-dry.

Ringgg. Ringgg. Ringgg.

Finally, an answering machine clicked on. The factory-installed automated recording was brief. "Please leave a message." It was followed by a long, loud beep. Charisma was caught up in the lavish lifestyles advertised on every page of the magazine she was thumbing through as she sat in a bathroom that was bigger than her entire bedroom at home. The smile on Charisma's face nearly enveloped her entire body.

"Motherfucker!" The irate voice belonged to a woman. "I told your ass last fucking night that li'l Rodney has a fever of a hundred and three, and I haven't heard one fucking word from your sorry ass. And you know that Mylow's christening is today, at noon. And your no-good, trifling ass isn't anywhere to be found. Don't fuck with me! I will *kill* you and the bitch you with. And . . . you know it!"

That smile dropped off Charisma's face as fast as a bitch could say, "He's married?" She wiped herself and bounded off the toilet as if it was on fire. Washed her hands, went back into the bedroom, and found her clothes. Then she nudged Roc awake.

"Your wife is looking for you."

Roc answered predictably. "No. Not my wife, but I can explain."

"She says that you have to be at a christening in a few hours." Charisma was calm. Cool. Collected.

"Oh, shit! I nearly forgot about that. Let me jump in the shower, and we can talk when I'm done. I promise you, I can explain this. It is honestly not as it seems."

Roc rushed into the bathroom. Instantly, she heard water beating against the marble floor of the monstrous frosted-glass shower stall.

Charisma got dressed. Found a pen and a piece of paper inside her purse, jotted something, and left Roc the note on one of the nightstands.

Good-bye.

CHAPTER 9
THE SHINING $TAR

Nine months later . . .

The news came as a surprise.

"I'm at the hospital. My water broke."

Fuck!

She wasn't supposed to give birth for another week.

Manny was exhausted. He was in the locker room. He'd just changed into his street clothes. His team had just finished the last game of a three-game series against the San Francisco Giants. It was an away game, so they were in the City by the Bay. His team was three games out of first place, so every game counted. After today, the team would be on a two-day break, but they had the Yankees on Tuesday. A tough matchup.

"Are you sure?" he said.

"Of course I'm sure! Are you coming or what?"

As if he would miss the delivery of his

firstborn. "Don't have my baby until I get there," he said.

Within five minutes he was on the highway, headed to the airport. An hour later he boarded the charter flight, and an hour and twenty minutes after it lifted off, it touched down at a small private airport in LA.

Manny's assistant, Janice, had booked a black Ferrari for him, and the guy driving the rental was supposed to meet him on the airstrip on which the plane was slated to land. However, the Ferrari wasn't on point when Manny exited the jet. He began to think that he wouldn't make it to the hospital in time for the birth. Then the driver of the Ferrari pulled up, and Manny dismissed the thought.

Manny threw his luggage in the backseat, hopped behind the wheel, and took off. On the trip from the airport to the hospital, God must've been rolling shotgun with him, thought Manny, because the normally gridlocked circus on the 405 was a breeze. His excitement over being a father surprised him. He felt the same way about the birth as he had a couple of years ago, during the World Series. It was game seven. They were in the eighth inning, and the opposing team was up by two. It was Manny's turn at bat. He stepped up to the plate, with two outs on the scoreboard. Underneath his gloves, Manny had sweaty palms. And although he didn't show it outwardly, Manny's heart was nearly beating out of his chest. He had to take a deep breath to calm it down. It didn't work, but he was ready.

He looked at the first pitch; it was wide and below the strike zone. But the ump called it a strike. Manny glared at the ump, stepped out the batter's box to readjust his grip, and then got ready for business. The pitcher threw that same pitch, a fastball outside the batter's box. This time the ball didn't dip; instead, it hung up. And Manny was ready for it. The ball came off Manny's bat like a bullet. It took off straight between the second baseman and the shortstop. A home run.

And that was the way he felt now, anxious but triumphant.

When he reached the hospital, he found a place to park, grabbed his camera from his carry-on, jumped out of the Ferrari, raced to the main entrance, then pushed through the doors of Cedars-Sinai Medical Center. He checked his phone for the time. Remarkably, it had been only three hours and six minutes since he'd got the call from Bing. Record time.

Cedars-Sinai Medical Center was the

number one ranked hospital in LA. Inside, one of the receptionists was available at the information desk when he approached it. He read the name tag pinned to her smock.

"Excuse me, Ms. Parker. Which floor is the maternity ward on?"

"Are you going to be a papa?" Ms. Parker asked without looking up from her computer.

"My first," Manny said proudly, flashing his pearly whites.

She feigned happiness for him as she lifted her head from the screen. "You look familiar," she said upon looking at him for the first time. "Are you someone famous?"

"Not really," he lied, not wanting any attention, especially from the media. "But I do get that all the time."

"Well, our maternity ward is on the third floor. If you give me the name of the mother, I can get the room for you."

"Bing Foo."

Ms. Parker punched Bing's name into the hospital's database. "She's in room three-twenty-three."

"Thanks." And then Manny broke for the elevator bank. He got on the next elevator and then got off on the third floor.

Being a professional baseball player sometimes took the front seat to everything in his life. But ever since he'd been ambushed by the news of Bing's unexpected pregnancy — due, apparently, to their one night of bliss — Manny had placed baseball second, after his unborn child. Manny and Bing were among the few people today who didn't opt to find out the sex of their child before it was born. They had chosen to wait and enjoy the surprise. Secretly, Manny hoped for a boy, but whatever God blessed them with, he would be ecstatic, as long as he *or* she was healthy.

"Manny Manifesto?" A fan stopped him in the hallway. "Wow! It's really you. Would you mind taking a picture with me?" Dude looked as happy as a kid at Christmas, except he had a pocketful of cigars with blue wrappings instead of toys.

"If you make it quick," Manny said.

"Say no more," the dude quipped.

Click. Click.

"Thanks, man. And good luck," the dude said.

Manny wasn't sure if the dude was wishing him good luck on the birth of his new child or in the upcoming play-offs. "You too," he replied absently.

Manny rushed through the corridors until he found room 323, and then he walked inside. Bing lay on her back on the hospital bed, with a huge smile plastered on her chubby face. She rubbed her stomach, as if she was checking to see if the baby was still in there. Then she pushed a lock of hair from her brow.

She lit up even more once she saw that it was him, and not another nurse or doctor. "Hey, Manny. I didn't think you were going to make it. We're about to be parents. How exciting. If I got any more excited, I think I might burst."

"I'm excited too," Manny said. "And you are going to burst any minute now. Is the baby kicking right now?" he added, placing his camera on a chair and walking over to the bed.

"No," she said. "Not right now." Then, "Hold up. Yes. Come and feel it. The baby must've heard your voice." She beamed, waving him over so that he could feel the little miracle before it stopped kicking.

Manny placed his hands on her swollen belly. He felt the baby kicking as soon as he touched her. It was the proudest he'd felt in a long time, maybe ever. He said, "Daddy's here, baby. I'm right here. Can't wait to meet you." He reached for the hem of Bing's nightgown, pulled it up, and kissed her on the stomach.

"Aw. That's so sweet, Manny. You're going

to be a wonderful father. I know it," Bing said. She placed her hand over his.

Manny asked, "What'd the doctors say?"

"That it'll be a while. My water broke, but I am not ready yet. The doctor just left. I've been having these monster contractions, though. Oh my God! That shit hurts so bad, Manny."

"It'll be over with soon, hopefully. My friend Marvin said that his wife was in labor for twenty-three hours. That's just crazy."

"Don't even say anything like that up in here, Manny. Twenty-three hours. Whew."

Manny spoke to her stomach. "Come on out here and meet your daddy. Daddy can't wait to meet you."

Bing's mother walked in while Manny was talking to the baby. "That's so very cute," she said. "Hi, Manny!"

"Hi, Mrs. Foo. I'm glad that you made it." Bing's mother didn't speak very good English, so Manny didn't expect her to have very much to say to him. He'd met her only a couple of times.

No response, but those Asian eyes watched every move he made. When Mrs. Foo sat down, the overstuffed chair nearly swallowed her tiny body.

Bing and Manny made eyes at each other. They both smiled, and then Manny ran his hand through her hair. He was more nervous than she, it seemed. He asked her if she needed him to get her anything.

"No. I have everything that I need right here. I'm just glad that you made it. I've been secretly surprised by how supportive you've been about the pregnan—" she said before a contraction cut her off. "Ughhh!" Bing clutched at her stomach. "Damn! These contractions hurt so fuckin' bad!"

Manny held her hand. She squeezed his so tight, he nearly pulled away. *Damn. She's strong,* he thought. But it looked as if the pain was getting unbearable. Manny pushed the call button right before Bing screamed. Manny had no idea what he should do. It was not like he'd taken any of the Lamaze classes with her. He hadn't even known she was pregnant until three months after she conceived, and the pregnancy had happened on what he thought at the time would be their last night of bliss. The call nurse bounced into the room about a minute or two after he rang the call button.

"Is everything okay, Ms. Foo?"

"The contractions are getting worse and are coming often now. Can I get something for the pain?"

"Sure." The nurse walked over to the IV and adjusted the release valve. "You should be okay, but we can't give you anything else for the pain, unless you want the epidural shot. The doctor will be back to see you soon."

"Okay. Thank you. I don't think that I'll be taking that shot in my back. I heard that if you move the wrong way, it could paralyze me."

"Don't worry. That almost never happens. But there is a record of it happening. But the chances are less than one percent. I used an epidural myself when I gave birth two years ago. Believe me, girl, it's safe. Some people just want to have their babies naturally, and there's nothing wrong with that, either. But, trust me, I know what you are going through." The nurse squeezed Bing's hand without the IV. "Hopefully, it'll all be over soon, and you'll be holding your precious gift from God."

"Thank you, Nurse Starling," Bing said, then laid her head back on the fluffy pillow, which her mother had brought from home.

Manny noticed that Nurse Starling was biracial. Maybe Indian and black. He wasn't sure. But she was very attractive, and she smelled like a bouquet of flowers. When he began to notice how tight her body was, even in the fitted scrubs she wore, he quickly turned away. He was there for one reason only, to see his baby being born. Besides, he hated hospitals.

Three hours passed.

Bing's contractions began to come more frequently, and each time they came, it was that much more intense for her. When Dr. Myers came to check on her, she cursed at him.

"What the fuck are you waiting for? Please! Get it out of me! Please!" she yelled.

Dr. Myers tried to calm her down. Once she had settled down somewhat, he lifted up the sheet and opened her legs to check how far along she was.

"You've dilated ten centimeters. It's time for you to have the baby now," he announced.

A team of nurses got Bing on a gurney and then pushed her over to the delivery room. Once she was situated in the delivery room, they quickly strapped her into the leg harnesses. Outside the room, a nurse told both Manny and Bing's mother that if they wanted to be at Bing's side during the delivery, they would have to wear paper footies, smocks, and surgical masks. Manny and Mrs. Foo both agreed and donned the paper items. Then they were ushered into the room.

"I need for you to breathe in deeply and

push," Dr. Myers told Bing. A nurse rolled a chair up behind the doctor, and he sat down.

Three hours later, after all the breathing, pushing, sweating, crying, and screaming from Bing, they hit the lottery. The top of the baby's head crowned. Manny, amazed by the sight of his baby about to come into the world, stood there motionless. Then, suddenly, he remembered his camera. He rushed out of the delivery room. Ran full speed down the hallway, back to the room that Bing had occupied. He got his camera, which was still on the chair, where he'd left it, and hightailed it back to the delivery room.

He rolled the video and filmed everything. The head coming out of Bing's prized snapper. Then he thought that it might not be that much of a snapper after this. Then the shoulders came through, followed by the torso, the legs, and feet. Dr. Myers turned the baby over and smacked it on the butt.

"Whaaain!"

The room erupted with joy once the newborn took its first breath. Their bundle of joy had arrived.

Dr. Myers said, "It's a girl."

Love at first sight. Manny felt a surge of warmth through his body, and at that moment, all his protective instincts kicked in. He reached for his baby. The nurse put her hand out, stopping him.

She asked, "Do you want to cut the umbilical cord?" The baby was covered in a slimy substance that they called afterbirth. After Manny did the honors of cutting the cord, the nurse cleaned the child up and passed the bundle to Manny. "Here you go."

Manny was afraid he would break her. She was so tiny. He looked down at her beautiful face and smiled brighter than the White House on a Christmas night. She had a head full of coal-black hair. He kissed her forehead, holding her close to his heart.

Bing asked, "Can I hold her, Manny?"

Manny walked the baby over to the head of the bed and laid her in Bing's arms.

"Isn't she beautiful!" Bing exclaimed. She had that new-mother glow. And it was bright. "Isn't she beautiful!" she said again. She answered her own question. "Yes, she is. Of course, she takes after her mommy." Bing kissed her itty-bitty baby girl on the top of her head.

Nurse Starling said, "Do you two already have a name for her?" She was looking over Bing's mother's shoulder.

Bing eyed Manny. "We're going to name her Star." She shifted her gaze to her newborn. "Hi, Star. Mommy loves you, little one," Bing whispered into Star's scrunched-up little face.

Manny smiled at his little angel, and the nurse noticed that the little angel already had her father wrapped around her tiny finger.

"You know what they say about men who have little girls, right?" Nurse Starling said.

Manny shrugged. "No. I don't know."

The doctor spoke up. "That's because they have given women hell, broken so many hearts, God makes them worry over their little girl's heart now."

"Well, I will have it easy. I was never a heartbreaker."

"All lies," Bing said in a joking way.

The doctor and all the nurses left the room. Then Bing's mother stepped out as well, giving the proud parents some time alone with their bundle of joy. Once they were alone, Manny sat on the bed, next to his baby and Bing. He played with Star's tiny fingers. Kissed them. Bing watched them bond. Then Manny reached down and removed a lock of silky hair from Bing's face. Bing's eyes filled with love.

Manny said, "I'm the happiest man on Earth right now. Thank you for giving me a baby. She stole my heart the moment I laid eyes on her. Damn." He almost couldn't believe it. "I'm a father. You already know that whatever you need, you got it. I love this little girl with all my heart, and she'll always come first in my life."

Bing asked, "Before baseball?"

Manny responded, "Before anything. I can't wait to show Marvin the pictures I took of her."

"You better not show Marvin the footage of her coming out. I don't want him looking at my stuff."

"Cut it out, Bing. I'm not showing him that. Just the shots of Star."

Bing grabbed her phone, which was beside her, and took a selfie of the three of them before Manny realized it. Then she took advantage and took more. "I'll send them to you so you can post them and let the world see your happy family and our little Star. We can take pics for the press release in about an hour. I have the makeup artist coming back to touch up my makeup for it."

Manny smiled, thinking how Bing had really caught him slipping, but he was grateful to her for his baby Star.

Batting her eyelashes, Bing said, "I can't wait for them to discharge us, and then we all get to go home and live as a family. It's going to be so wonderful." Bing radiated excitement.

Then came the bombshell.

"Come on, Bing. Give up the fairy tales. You know good and well that there isn't going to be any *us* living together as a family. It ain't fucking happening. But the one thing I'm absolutely sure about is I'm going to be there for my daughter, and you and I are going to co-parent. But other than that, there will be no us."

Bing felt like a mugger had ambushed her in a dark alley. Except, instead of her purse, this mugger had stolen her life, the life that she had plotted, using Star as security with the help of a turkey baster. She wanted to cry but refused to give Manny the satisfaction. Nor did she want Star's first impression of her mother to be of a weak bitch crying for a man. She would not do that to her child. Plus, she knew that the false eyelashes she had applied a couple of days ago would cause her eyes to burn if she let her tears out. Bing blinked her tears away. But she couldn't extinguish the emotional storm brewing inside of her. It just came out.

"What the fuck do you mean, Manny? Really? Really, Manny? Why you keep playing with my fucking heart like this Manny?

Just answer me that one question. You always find a way to fuck up my mood. I can't believe this fucking shit!"

Star began to cry.

"Bing, calm down. You are upsetting Star."

"No. *You* are fucking upsetting her."

Manny took the baby from Bing and began to comfort her, and she stopped crying right away. Manny handed the baby back to Bing. There was silence for a few minutes. Then Manny spoke and tried to set the record straight.

"You act like we are together. Shit. You just told me five months ago that you were pregnant. You think I'm a lame or something. I'll play my part to the fullest. The baby will not want for anything. Point-blank. Period."

"Manny . . ." Bing's voice was gentle as a summer's breeze now. "Get the fuck out. I don't even want to look at you right now! You get on my last damn nerve. I've done everything to please you, and that shit you pulled at the hotel the last time we were together . . . Oh, my God! I don't even know why I'm still talking to you! Get out! Get out! Get out!" she yelled.

He didn't budge.

"Fucking leave, you sorry sack of shit!" she screamed at the top of her lungs.

Manny bent down and kissed his daughter once more, then grabbed his camera and cell phone and headed toward the door. Then he walked out without saying a word. As he walked out the door, Bing picked up a vase with flowers in it and pitched it across the room at him. Too bad her aim was way off.

"Bastard! Fucking . . . asshole!" she yelled.

Bing lay in the bed, feeling empty inside. She could not believe that after all she'd been through with Manny, it would be this way. She wanted Manny to suffer the way she was suffering at that moment. Alone with Star, Bing sobbed loudly. Her eyes burned like they were on fire from the false eyelashes. She eventually managed to pull herself together. Afterward, she gently rocked her baby in her arms. Star had all of Manny's features. Holding Star to her chest, Bing began to talk to her.

"Star, I gave him you, but he doesn't want me in his life. He's a bitch-ass nigga for that! I swear on everything I love, I am going to make your daddy's life hell."

CHAPTER 10
EARLY PREGNANCY TEST

The gentrification of Locust Point, a neighborhood in Baltimore, began in the nineties. Today most of the old residents were long gone. They hadn't been able to afford either the continuously rising property taxes or the ballooning rent. Even those who had lived in the same house their entire life had been forced to move to a new neighborhood. One they could afford. The few who had been lucky enough to own their own home had sold their properties for a huge profit.

Uncle Vess was one of the few who could afford to stay. His four-story family house was in pristine condition as he had renovated it, turning each floor into an individual self-sufficient apartment. Uncle Vess had kept the first floor for himself. It had the biggest master bedroom, and there were no steps to walk up. He had given Charisma the third-floor apartment. After finding out that her husband was cheating on her with a coworker, Charisma's cousin Wanda and Wanda's two children had moved into the second-floor apartment. And her cousin Marcus, Uncle Vess's only son, lived on the fourth floor — when he wasn't locked up for doing something foolish.

On the third floor, Charisma sat on the edge of the tub in her bathroom, her thoughts running wild.

What the hell had she done? Charisma couldn't believe she had put herself in this situation. The man she had shared a night of hot, incredible, mind-blowing sex with was married. And she was sure he had children. Charisma couldn't stop beating herself up. It was so unlike her to go to bed with a man whom she knew nothing about. It was like someone else had taken over and possessed her entire being.

Sure, she thought. *Blame it on aliens. It's another* Invasion of the Body Snatchers.

Since that unearthly night, Roc had called her every day, usually more than once and sometimes as many as twenty times. Frustrated but sticking to her guns, Charisma had not answered or returned any of Roc's calls.

It would've been nice to have mind-blowing sex with a drop-dead handsome single man. Lord knows every girl needed that in her life. . . . That fantasy was nothing short of amazing, but Charisma snapped out of it quick. She did not need a sexcapade with a man who was already taken and who wanted to have his cake and eat it too.

She'd made one mistake. At this very moment, there was honestly nothing that she could do about that, but choosing not to perpetuate that mistake was in her power. And she had made an executive decision to exercise that power, and it had started with refusing to have any communication with this man.

However, Charisma had other problems, potentially, besides Roc's constant calling. The Walgreens bag that sat on the bathroom sink, where she'd put it, would determine whether she faced a large problem. The moment she removed the purple box from the plastic bag, she felt overwhelmed, filled with so much anxiety. If one more emotion crammed into her body, she might explode.

Charisma sucked in a deep breath and then read the directions on the back of the box. It was pretty simple. She had to take the stick out of the box and urinate on it. Then wait for the results. If the results of the test were positive, the simplicity of her life would be a thing of the past. *Lord, give me the strength,* she thought, but she had no idea what that really meant.

She took another deep breath, wanting to put off the answer, but her procrastination only made her feel worse. She followed the directions, then laid the urine-saturated stick on the edge of the sink and took another deep breath. The directions said that she would have the results in two minutes.

She waited. . . .

"Charisma!" one of the kids yelled as he knocked on her apartment door, startling her so much that she nearly knocked the stick on the floor.

The seconds crawled by as slowly as a sixty-year-old, arthritic turtle. She considered ignoring the test results, getting up and going about her business. She could always come back later. But Charisma was glued to the toilet seat, unable to move until she knew the results. Twenty-three seconds had passed when she heard another knock on her apartment door. She wasn't expecting anybody, nor did she want any company right now. So she ignored the knocking and the uninvited guest. But the knocking continued.

Those damn kids, she thought to herself.

They won't let me get a quiet minute to save my life.

And then a little voice, which was barely audible through the wooden door, called, "Charisma? Charisma? It's me."

Wanda's oldest boy, Kendall. He was seven years old.

She yelled from the bathroom, "I'll be downstairs in a minute, Kendall. Okay? I'm busy right now."

"Okay." Kendall sounded disappointed. He added, "Can we play video games when you come down?"

"Sure." He was crazy about the game *Lego Marvel Super Heroes.* She said, "Just wait for me downstairs." She heard him drag himself away from her door.

A minute had passed, but it seemed like an eternity had elapsed since she'd peed on the stick. Taking another restorative breath, she continued to wait, attempting to contain the tangled web of thoughts twisting through her head. She thought about her past and her future. How would her life change?

She remembered being nine years old and her fourth-grade teacher asking everyone in the class what they wanted to be when they grew up. Most of the kids had hunched their shoulders. Some had shouted out the usual answers that kids spewed at that age. A fireman. A policeman. A nurse. A doctor.

Charisma remembered that Chucky had said that he wanted to be a superhero when he grew up. The class had laughed at him, including Mrs. Clark, their teacher. And when it was Charisma's turn, she'd declared — in a matter-of-fact tone — that she was going to be a best-selling author and would tour the world, meeting people with her knight in shining armor. The only thing that she had ever put ahead of that goal was working at Legacies.

Another forty-five seconds had crept by.

So, how had she got herself into this position? Well, of course she knew *how* it had happened. A better question, she guessed, would be, why had she allowed it to happen? She knew that nothing would come from beating herself up, but there was no one to pummel with guilt but herself.

With only five more seconds to go for the test results, someone belted out the loudest cry for help Charisma had ever heard. And the owner of the bloodcurdling bellow was her cousin Wanda.

"Nooo! *Nooo!*" Wanda screamed at the top of her lungs. *"Nooo! Help!"*

"What the fuc—" Charisma began, but before she even realized she was going to

123

do it, she jumped off the toilet, ran out of the bathroom, and scurried down the steps, taking them two at a time.

When she got to the second floor, Charisma heard Wanda's cry for help again. "Nooo! Help!" she screamed.

The screams came from the first floor. Charisma picked up a baseball bat that was leaning against a wall outside the door to Wanda's apartment and then shot down the steps. Uncle Vess's door was open. She darted inside his apartment and was hit by a thunderbolt.

"Charisma!" Wanda looked up at her cousin. "He's not breathing."

This time Charisma was the one screaming. "Call nine-one-one!" She ran to Uncle Vess's side and began to listen for his heartbeat. Then she reached for his wrist and searched, praying for a pulse.

Little Kendall was in the corner, crying. "I already did that," he sobbed.

Seconds later Wanda began pushing on her father's chest, administering CPR. She'd learned CPR one summer at swimming camp. Uncle Vess didn't move; he just lay still on the floor. Wanda continued to pump his chess rapidly until paramedics arrived a few minutes later. They took over.

As the paramedics loaded Uncle Vess onto

a collapsible gurney, one of them asked a series of questions. "Does he have a history of heart problems? Is he on any medication? Does he have any allergies?"

They answered as best they could. Then both Charisma and Wanda asked a question of their own.

"Is he going to be all right?" they said in unison.

The paramedic who had asked the questions ignored their desperate need for assurance and simply said, "I don't know."

They rushed Uncle Vess out the door and into the waiting ambulance. Wanda took it upon herself to ride in the back of the ambulance with her father. Then they peeled off, heading to the emergency room with red lights flashing and the siren blaring.

After corralling Wanda's kids and situating them in her little car, Charisma drove as fast she could to the hospital so that she could be by her uncle's side. It was a miracle that she wasn't in an accident on the way. The kids thought it was fun, oblivious both to the danger speeding presented and to their grandfather's serious condition.

The emergency room at the hospital was a madhouse. One crisis after another poured through the sliding doors at the hospital's emergency entrance. The sight of all the victims of gunshots, stabbings, and car accidents only made Charisma more anxious. When she learned that a man had been hit in the head with a sledgehammer and a little boy had eaten rat poison by mistake, she realized there was no end to the emergencies. But she had only one person on her mind: Uncle Vess. Wanda rushed up to Charisma and the children the moment she saw them. The nurses at the reception desk had told Wanda that everyone would have to wait in the waiting room until Uncle Vess was stabilized.

As Charisma, Wanda and the children waited, other family members arrived one by one. They took turns pacing the floor and going to get coffee just to break up the tension in the room. Six hours passed without any word. The waiting was the worst.

At least they thought that was the worst part until a doctor appeared with news about Uncle Vess.

"I'm sorry, but he didn't make it." He'd had a massive heart attack.

The kids kept asking for their grandfather. Wanda looked blankly at the pale green walls. And Charisma's silent tears wouldn't stop coming, although she tried her best to keep herself together. She was always trying her damnedest to be strong for everybody else.

That night, back at home, Charisma dragged herself into the bathroom to take a shower. Hot water and sadness beat on her mentally and physically drained body. When she stepped out of the shower, she felt no better, but it was then that she noticed the pregnancy test on the edge of the sink. She picked it up and read the results.

Positive! Fucking positive.

How can this be positive when everything else seems so fucking negative? she thought.

CHAPTER 11
POUR OUT A DRINK

Green Mount Cemetery's grounds crew lowered Uncle Vess's coffin into a freshly dug resting place — next to his wife — at exactly 1:15 p.m. Charisma imagined Aunt Sandra's first words to her husband in the afterlife. *Can a lady go anywhere by herself?* Aunt Sandra had had a great sense of humor, especially when it came to Uncle Vess. They were one of those couples who were born to marry and spend their lives on earth together. And now they would finish the journey, together, in heaven.

After the funeral, friends and family congregated at Legacies to get some closure. Surprisingly, Wanda had taken control of everything and had personally handled all the arrangements for the funeral and the repast, including the decorations and the food catered at the bar.

Closure? Whatever that means, Charisma thought as she stood inside Uncle Vess's office, where she had been hiding out all evening.

How did one close the book on someone one loved? A parent? A brother? A sister? A child? Or even a dear friend? To Charisma, the term seemed barbaric. It had been repeated so often over time to those in mourning that it had become hackneyed. As far as she was concerned, there was no such thing as closure after the loss of a love one. There was only pain, and then, if one was lucky, there was learning to live with the pain.

"Charisma?"

Did someone call her name?

"Charisma?"

She heard it a second time, or was it the third? Charisma wasn't sure. Then she looked up and saw Wanda standing in the office doorway.

"I'm sorry, Wanda. My mind is just somewhere else," she said. Impressed by her big cousin's resolve, Charisma mustered a smile.

Maybe she could take a lesson or two from Wanda, she thought. Wanda had put all her own emotions to the side to handle things and had thrown herself into her father's affairs. This was a new leaf that she had turned over after her father passed away.

Friends and other folks in the family had been whispering that Wanda was doing so much because she felt guilty about her father's death, but Charisma saw it merely for what it was: Wanda stepping up to the plate. And with all that Charisma had going on, she was glad Wanda had.

Wanda stepped inside the office and put a hand on Charisma's shoulder. They shared a brief moment, letting the hurt resonate from one cousin to the other. "Everyone keeps asking about you," Wanda finally said. "Are you okay? You need to get out of this office and mingle. Being locked away, left to mourn alone, is not good at all."

Charisma felt a lot of things, but okay definitely wasn't one of them. In fact, she felt horrible. "I'd rather not be bothered," she said. "Not right now, anyway."

Wanda really understood. Charisma and her uncle had had a truly unique relationship. Though Wanda was Vess's daughter by blood, Charisma had always been bound to him in his heart. Charisma had been very much Daddy's little girl to her uncle Vess. And this had been perfectly okay to Wanda. There had been no jealousy between the cousins. Wanda knew that she had slacked on her responsibilities to the family business and was grateful that Charisma had stepped in.

"Maybe later," Charisma added.

"Can I get you anything?" Wanda said.

"How about a hug?" Charisma extended her arms.

"Sure, cuzzo. I can use one myself."

They squeezed each other as tight as they could stand. Then squeezed a little tighter before finally stepping out of the embrace. The two of them used to be as thick as thieves. But when Wanda got married and started having babies, they sort of drifted apart. Until now, Charisma hadn't realized how much she missed their friendship and sisterhood.

Wanda peered at her. "Better?"

"Yes." Actually, she did feel better. Not a lot, but some. And that was better than nothing at all. "I'll be out in a minute." She took a deep breath and tried to shake off her despondency, but for the life of her, she just couldn't.

"No hurry," Wanda said. "Those people are getting so drunk, they probably won't remember seeing you, anyway." Wanda looked back once before leaving the office, then shut the wooden door behind her.

Charisma sighed. She felt lifeless. Which was ironic, because at the moment she a carrying a potential life inside of her. She

131

wondered if it was some type of sign that she found out that she was pregnant on the same day that her uncle died. *One for one.* Then she shook the thought away. Because if she believed in the symbolism of the two events, then, by default, she would also have to believe that Uncle Vess's death was somehow connected to her. And she wasn't prepared to bear that type of burden on her shoulders. The weight on her heart was heavy enough as it was.

Charisma closed her eyes, lowered her head, and mouthed a prayer — Psalm 23 — to evict the unhealthy thoughts that were trying to rent space in her head. Then she fished her phone from her pocketbook and did something that she should've done a week ago — call Roc just for the fuck of it. Honestly, she didn't care what Roc's opinion was of the "situation" they had created together. Her mind was already made up, and there was nothing Roc could say to change it.

She said, "We need to talk," when Roc answered the phone.

"Sure!" He sounded upbeat. "I've called you every day since . . . ," he said, his voice trailing off.

"Since you lied to me," she said, finishing his sentence for him.

He was probably wondering which lie she was referring to. The wife, the child, the mistress? The morning after their tryst, Charisma had Googled the man whose bed she'd shared for a night. And according to the ESPN Web site, Roc was a big-time basketball player, one of the best in the NBA, if not *the* best. A few years back, he'd won the scoring title and the MVP Award. Walt Wonderland had signed him and his family to an enormous endorsement deal; it was rumored to be worth more than one hundred million dollars. They were the poster family for happiness and unity. And for years that had always been his image and what he represented.

Charisma thought, *God knows what other skeletons he has in his closet.*

There was a brief pause. Then he said, "Let's start over. Everything on the table this time."

How convenient.

"It's too late for that," she told him. "Some fires can't be put out once they've started. And what we have on the table are wildfires."

"That's true with other things also," he said. "Love can't always be extinguished so easily, either. If it means anything to you, everything I said about the way I felt about you was the truth. And still is."

"It doesn't."

"What? Huh? Sure it does."

"No, it doesn't mean shit to me, not now, not ever," Charisma shot back.

"Then how come you called, Charisma? We can't undo the past. We can only live in the present and prepare for the future. Nothing else matters. We have to push forward." Roc was confident that he had won Charisma over.

At that very moment, Charisma figured out how Roc was able to seduce her the way he had. He had a silver tongue. And a banging body. And in the bedroom, he was expertly skilled at using them both. Charisma then thought about what he'd said about not being able to change the past and about having to prepare for the future. That was exactly why she'd called.

"You are right. We can't go back and live in the past," she said.

"That's right, baby. I'm glad we are on the same page."

"Presently," she said, "I'm pregnant."

The phone went pin-drop silent for a few beats.

Then Roc gasped, "Can you repeat that? I'm not sure I heard you correctly."

"I said that I am pregnant with your bab—"

Click!

The line went deader than Uncle Vess.

CHAPTER 12
SERVED

I know that lying mofo didn't just fucking hang up on me!

Charisma side-eyed her phone just as a snake was slithering from the screen. And the head of the serpent strongly resembled Roc's no-good ass, beady eyes and all. Charisma was two snaps from cocking back and slapping the scales off the slimy bastard when she suddenly blinked away the repulsive figment of her imagination. *Damn!* she thought. She was so furious, she'd started seeing things. Roc was a bona fide king cobra, all right, but he wasn't slithering from her iPhone. She tossed the phone on the desk.

Fucking bastard!

Charisma took a second to breathe. She took a few deep breaths. She needed to calm herself down. Being this angry was neither healthy nor helpful. If her body temperature rose any higher than it was right now, her weave would catch fire. She imagined her 'do spontaneously combusting. The silly image brought a much-needed smile to her face. She was starting to feel sorry for herself for being a jump off, a one-night stand, and, most of all, for sleeping with a strange man whom she knew nothing about, someone who had just inserted a baby inside of her during one solitary fuck. But then it got more real when she thought about what else he could've left behind. She could get rid of a baby, but what about the shit she couldn't?

Just then she heard the door to the office creak open. It was probably Wanda again. She was determined to make Charisma socialize with the mourners. But when Charisma looked up, she saw that it was Marcus.

"What's up, cuz?" he said.

"Hey, Marcus. I was just thinking of something stupid. Letting my mind run wild, go to a place it should never be."

Marcus stepped into the room, reeking of pot and booze. When he closed the door behind him, the smell grew more intense. "Wanda told me you were hiding out back here." His eyes were puffy and red, like two ripe cherry tomatoes. Charisma wasn't sure if his eyes had got the way because of all the vodka and weed in his system or from the stream of tears he'd shed when he thought no one was watching. "I've been assigned the task of getting you out of this . . ." Marcus' bloodshot eyes surveyed the items in the room: the imitation Persian rug underneath the scarred oak desk, the framed photos of his father posing with celebrities, the antique wooden file cabinets. "This shrine," he finally said. "Come have a drink."

"Fine," she said. Between her grief over the loss of her uncle and the rage she felt for Roc, a drink didn't sound like a bad idea at all.

Before leaving the office, Charisma scooped up her phone from the desk. "Okay. Let's go." She locked the door behind them after they exited the office, and then she took her cousin's hand as she followed him down the narrow hallway.

In the bar the atmosphere felt more like that of a wedding than a repast. "Happy," by Pharrell Williams, boomed from the sound system. Vanessa spotted her and Marcus.

"About time you got your butt out here, girl," Vanessa said once she had made her way through the crowd and reached their side. She handed Charisma a Blue Motorcy-

138

cle. "Drink this. It'll make you feel better."

Charisma took a sip. "Thanks." All over the place, people were drinking, eating, and conversing. A few were dancing. Charisma hadn't seen the bar this turned up since the New Year Eve's bash, the one with the liquor that had landed Chucky in prison.

Marcus said, "I'm going to go get me something else to drink, cuzzo. I'll be back in a sec." He slipped away.

Charisma said to Vanessa, "Wanda did a good job putting everything together, didn't she?"

"The bitch makes me mad sometimes, but, yeah, she did her thang. With everything. Funeral and all." Vanessa took a big sip of her own mixed drink. "I don't know how she did it." She took another big sip and drained the glass. "Well, I need a refill. Be right back."

After Vanessa left her side, guests kept walking up to Charisma and offering their condolences. When one guest walked away, another would take his or her place. They all said things like "Where have you been?" and "How are you doing?" and "He's in a better place." Now Charisma understood why her cousins had been urging her to show her face. They were probably fed up with juggling questions about her.

139

By the time Vanessa got back with her cocktail, the third of the night, R. Kelly's "Step in the Name of Love" was playing. Instantly, a line dance broke out. "Come on, Charisma. Let's join in. It'll be fun." She bounced her shoulders in time to the beat and pulled Charisma by the arm.

Charisma gave in. "Okay. Why not?"

The impromptu dance troupe was four lines deep, with at least six tipsy guests in each line getting their boogie on. She and Vanessa wedged themselves into a spot in the front, between a guy who reeked of Brut cologne and a woman who sported a red bob wig. They both looked to be in their midsixties and were full of energy. But what was that smell? Charisma looked around and found the source of the odor. A woman in the second line had kicked her heels off, and her feet smelled like spoiled chicken.

R. Kelly's voice, blaring from the Bose sound system, was infectious. "Said I know that it's somebody's birthday tonight somewhere, and I know somebody's gonna celebrate tonight somewhere. . . ."

Once Charisma got past the god-awful odor of the Brut cologne and the rotten chicken, the situation with her and Roc began to fade to black in her mind. She stayed step for step with the line, actually

140

enjoying the moment. The moment was all that mattered.

The moment . . .

And at the moment, someone was shouting her name.

"Charisma!" It was Wanda. "These people need to see you!"

Charisma looked up. A man and a woman whom Charisma had never met were standing next to Wanda. The lady — probably in her thirties and wearing an expensive dress and heels — had her hands propped on her hips. And Charisma felt like she was side-eyeing her. The man was old enough to be the woman's father.

What was this about?

Charisma excused herself from the line dance, then eased her way through the crowd over to where Wanda and the two strangers were standing.

"My name is Jasmine Albright," the woman said once Charisma reached the little group. "And my husband's name is Jason." The confusion must've shown on Charisma's face. "You probably know him by Roc."

An "Oh shit" look was on Charisma's face now.

"And this is my lawyer." Jasmine Albright nodded at the older man next to her. "Jonathan Boatwright." She let her fingers do the talking in regard to the introductions, making sure she displayed the rock she was rocking on her wedding finger.

Jason Boatwright — a senior partner at the law firm of Boatwright, Walker, and Spencer — took the baton from there. "Ms. Bland, we have a nondisclosure contract from Mr. Jason 'Roc' Albright. It's in the amount of one million dollars." The lawyer handed Charisma a manila envelope. "All you have to do is have an immediate abortion at the specified clinic where we've set up an appointment for you and have a doctor waiting for you. And you must never mention the procedure, the pregnancy, or who the father may or may not be. Mr. Albright is a very well-respected man in the sports world, and the world in general, for that matter, and he would like to keep this . . . this foolish encounter out of the public spotlight." He spat the words out as if they left a bad taste in his mouth.

What Boatwright didn't mention was that if the scandal got out about Roc having a child with a mistress, and not with his wife, it would destroy his all-American, family-man image and cost him tens of millions of dollars in endorsements. So, in the scheme of things, the million dollars the Albrights

142

and their high-powered lawyer were offering was merely a drop in the bucket.

A little more than thirty minutes had passed since Roc banged the phone on her. She had given him a courtesy call only because she thought that it was the right thing to do. She had no intention of having Roc's baby. With this in mind, Charisma said, "I'll agree to those terms." Why not get paid a million dollars to do what she was already going to do? This was truly a blessing in disguise, she thought.

Wanda, who had been listening to the entire conversation from a spot a few feet away, said, "Let's be clear. You don't fucking waltz into our family's place of business on the day my father is buried and try to insult my cousin. Bitch, I don't know you or your cheating-ass husband, but you must be out of your fucking mind. My cousin doesn't have to do nothing she don't want to do." Wanda wasn't sure about all the details, but she was quick on her feet. And even more importantly, she had her cousin's back. "You think you can force her into having an abortion?" Wanda cut Jasmine with the same disgusting look that her high-powered lawyer had sliced Charisma with.

"Okay," Boatwright quickly interjected. "I see we have a greedy one. My client is

143

prepared to offer another half million to make it more worth your while. All we have to do is get your signature on the dotted line and we're out of here. Your appointment at the clinic is scheduled for tomorrow."

A few words from Wanda, and the offer had gone up by 50 percent. Everything was moving so fast, Charisma was having trouble thinking clearly.

Wanda spotted the indecision in her cousin's eyes and said, "Excuse us. Let me speak to Charisma privately for a moment." Wanda took Charisma's hand and led her to the office.

Once they were alone behind the closed door, Wanda said to Charisma, "You don't have to do this."

"But you don't understand."

"I don't need to. If you want to have your baby, then fuck them motherfuckers. We'll figure it out. I will help you. We're family. We don't let no bitch and tired-ass lawyer come in here, demanding how you going to live your life. Girl, I got your back. You do whatever it is that you want to do, not what these muthafuckers want you to do."

Finally, Wanda shut up.

"I appreciate everything you said, Wanda. It means a lot to me. But I had one night of amazing sex with this guy, and he never told me that he was married. And I'm not interested in having nobody's baby. I was going to have an abortion in the a.m., anyway. These people just made it a lot more enriching."

Vanessa barged into the office. "What the fuck do those two snobby assholes want with you, Charisma? I'm telling you, I'm 'bout to curse that ho out, coming around here, acting like she too uppity for our drinks."

"We got it under control," said Wanda.

Vanessa calmed down. "A'ight. But I'm one milliliter of a second from puttin' my foot up her ass."

Wanda told Charisma, "Big cousin got you. When we go back out there, just let me do all the talking."

Charisma agreed. "Thanks, Wanda."

They met back up with Jasmine and her lawyer at a back table that Vanessa had seated them at before coming into the office.

Wanda addressed Jasmine, ignoring the lawyer. "So you are offering one-point-five million dollars, huh?"

"Correct," Jasmine said through pursed lips.

Wanda got straight to the point. "Make it

two-point-two million and you have a deal."

"You greedy, opportunistic bitch!" Jasmine growled.

Wanda put a finger in her face, silencing her. "Watch yo' mouth in my place of business, lady. And let's not forget that your husband is the low-life, irresponsible one. Sticking his dick in places where it doesn't belong, sending you out the house with hush money, humiliating you. What does that say about you, bitch?"

Wanda and Jasmine stared dead into one another's eyes, neither woman backing down.

Seeing that the negotiations were going straight to hell, Boatwright intervened. "Two million," he said. "Not a penny more."

There was an "inflated bubble" silence.

Then Wanda stuck a pin in it. "Deal. We want half now and the other half the morning she gets on the table at your clinic."

Boatwright nodded and said, "Agreed. We have a deal."

Everyone shook hands. Then Jasmine sat there with her arms folded, sucking her teeth, trying not to lose her composure while Wanda, Charisma, and Boatwright went over the fine print of the contract.

Once all the paperwork was done, Wanda

looked Jasmine in the eye and said, "Now cut the check, bitch!"

CHAPTER 13
DINNER FOR ONE

Manny had reserved his usual private table in a secluded area near the back of the Miami restaurant. He was there to meet a couple of good friends — Raheem and Jamar — who were already seated when he arrived. Three humongous, vigilant bodyguards watched Manny's every move as he headed toward his table, making sure no potential troublemakers got too close. Manny was far from a punk, but professional athletes seemed to attract bad seeds looking for a few minutes of fame and a quick come-up.

Before copping a seat, Manny slapped hands with his two partners. He said to Raheem, "Nice game last night." Raheem Slaughter was the backup power forward for the Miami Heat. He and Manny went back like G.I. Joes with the Kung Fu Grip. They had both scraped by in the trenches of LA, where you were tested as soon as your lips left your mother's tit, if not sooner. They had held it down in the same junior high school. When Manny was in the eighth grade, Raheem was in the sixth. Both were standout star athletes who played everything. Football. Basketball. Baseball. And the honeys . . . Girls were their second priority, after sports.

Raheem thanked Manny for noticing. The pros hadn't been as easy for Raheem as high school and college had been. "I'm just happy to have got some burn." He'd dropped eight points and six rebounds against the Bulls in a home game, in seven minutes of playing time. "What about you, superstar?"

"You already know how I do. If it don't make dollars, it just don't make sense, playa."

"I know that's right," Jamar said. "Well, I'm glad we finally on the same coast again." Jamar had recently been traded to the Marlins from up north.

"Man, you know I wanna know if you hit that bitch or not," Manny told Jamar.

It was rumored that Jamar had slept with the wife of the starting pitcher from his previous team. But Jamar had said he wouldn't have fucked the ugly bitch even with Lucky's dick. Lucky was his 120-

pound rescue rottweiler.

"Hell naw, man. I only fuck with dimes."

Just then a waitress came to take their orders. She wore a tight black skirt, a snug white blouse, black kitten pumps, and a bright smile. "Are you guys going to be drinking anything tonight?"

Manny thought the smile alone was well worth the 30 percent gratuity that he customarily doled out for mediocre service. "We'll have a bottle of your best champagne," he said. "And as an appetizer, the biggest lobster you can find. With a bowl of cognac butter."

Raheem ordered sparkling water. He never drank alcohol during basketball season. Not even during his days in college.

Manny tapped Jamar on the leg to grab his attention on the low. "You peep that honey sitting over there by herself?"

"Who? The one that just stood up and is wearing the green jumpsuit?"

"I think I need to meet her," Manny mused.

Jamar did a double take. "She does have a boatload of sex appeal," he remarked as the lady in question walked by. It also didn't go unnoticed that she refrained from making eye contact with any of them as she passed by.

Manny watched how her lady humps wiggled and bounced underneath the delicate material of the romper she wore. He wasn't sure what it was, but there was something about this anonymous chick that made him want to get to know her better. Once she was out of sight, he turned back to his boys. At that moment the waitress returned with a chilled bottle of Ace of Spades and a bottle of sparkling water for Raheem.

She said to the group, "Your lobster will be here shortly. Have you decided what else you'll be having?"

They couldn't make up their minds, so they ordered a little of everything.

"My treat," Manny magnanimously announced.

Moments later the chick in the emerald-green jumpsuit returned from the restroom. Manny's eyes were glued to her body as she glided across the hardwood floor to her table. Once she sat down, Manny glanced over in the direction of one of his trusted bodyguards. Big Dre lumbered over to his employer.

"You need something, boss?"

"Yeah, big fella. Go ask the young lady if she would like to join us for dinner."

"Say no more." Big Dre tromped over to

the woman's table. She sat alone, eating roasted salmon with lemon.

Charisma used one hand to sip from a glass of red wine while she texted her cousin Wanda with the other. Since she was dining alone, Charisma kept thinking that relocating to a city where she had no friends and family might not have been such a great idea, after all.

Wanda: Did you get out of the house?

Charisma: Yes! At the restaurant now. How are things at the bar?

Wanda: SMH. Great. But didn't I tell you not to worry about the bar?

Charisma: LOL. I know, cousin. But old habits are hard to break. J

Wanda: You have to mingle.

Charisma knew that she really did need to stop thinking about the bar so much and concentrate more on the book she wanted to write. As she was contemplating this, her phone chirped. She had an incoming call. The number was one that she didn't recognize.

"Hello?"

A recording on the other end said, "This is a collect call from . . . *Chucky.*" Then the automated voice gave her instructions: "If you want to accept this call, push zero. To refuse this call, push one."

"Hey, Chucky."

"Damn. You sound good, girl. How have you been doing?"

Charisma had to admit that he sounded good too. She and Chucky had been friends for a long time, almost her entire life. And she'd forgotten how much she missed having him around. If it weren't for Chucky, she probably wouldn't even be alive. "I'm glad you called. I never got to let you hear me say, 'Thank you for the flowers you sent to my uncle's funeral.' "

"Well, I never got a chance to thank you for the money." Since the day Chucky was arrested, Charisma had put fifty dollars on his books each and every week. And when she got her big payoff, she'd put aside a nice piece of money for him so that he would be okay when he came home. "Even after the bullshit I put you through in the visiting room with Donna, you still fuck with your boy."

Charisma and Chucky might not have spoken to each other since Charisma was escorted from the jail that day, but in her heart, they had never stopped being friends. As far as Charisma was concerned, that was something that would never change. "That's what friends are for," she reminded him.

"But I know you didn't call me to remind me about that trick Donna. I'm just saying."

Chucky's laugh was contagious. "She's history. I got a new friend, though. Well, she's not exactly new. You remember Tina Brooks, don't you?"

"Big-booty Tina from Division Street? Doesn't she have a boyfriend?"

"Yeah, that's her. And no, she doesn't have a dude. Not anymore."

"I like Tina." That was kind of true. "And if you're happy, I'm happy for you."

"You know me, Charisma. I just go with the flow."

She did know him. Chucky was the type of dude that could take it or leave it. He never sweated anything. Big or small. Not even killing two people and going to prison for a friend. That was the type of guy he was.

"Well, I got a li'l something for you when you get home, so you can be good . . . so you don't have to get out and do anything crazy to get money."

"You ain't have to do that."

"Yeah, well, you know, if I'm good . . . you're good." That was the way she rolled.

"You don't have to do it," he said, "but I appreciate it. More than you know."

154

Charisma could feel his smile through the phone, prompting her to glow. They kicked it for a few more minutes before their time was up and the call was promptly disconnected. The last thing Chucky said was that he "missed her smile." Not his freedom. Not his favorite food. But her smile, and that made her smile even more.

A few seconds later, a huge dark-skinned dude headed toward her table. Charisma gave him the side eye. Her expression said, "I don't want to be bothered! Get away," but he ignored her telepathic stop sign and proceeded to blow the light.

"Can I help you?" she asked once he reached the table.

"Good evening, miss . . ."

"Charisma," she said. "My name is Charisma." She didn't have time for strangers who were trying to hit on her, so she added, "And I'm married."

The black Hulk Hogan glanced at her empty ring finger and disregarded her last remark. "I came over here because my friend Manny Manifesto" — he pointed to a guy at a table near the back of the restaurant — "would like for you to come over and dine with him."

The man whom the giant had identified as Manny waved when he saw her look in

155

his direction.

"I know damn well your boy didn't send you here to do his talking for him. Where they do that at?" Charisma said, casting hella shade.

"Listen . . . It's Charisma, right? Don't shoot the messenger. Manny Manifesto is my boss, and he asked me to offer you his invitation to dine with him and his friends." Hulk Hogan seemed contrite about bothering her, but he was also hell-bent on carrying out his boss's command.

"You keep dropping his entire name like it should mean something. Who is Manny Manifesto? Is he from Baltimore?"

Hulk Hogan acted surprised by her questions. He smiled. "Manny's the shortstop for the Marlins."

Charisma cut her eyes over to where Manny was sitting with his two friends. She had to admit, he was kind of cute. Manny was light skinned and had curly coal-black hair, the prettiest white teeth, and a smile that lit up the entire restaurant.

She asked, "Is he mute or something?"

Hulk Hogan's eyebrows — which looked like two bushy caterpillars — crawled closer together. "A what?"

Charisma rolled her eyes. "Is he incapable

of speech? Or are you paid to do all his bidding?"

"Hold up, shorty! You don't gotta get all crazy. Hell naw. My man ain't no mute or no dumb-ass jock. He's a college graduate and a businessman."

"I'm glad that you think so highly of Mr. Manifesto. But if he wants to talk to me, he can come over and do it himself. Tell Mr. Manny Manifesto that I don't bite on Saturdays, unless I'm provoked."

Big Dre flashed two rolls of pearly whites before lumbering back toward his employer. He'd never seen a chick act that way once he told them who Manny was.

Manny hunched his shoulders, eyeing Big Dre. "So . . . ?"

Big Dre said, "Her name is Charisma. And she said that if you want to say something to her, then you gotta get up and do it yourself."

Manny cut his eyes back toward Charisma. She was obviously playing hard to get. "Did you tell her who I am?"

"Of course," Big Dre said. "But she acted like she'd never heard of you."

Manny managed a tight laugh. "Are you serious, man?"

"As cancer, boss. She wants you to come holla at her yourself."

"That ain't going to happen," Manny replied, looking at Jamar and Raheem. He was an all-star Major League Baseball player with more endorsement deals than a junkie had excuses to quit using. Shit! He had a reputation to uphold.

Jamar cut a bite-size square from his filet mignon and put it in his mouth. "Fuck that, chick," he said through a mouthful of the best-tasting Kobe steak he'd had in a while. "Women are like busses. . . . There's another one — two, three, or four — every fifteen minutes, bruh. Especially in Miami."

Raheem shoveled a forkful of the jumbo crab cake in his mouth and nodded. Manny wasn't sure if his boy was agreeing with Jamar's bullshit or liked the flavor of the shellfish. Either way, he'd already forgot whatever it was he was talking to Big Dre about.

"How 'bout that ass whipping Mayweather put on that boy Pacquiao the other night?" Jamar said to change the subject. He knew how his boy felt about rejection.

Raheem looked indifferent. "If that's what you want to call it. That shit wasn't much of a fight to me."

Jamar put his fork down. "Hold up, bruh. Money is pound for pound the best boxing technician in the world. Flat-out."

Raheem had heard it all before. "If I wanted to see a technician, I would've called the cable man and watched him add more bandwidth to my Wi-Fi. I wanted to see a fight. That shit was some bullshit."

Because he and Floyd Mayweather were boys, Manny was biased on the subject, but he tried to keep it real. "You know what you going to get when you watch a Money fight. Cats watch because they believe the next muthafucka is going to be the one to shut his mouth. But it never happens. Forty-nine to zero. That's undeniable."

"Like I said," Jamar cosigned, "pound for pound that nigga Money Mayweather is the best to ever do it. Flat-out."

"That's some blasphemous shit right there," Raheem said. "So you trying to say that Money is a better fighter than Muhammad Ali in his prime? Muhammad Ali? People be acting like they forgot about my dude Muhammad." Raheem hadn't yet been born when Ali last stepped into the ring, but he'd watched all the old footage on YouTube.

"He got you there," Manny said to Jamar.

"I give 'im that," Jamar retorted. "No question about it. Muhammad was the god-father of the ring. Straight warrior. But

Money is God with the gloves, yo. Flat-out. God!"

Raheem shook his head. What else was there to say? Jamar had obviously been hit in the dome with one too many fastballs, he thought.

Manny echoed Raheem's thoughts. "You done jumped slam off the cliff with that one. Money is a bad dude, but he ain't nobody's God, my dude."

Realizing how crazy he sounded, Jamar tried to back it up a little. "I meant a boxing god, that's all."

"Whatever," Manny mumbled.

They all cracked up, even Jamar. As the evening progressed, the debates continued, with the topic flipping several times throughout the meal.

When it was over, Manny ate the check, giving the waitress one of his Black Cards. He said, "Give yourself a thirty percent tip." Then he winked. The bill was $5,235.17.

Raheem offered to pay the next time. Jamar, a natural cheapskate, stuffed his paws in his pockets and kept his mouth shut for the first time all night. Manny knew that neither of them was making the type of bread he was taking down.

"Don't worry about it," he said. "It's only money."

They left the restaurant together. Outside, it was a dark, starless night. And Mother Nature was dropping rain on the city, as if she was trying to extinguish a five-alarm fire. Valet attendants hustled to get their cars. Manny overheard a woman asking one of the attendants if she could borrow an umbrella. Apparently, she'd parked around the corner. The valet attendant was un-moved.

"Sorry, miss. These umbrellas are only for our valet customers."

When he looked closer, Manny saw that the woman was the same chick whom he had wanted to have dinner with. "Excuse me," he said. "I'll be happy to give you a ride to your car."

Charisma looked up. After the giant bodyguard had left her table, for shits and giggles, she had called her cousin Marcus and had asked him if he had ever heard of Manny Manifesto. Marcus had acted as if he was one of Manny's biggest fans. So she had Googled Manny, and then she had secretly wished that she'd taken Wanda's advice to be nice and mingle. But Charisma wasn't about to bow down now because Manny had one of the most lucrative base-ball contracts in history. No vapor catching for her.

With a slight smile, Charisma refused his generous invitation. "I don't eat or ride with strangers," she said with a little too much pride. She'd just wait until the rain slowed down, she thought.

When one of the valet attendants pulled up with Manny's Car, Manny offered the attendant one hundred dollars for his umbrella.

"It's yours," said the attendant.

I bet it is, Manny thought. The umbrella was a ten-dollar piece of crap. "Do me a favor. Give it to the lady over there." He pointed to Charisma. "But don't tell her that I gave it to her." Manny figured if she knew that it came from him, she might not accept it.

The valet guy said, "No problem."

Charisma was suspicious about the valet's sudden act of chivalry, but she accepted the little umbrella all the same. It was one of the little, flimsy fold-up ones, but it was better than nothing. "Thank you," she said. "I'll bring it back once I reach my car."

"That won't be necessary," the attendant said. "I have another. You can have it." A gust of wind blew through, almost ripping the umbrella from her hand. "You might want to hold on to it a little tighter," the attendant called out before going to retrieve

162

another car.

The rain came down in buckets. Charisma cursed herself for not paying to have her car valeted, then took one last deep breath as she prepared herself to trudge through the awful weather. The wind pushed at her face, making it difficult to walk. But she held the umbrella with both hands and pressed on. After all, she was from Baltimore; she'd walked through three-plus feet of snow before.

As if Mother Nature had read her thoughts and rose to the challenge, a strong gust of wind came from Charisma's left side and snatched the umbrella from her grip. The umbrella flew into the air and down the block like a runaway kite. A bolt of lightning lit up the sky and was so close, she could almost feel the heat. A second later came an earsplitting clap of thunder. Shit was getting real. Her car was still a two-and-a-half-block hike away. Right at that moment a powder-blue Rolls-Royce pulled up beside her. The windows were tinted, so she couldn't see inside. The back passenger glass glided down, giving her a view of the car's interior.

A man's friendly voice said, "That offer of a ride is still on the table." It was Mr. Manny Manifesto, and he was sitting in the backseat. "I know you said that you didn't ride with strangers, but I feel like I've known you for forever. This is our third encounter." The Rolls's back passenger door opened. He assured her, "I promise to be on my best behavior."

In no position to look a gift horse in the mouth, Charisma was forced to reconsider. She acquiesced. And climbed into the back of the Rolls.

She was soaked.

Manny offered her a silk handkerchief. "My name is —"

"Manny Manifesto. I know." Hulk Hogan, the guy Manny had sent over to her table to fetch her, was driving the car. She said, "I'm —

"Charisma," Manny said, finishing her sentence for her. They both chuckled. "Where are you parked, Charisma? That, I'm afraid, I don't know."

Charisma said, "Make a right down here at the corner."

Manny passed the directions on to Big Dre.

Charisma asked, "Do you always pick up strange women?"

"Only on Saturdays. And only during the off-season," Manny said with a slight laugh.

Charisma, trying not to blush, thought

that his laugh was nice . . . and sincere. Could this man possibly be a wealthy ballplayer who wasn't an asshole?

"What about you?" he asked.

"What *about* me?"

"Do you always eat out alone?"

"Say what you really mean."

Manny raised an eyebrow.

"You really want to ask if I always act like a bitch toward strangers. Admit it," she explained.

"Do you? Or do you think I'm a special type of stranger?"

Oh, you're special, all right.

CHAPTER 14
FRESH START

American Airlines Arena . . .

"You sure you want to be in a place this public on our first date?" Charisma asked.

It was the last game of the regular season. The play-offs were right around the corner. The Heat was a number one seed going in, win or lose. Their seats were amazing. If they were any closer to the action, they'd have to check into the game.

Manny looked directly into Charisma's oval hazel eyes. "Besides wanting to be a Major League Baseball player, I'm as sure as I've ever been about anything."

Ever since he'd given her a ride to her car, Charisma and Manny had talked on the phone, texted, or had face time every morning, noon, and night. Sometimes the conversations rolled on for hours. Day or night, it didn't matter. They had kicked it about everything under the sun — favorite foods and colors, likes and dislikes, dreams and aspirations. They had even reminisced about their favorite childhood pets. Manny's was a red-nose pit bull named Reggie Jackson. And Charisma had cherished a fish named Wanda. Her cousin Wanda hated that fish.

In the brief time she'd known him, she'd opened up her life to Manny. The only things she had kept to herself were the one-night stand with Roc, the abortion, and the hush money. She'd buried those bones deep down in a dark place, vowing never to let them see the light of day again. As her uncle used to say, "Some things are meant to take to the grave." She'd told Manny, and everybody else who wanted to know, that her sudden riches had come from her uncle's life insurance. No one needed to know any different.

Manny put his hand on her knee. "I also wanted to support my homeboy," he said. "He's starting tonight. I hope you don't mind me having ulterior motives."

She blushed. "I would be upset if you didn't have ulterior motives." Charisma knew that Manny and Raheem were close. And she liked basketball, so it was all good.

The game was amazing, and so was the vibe in the arena and the chemistry between the two of them. They held hands for most of the night. When the game was over, they went onto the floor to congratulate Raheem. He'd scored twenty points, with ten rebounds.

Manny gave his boy dap. "You did yo' thing tonight."

Raheem was sweaty and was still breathing heavily. He said, "We're having a party at LIV, the nightclub at the Fontainebleau Hotel. You coming through, aren't you?"

Manny looked at Charisma for approval.

"If my baby feels like it, then we coming through." Charisma smiled. That was good enough for him.

"For sure," Manny said. "We'll be there."

By Miami standards, they arrived at the club early — around 1:30 a.m. — with plans to roll out before it got too late, or too early in the morning, depending on one's perspective.

Walking past the organized mob of people in the lobby of the Fontainebleau Hotel, through the velvet ropes, and straight through the entrance doors to the hottest party on this Sunday in the entire country — while on the arm of one of the highest-paid athletes in the world — felt damn good. LIV was in full-blown party mode. Confetti fell from the ceiling, landing on the crowd of beautiful people who were partying to the intoxicating music. It was everything she had never dreamed of. Charisma tried not to come off like it was her first time partying like a rock star, which it was.

"Here, babe." Manny handed her a glass of champagne. He put his mouth close to her ear and gave a toast. "To us, baby!" They bumped glasses.

"This place is off the meds!" Charisma exclaimed after being inside for a short time.

And it only got crazier as the night progressed. Manny knew all the athletes on a first-name basis, and most of the celebrities as well, it seemed. A who's who of famous people stopped by their table. And champagne flowed like groupies at a rock concert. Manny was a great host. He introduced her to everyone. He didn't even get upset at the throngs of people asking for a selfie.

"Is that Ice Cube over there, sitting with Kevin Hart?" Charisma was beginning to feel like a groupie herself. "Are they as funny in person as they are in their movies?"

Of course, Manny was cool with them both. "Funnier," he said. "But no one in the world is as funny as Kevin. You'll see." Manny must've been prophetic, because no sooner had he said this than Kevin came over and cracked on his shoes.

"What the fuck you doing with purple alligators, man? Tell the truth. You got them muthafuckas from Prince's house, didn't you? Those muthafuckas are from Prince's *Purple Rain* collection. Whew-ewww! I bet you got that bitch Apollonia's number while you were there, too. I know you got the digits. You know how I know you got the digits? I'll tell you how I know. Because you're a pussy purveyor who collects old pussy. That's how I know. I bet you got old, vintage pussy stowed away in your closet and shit. Pussy that should be in a museum, for the world to see, and you got that shit locked up in your closet. . . ."

Manny took the ribbing like a champ, allowing Kevin to finish his monologue before he, Manny, introduced Charisma.

Charisma shook his hand. "Nice to meet you," she said.

Kevin looked at Charisma, Manny, and then back at Charisma. "The pleasure is mine. You fine as shit, girl. You know I was joking about his closet, right? He don't really keep museum pussy in his closet." Kevin then brought his mouth so close to Charisma's ear, she could feel his breath. He whispered, "Not anymore," and then he winked.

Raheem showed up around 2:00 a.m.,

wearing Robin's jeans and Louis Vuitton sneakers, drinking Welch's grape juice. "Glad you came," he told Manny and Charisma. He and Manny did that man hug thing. "You guys enjoying yourselves?"

Charisma couldn't stop smiling. "We're having a blast." She was nodding her head to Rihanna's "Bitch Better Have My Money." And, of course, RiRi was also in the club, partying.

Raheem said, "Good." He did a little two-step, drank a sip of his juice. "I can't wait until we win it all, so that I can really get turned up. I have to keep it simple during the season." He held up his cup. "No alcohol."

Later Charisma and Manny danced to Chris Brown, on the floor with Chris Brown. Rick Ross performed live, along with members of his label. When they were done, the crew popped bottles like they were in the winning locker room of the World Series.

At three in the morning everything was still in full bloom, with no signs of slowing down.

Charisma came clean. "I've never partied at this level," she said.

"This is nothing," Manny assured her.

"The parties after the club are when it gets crunk."

"No way."

"Way."

"Well, this is more than enough *crunk* for me."

"You sure? Because I got several invites — Chris Brown, Rick Ross, DJ Khaled. Khaled always throws a good party," he said.

It sounded good, but Charisma was past her limit for one night. "Maybe the next time," she said.

Focusing on the "next time" part, Manny said, "I'm going to hold you to that, you know?"

Charisma couldn't wait. For the first time since she arrived in Miami, she hadn't thought about Baltimore, the bar, or her cousins for one moment.

"I have to use the little girls' room," she announced. She had to dispose of some of that champagne she'd drunk before she had an accident.

"You want me to walk with you?"

The man was so thoughtful. She'd never had a guy offer to walk her to the restroom before. Unless he was trying to do the dirty in the stall. Which wasn't happening.

"Thanks. But I'm a big girl."

"You certainly are that," Manny quickly

quipped and grabbed her hand. He said something to Big Dre. Then the bodyguard began to part the crowd with his huge girth, providing them a clear path to the ladies' restroom.

The restroom was packed with chicks who were checking their makeup and comparing notes. Charisma took care of her business, washed her hands, and was on her way out the door when her phone vibrated. She'd been ignoring the incoming calls the entire night. She didn't recognize the number but answered the call, anyway. People changed numbers so often nowadays, it could be anybody.

"Hello?"

"Charisma?" She could barely hear over the music but made out that it was a man's voice.

"Who is this?"

The man on the other end said, "If I can't have you, then nobody can." He was whispering, but Charisma was sure that she recognized the voice.

"Roc? Is that you?"

He repeated that same creepy shit. "If I can't have you, nobody can."

Charisma wished she'd never answered the phone.

Click!

After hanging up, she blocked the number, her heart beating a little faster than it had before she received the call. *Calm down, girl. You're going to be all right,* she told herself, hoping it wasn't a lie.

When she stepped out of the restroom, Manny quickly picked up on the change in her vibe. "You all right? What's wrong?" he asked.

"Nothing," Charisma lied. She grabbed another glass of champagne from a server walking by with a loaded tray and downed the contents. "But I'm ready to leave whenever you are."

Manny didn't press her. Instead, he said, "Okay. Cool. Whatever you want."

On their way out of the club, a white guy pressed up on them. "You're Manny Manifesto, aren't you?" he said. "I don't mean to come off like a lame, but you're my favorite ballplayer, man. Can I get an autograph?"

Dude is old school, Manny thought. Most cats today asked for selfies. Autographs were a relic of the past. Unless they were memorabilia. But Manny, always cordial with the fans, said, "Sure. I think I have a napkin or something in my pocket."

The fan whipped out a baseball card. It was from Manny's rookie season. "You can sign this," he said, cheesing.

Manny was impressed. His rookie card was almost impossible to come by. "You prepared, huh?" Manny scribbled his signature across the rare card. "You must've been a Boy Scout back in the day."

The fan said, "Thanks. And one more thing."

"What's that?" Manny asked. Dude was pressing his luck now. That was the problem with being nice to people. You gave an inch, they shot for a mile.

"I just want to give you this." He handed Manny a manila envelope. "You've been served." And then he walked off as photographers and paparazzi popped pics.

"Sneaky son of a bitch!"

Manny ripped open the envelope, pulled out a letter, and read it.

The state of California hereby summons you to court to settle a dispute over child support with Ms. Bing Foo for one baby, Star Foo, in the amount of $150,000.00 per month.

Manny was outdone, but he didn't let it show on his face. However, once he was inside the car, away from the cameras, Manny mumbled to himself, "That petty, greedy, worthless bitch!"

CHAPTER 15
REALITY CHECK

Los Angeles, California . . .

Bing woke up feeling as if she was on top of the world, and to celebrate, she danced and sang, doing her best Rihanna imitation. "Bitch better have my money. Y'all should know me well enough. Bitch better have my money. . . ." She sang and danced her way into the kitchen. "Pay me what you owe me! Ballin' bigger than LeBron . . ." There she found her mother warming milk for the baby.

Her mother asked, "How come you're so happy this morning? You haven't been up this early since high school." Mei Foo's English was excellent, almost as good as her daughter's. "I haven't seen you this jubilant since . . ." Mei swallowed her words. Bing was her only child, and no decent mother ever wanted to see her child in pain. A couple of beats passed before she spat out, "Since before Manny abandoned you and the baby."

Mei was right. Bing had been in a funk ever since Manny had treated her like a used-up whore and dumped her. She had thought that he would come around once he found out that she was pregnant with his baby. But he hadn't. Instead, he had acted like a dick, offering her some crackhead means of support while she was pregnant and couldn't work. Actually, Bing had never worked a real job a day in her life. And if she could help it, she never would.

Once Manny found out she was pregnant, there wasn't much conversation between the two of them. It went without saying, he would provide everything his child needed, and he'd already gone far beyond what was required when it came to the preparations for the nursery, purchasing all the latest gadgets and the very best of the best. He'd also set up what Bing considered a small monthly allowance for her. Any other expectant mother would have been elated at how Manny had laid everything out, but not Bing. It just wasn't enough. Nothing was ever enough. That always seemed to be the problem with Bing.

She was convinced that when the press found out about their child together, he would definitely turn things around with her, since he wanted to maintain his image. He would marry her for sure. That was why yesterday morning, before having Manny served, she'd leaked the paperwork to TMZ. Bing knew that within forty-eight hours, all the major media outlets would jump on the story. And drag Manny through the mud, like the dirty pig he was. Two could play at this game.

She pirouetted in the middle of the kitchen and continued to sing. "Bitch, give me your money. Who y'all think y'all frontin' on?" The baby just laughed and farted, while her mother just looked confused. Bing danced out of the kitchen and over to the coffee table in the family room. She picked up the remote, then clicked on the TV to watch the morning news.

Damn right, she was happy. And once she began getting that child support paper, she would be a whole lot happier. Believe that. Nothing in the world made her feel better than spending money. Nothing — not sex or food, not even family. She looked over at her mom and silently apologized for her thoughts. But she couldn't help herself. Money was the only thing that made her happy.

Sorry, Mom. Just being honest.

When she found nothing on the TV about

her and Manny, Bing sat down on the couch, grabbed her iPad from the coffee table, and powered it up. The tablet yawned to life.

Bingo.

It didn't taken long to find what she was searching for. All the sports and gossip blogs were buzzing like a hive of hungry wasps about the Manny Manifesto news. Everyone had an opinion. Bing read it all. She was really taken aback by what Media Take Out had to say.

Manny Manifesto, Marlins star shortstop, is being sued by his ex, Bing Foo, for $150,000 in monthly child support payments. I'm sure it won't hurt his bottom line. The man just signed a two-hundred-fifty-million-dollar contract. And let's just be real. That girl he was out with last night was drop-dead gorgeous. Video vixen Bing Foo may need to visit another plastic surgeon if she wants to compete with that. And we're told that this other chick is 100 percent natural. How refreshing. Real is making a comeback.

"Bitch!" Bing yelled.

That's why I never liked Media Take Out. They're a bunch of gossiping haters. Fuck them.

She went to another site, Baller Alert, but the post was no better.

179

It's a Girl!

Star shortstop Manny Manifesto knocked up his ex Bing Foo. She alleges that Manny's a deadbeat dad. Manny was photographed last night at LIV with a new boo. And by the looks of her, if I were Bing, I would be worried. That chick is fine.

The next site she visited, TMZ Sports, was even worse, owing to its pictures of Manny and Charisma hugged up at LIV.

Manny Manifesto Really Does Have Game!

Manny has more on his mind than his gold-digging ex Bing Foo and their alleged new baby girl. He's got a gorgeous new mystery woman on his arm and an even better game. Congrats, Manny!

Who the fuck is this mystery woman? Bing wondered. She shrugged and continued on to the next site. ESPN offered her a little bit of solace.

Manny Manifesto may or may not be trying to step up to the plate. But is it a surprise that another star athlete has a baby out of wedlock?

But the Shade Room took that solace away.

Gold-Digging Karma.

Isn't Bing Foo the same chick who says a broke man can't do anything for her? Well, it looks like her alleged baby daddy, Manny

Manifesto, isn't trying to do anything for her, either. She's begging for money already, and her baby is not even two weeks old yet. Karma is a bitch. And, according to sources, so is Bing Foo.

"Bitch! What the fuck?" Bing was pissed beyond pissivity.

Mei called out from the kitchen, "What did you say, dear?"

"Nothing, Mom. Just thinking out loud, that's all." Bing's attention went back to the photo of Manny all hugged up with his Tuesday bitch. That was what Bing called random chicks whom guys slept around with on the low. She ignored the fact that the photo had been taken on a Sunday night at the hottest club in Miami. And Bing had to admit that the girl was attractive, but she wasn't all that.

And she damn sure is no me.

Mei walked into the family room with Star and a baby bottle in her arms and sat on the opposite end of the couch from her daughter. After making herself comfortable, she fed the bottle to Star. "You know you really should be breast-feeding."

That was the last thing that Bing wanted to hear. She wasn't concerned about her motherly duties. "Ma, please don't start. She won't connect to my breast."

"Well, you have to cuddle her and keep trying."

"Yeah, I hear you," she mumbled, shooing her mother away from the topic. "We not talking about this. I got bigger shit on my mind than this."

"Talk to me, baby."

"It's just Manny. I had him served child support papers, and I haven't heard from him. Instead, he's running around Miami with some chick."

Mei was quiet for a minute. She chose her words carefully when she did finally speak. "Well, baby, I don't like to say I told you so, but I told you, you had to be smart about this. And not evil spirited. Let's pray that he comes around."

Bing took a deep breath and gazed back at the picture of Manny and the new girl smiling on the iPad screen. "Look, Ma, no disrespect, but the only thing I'm going to pray for is the fire to fight him with."

CHAPTER 16
GOOD MORNING, BEAUTIFUL

Las Olas Boulevard, Fort Lauderdale . . .
A cell phone rang.

The unwelcome ring reached into her bed, shaking her awake from a wet tropical dream on the beach.

Ringgg! Ringgg! Ringgg!

Charisma took a peek at the clock: 1:07 p.m. Judging by the ringtone, she ascertained that it was the doorman downstairs. Since it wasn't a fire alarm, she would call the doorman later.

After leaving LIV, she and Manny had gone out for breakfast. When she'd finally made home, it was somewhere north of six o'clock in the morning. Now Charisma pulled the sheets over her head, ignoring the obvious conspiracy to deprive her of her beauty rest. The call eventually got transferred to voice mail, and Charisma tried to slip back into the dream she was having before the interruption. Maybe if she slid down the right rabbit hole, she'd find that exact picturesque spot on the white sand, the one next to that forty-foot waterfall.

But instead of hearing the cascading seawater beat against the jagged rocks, she was jarred back to reality by the screaming cell phone.

Ringgg!

I might as well answer it, she thought.

"Hello . . ."

"Hey, beautiful!"

It was Manny. The sound of his voice did something to her. It made her glad to be alive.

"Hi, handsome."

"Listen," he said, "I apologized for what I've got you into." He sounded genuinely contrite about something. What, Charisma had no idea. She was confused.

"You have nothing to apologize for. I had one of the best times of my life last night. Except for this headache I have, last night was the best time I ever had."

"I'm talking about the child support papers by my ex. And all the attention you're getting in the press. But I did tell you in advance that my ex was crazy. I have no secrets, Charisma."

"You did." Charisma didn't really think it was a big deal. A girl had to do what a girl had to do. And obviously, Manny's ex wanted what she thought she deserved. And, Charisma mused, if she could get paid two million dollars *not* to have a baby, who was she to tell another woman that they shouldn't get paid for having one. "But what does that have to do with me . . . and the press?" she asked.

"I take it that you haven't been on the Internet today."

"I haven't been out of the bed. Why? Is there something that I should know about?"

"I've already sent flowers in advance. They should be there shortly. And I want to apologize for putting you under the spotlight."

"I love flowers!"

"I won't forget that."

"But what do you mean about being 'put under the spotlight'?

"I live in a fishbowl, Charisma. Unfortunately, it comes with the job. The cost of being famous. Nothing is off limits," he said, "including my personal life."

Charisma was already reaching for her iPad so that she could scan the gossip blogs while Manny apologized for being rich.

"It can't be that bad," she said.

"Which?" he asked. "Being famous or what the press is saying?"

185

Charisma laughed. "Both."

"As far as being famous, like anything else, it has its ups and downs. But the ups far outweigh the downs. And as for the latest headlines, you tell me."

"I'm reading some of it now. Mystery girl, huh? They think I'm pretty too."

"The tabloids and blogs aren't the only ones that think you're beautiful."

She was blushing. "Compliments will get you everywhere."

"That's good to know, because there's lots of places I want to take you," he said. "But right now I have to go. I have to attend this meeting with my agent. I'll call you back later, okay? Enjoy the flowers."

"Okay, sure. Take care."

The doorman called again as she was hanging up with Manny. He alerted her that he was escorting up a delivery person.

"We know you are still kind of new to the building, and under normal circumstances, we wouldn't let him up. We'd just accept your package and deliver it to you. However, these are not normal circumstances," he said.

Whatever that meant. She didn't ask; she just agreed and threw on a housecoat and hurried to the door. When she looked through the peephole, she saw the doorman.

She opened the door.

The doorman greeted her, motioned to the delivery guy behind him, and then headed back to the elevator, eager to return to his post.

"Ms. Charisma Bland?" The delivery guy wore a uniform with a name tag that read STANLEY.

And the hallway was filled with roses of every imaginable color.

"Yep. That's me." The smell of the budding beauties was intoxicating.

Stanley asked, "Where do you want me to put them?"

"Anywhere you can."

When Stanley was done unloading his delivery, bouquets of roses took up every unoccupied space in her living room, and then some.

"I'm going to need for you to sign here." Stanley handed her a proof of receipt form and a pen. Charisma scribbled her name along the bottom. "That'll do it." Then he gave her a hard stare, as if he'd just remembered something. "I know it's none of my business, but aren't you the girl that's in the photo with Manny Manifesto that's being talked about everywhere?"

This was getting strange. And she was wearing a big housecoat, with a silk Louis

Vuitton scarf wrapped around her head. So she had no idea how the man had recognized her.

And if you know that it's none of your business, then why ask? she thought.

"I'm afraid so," she said, feeling a little uncomfortable.

"Well," Stanley said, "Manny has very good taste."

"Thank you."

She showed him to the door. After he left, she closed the door and locked it behind him. Afterward, she inhaled. The house smelled and looked like an exhibit at a botanical gardens. She was searching for a card that came with the flowers when the doorman rang again. What was it now? She wasn't expecting anyone.

"Another delivery for you, Ms. Bland."

Another delivery?

"You can just send him up this time."

A few minutes later Charisma looked through the peephole. There was another flower guy in the hallway, but this one wore khakis.

"Are you sure it's for me?" she asked through the door.

"Are you Ms. Charisma Bland, seventeen hundred Las Olas Boulevard, thirty-three B?"

Charisma opened the door.

The delivery guy's eyes doubled in size when he saw the army of roses that stood sentry around the living room. "Is it your birthday?"

"Not for another couple of months," Charisma said.

The new delivery guy handed her a crystal vase filled with a dozen of the most beautiful sunflowers she'd ever seen. Sunflowers were her all-time favorite.

After the delivery guy left, she searched for a card. When she found one, she plucked it and immediately read the message. It was simple and thoughtful.

I hope you enjoy the sunflowers as much as I enjoyed being with you last night.

Manny

Charisma's eyes surveyed the living room of her new condo. It was teeming with fresh flowers. It felt like something she'd witnessed in a romance movie or read in a fairy tale —

Hold up.

Wait just a minute.

Something wasn't right.

If Manny sent the sunflowers, then who in

the hell sent all those roses?

She searched for a card among the roses. As she searched each of the vases, Charisma began to feel more and more uneasy. She couldn't find the damn card anywhere. Maybe she should call Manny and just ask him if he sent the roses too. But what if he said, "What roses?" What would she say then?

No, she thought. *That isn't a good idea.* It wasn't good to tell lies, because they always somehow found a way to come back and bite you in the ass.

She thought she might have spotted it.

On the floor, in the corner, stood the biggest vase of them all. The crystal vase was packed with long-stemmed hybrid tea roses. They were all bloodred and in full bloom. Charisma plucked the card from the bouquet, pricking her finger on a sharp thorn. Blood trickled from the puncture. Charisma licked the small wound and read the card.

If I can't have you, then no one can.

The phone rang.

Ringgg!

Her cell phone was in the bedroom. She hurried to the room to grab it before it stopped ringing. It was probably Wanda.

They hadn't spoken since last night. They'd only exchanged a couple of brief texts. But Charisma knew that it wasn't her cousin calling when she read the caller ID.

Private.

"Hello?"

"Did you get my message?"

Roc.

Aw, hell naw!

CHAPTER 17
FLOWERS & MORE FLOWERS

Charisma banged the phone before Roc could utter another disgusting syllable. Then she called her cell phone service provider and changed her number. She had had that number for seven years, but it had to go. Once she was done with the phone company and had a fresh new number, she e-mailed it to a few friends and family. Then she called Manny.

"Hi. It's me. Charisma." Before he could ask, she said, "I changed my number, so please lock it in."

"I just tried to call you. Don't tell me the paparazzi are already calling you for comments? They can be such a pain in the ass. I'm sorry about all this."

Charisma chuckled. "No, not yet," she said. "I've just been meaning to let the old number go since I have left my old life behind. You know . . . a fresh start." She hated lying to Manny. But she had been paid two million dollars to play a certain role. So she stayed in character. That was the way she rationalized lying. It was easier to deal with the deception that way.

Manny asked, "Did you get the picture I sent you?"

"Let me look. . . ." She navigated through her phone messages. She smiled when she saw the picture of a pair of Chanel sunglasses and a box of Tylenol. The caption read *Just what the doctor ordered.* "Thank you so much."

"You are very welcome," he said. "I was thinking that I should be over in about an hour. I'll have the glasses for you when I come. Maybe we can catch a movie. Or if you don't want to go out — I know last night was a lot to take in — maybe we can just chill inside and watch a movie. It's whatever you want to do, baby. I just want to spend some quality time with you."

"Sounds good to me," she said.

"So," he asked, "is an hour enough time for you to be ready?"

"An hour will be great."

She hung up the phone as butterflies danced around in her stomach. It was hard to imagine that this was her new life. . . .

A new city.

A new bank account.

A new hairdo.

New clothes.

And a new guy friend who was not only rich but famous too.

She pinched herself to make sure she wasn't dreaming. She wasn't. *And that's going to leave a mark,* she thought. Thinking how quickly her life had changed, she sucked in a deep breath and inhaled the sweet fragrance of the flowers. . . .

Oh shit!

The flowers.

They were everywhere. How was she going to explain a houseful of roses to Manny? There was no way that she could let Manny see them. What was she going to do? Nearly in a panic, she looked out the window at the Nu River, thirty-three stories below. For a split second, she thought about opening the balcony door and tossing the flowers over the railing. Maybe in Baltimore she could get away with some messy shit like that, but not here. She had an hour to shower, get dressed, and find a way to dispose of a small florist's shop.

One moment before totally losing it, she was hit by a bright idea. And with any luck, it just might work out. She started by picking up the phone and calling the building's concierge.

When she got him, she asked, "Is it possible for me to reserve the movie room downstairs for tonight?" Her building had a game room, a gym, both an indoor and an outdoor pool, a party room, and a theater room. She just hoped that she could book the theater room on such short notice.

Tom, the concierge, said, "Let me check." He took a few seconds, then said, "Sure. No problem, ma'am. It's available all evening."

"Thank you so much. You're a lifesaver." She gave him her name and apartment number.

One phone call, and it was done. As long as she could keep Manny out of her apartment, things would be fine. So maybe they could walk to the strip on Las Olas to get some food after they watched the movie and then call it a night there. She could say that she was still tired from last night. She had a plan, and now it was time to get dressed and pretty.

Not only was Manny generous; he was also punctual. He arrived at her building in exactly an hour. She met him downstairs and escorted him to the theater room. They watched a DVD screener of the new Tyler Perry movie. They both thought that the movie was okay. Afterward, Charisma suggested that they get something to eat at one of her favorite restaurants.

"I'll drive," she said. "It'll be easier for me to get my car in and out of the residential parking lot. The valet here sometimes takes a minute."

Manny said, "Cool." He was good with whatever she wanted to do.

When they arrived at the restaurant, the manager immediately got them seating in a secluded room. The room was private, and the ambiance was nice. A waiter came right away and took their order.

Charisma reached out for Manny's hand. "Are you okay?"

"Of course," he said. "I couldn't be better. I'm with you."

"That's nice to know, and flattery will get you everywhere. But I mean with the baby mama stuff you're going through."

Manny let out a little sigh. "Once I got home, my lawyer came over, and we looked at the document together. Do you know that Bing filed for child support three days after my daughter was born?"

From what Charisma had heard about Manny's ex, she wasn't surprised. "Wow! She didn't even let the ink dry on the birth certificate. Or give you a chance to offer an agreement in regard to support."

As the waiter quietly placed their drinks in front of them, Manny said, "That's Bing for you. Greedy. It's just sad to know that my daughter means nothing to her but a paycheck. Another object to secure a dollar. It really hurts me."

Charisma felt sorry for him and the innocent baby girl. When she gazed into his eyes, she could see the pain he felt. She asked, "Was Bing like this when you two were together?"

"Not at first. Well, it wasn't as bad at first. But she has always been selfish and greedy. That was the reason we broke up. I've been wiring her thirsty ass fifteen thousand dollars a month since she found out she was pregnant. And the second she went into labor, I was at her bedside, and I prepared for my daughter, Star, to enter the world. I swear . . ." His eyes took on a steely glare. "I'm not going to let her exploit my daughter."

They were quiet for a moment, both soaking in their individual thoughts. A moment later the waiter arrived with their entrées.

After the waiter left their table, Manny spoke first. "No more talk about Bing, okay? I want to enjoy my time with you." And to show that he meant it, he asked, "How was your day?"

"Amazing. The past two days have been amazing." It sounded corny, but *amazing* was the only word that she could think of to describe how she felt. Things couldn't be any better, she thought.

Manny cut a piece of his steak and ate it. "I'm glad," he said. "I hope I have a little something to do with you feeling so . . . amazing."

Charisma put her hand on his knee. "Sorry to disappoint you, but you don't."

"Damn, girl. You can let a brother dream, can't you?"

She said, "You have *everything* to do with the way I feel right now."

For the rest of the meal, they talked only about themselves. Manny was excited about spring training, which was coming up, and Charisma went on and on about the novel she was writing. The food and the conversation were both organic and filling.

Chapter 18
Please . . . Not the Fiat

The next day . . .

The next day pictures of Manny riding shotgun in Charisma's convertible Fiat were posted all over the gossip blogs. As she sat on her bed, checking out the blogs, Charisma was especially riveted on the gossip on Bossip.

Mystery girl strikes again. Who's the mystery chick that has superstar Manny Manifesto rolling in a Fiat? Everybody knows that Manny loves his expensive foreign cars. Isn't he the same brotha who said in an interview with Elite Sports that he wouldn't be caught dead in a car that cost less than a hundred thousand dollars? I'm no car aficionado, but that Fiat ain't worth nowhere near a hundred stacks. . . .

Charisma was thinking, *I can't read any more of this shit,* when her phone lit up.

"Hey, cuz. What's up?" Charisma said after she picked up. She really didn't feel like talking. Everybody she had spoken to so far today had asked her the same thing.

"Don't 'what up' me, cuz." Wanda sounded upset. "How come you're on TMZ and every other blog with Manny Manifesto, and I don't know about it? The whole fucking Baltimore is ringing my damn phone."

Her name hadn't been mentioned on any of the blogs. They referred to her as the "mystery girl."

"How do you know it's me?"

Wanda smacked her lips. "Girl, please! We shared the same fucking bed for two years. And who else would get a come-up for two mill and would drive a fucking Fiat?" She chuckled.

Charisma searched all over, but for the life of her, she couldn't find anything funny. Besides, she liked her convertible Fiat. "So you going to rag on my car too?"

"That's all people are saying. . . . 'Who is the chick that got Manny riding in a fucking Fiat?' "

"At least I'm riding," Charisma retorted, defending herself.

"Pump the brakes, cuz. Don't try to change the subject. This ain't about no car. What's up with you and Manny? And how come you're keeping all the tea to yourself? If I were fucking with a brotha like that, I'd be shouting it from the rooftops. So are you going to spill the tea or what, girl?"

Since they were teenagers, they'd kicked it about boys. Who they thought was cute and whom they wanted to do the do with.

Charisma thought about last night. It had been wonderful. But she hated keeping secrets from Manny. And if he wasn't such a gentleman and had pressed her to come up to the apartment, she didn't know what she would've done. The place still looked like a branch of Flowers.com. She made a mental note to throw out the damn roses the second she got off the phone.

"There's nothing to spill, Wanda. We've been out a few times. That's all. If it was anything more, I'd tell you."

"Bitch, you lying like this damn Persian rug on my floor. I can hear it in your voice. Can the nigga fuck or what?"

Charisma said, "What's got into you? That's some shit Vanessa would ask."

"Uh-huh. And that's not an answer," Wanda made sure to point out. "Spill it, cuz."

"We haven't had sex, but . . ." Charisma didn't know how to describe her and Manny's relationship. They hadn't had sex, but they'd been intimate, if that was even possible. "We're just kickin' it," she said.

There it was.

"Wow!" A momentary silence came over the phone, until Wanda said, "My little cousin is banging Manny Manifesto. Like what the fuck, man!"

"See?" Charisma said, chastising her older cousin. "That's how rumors get started. Shit like that. I'm telling the truth. The furthest we've got is a kiss on the cheek and a few hugs . . . like, that's it!"

"I'm not trying to start anything, girl. Certainly not any rumors. But when he do bust that cherry, you have to promise to give me all the salacious details."

"You got it. You will be the first one to know."

"However," Wanda said, "those gossip columns are right about one thing."

"And what might that be?" Charisma asked, not sure if she really wanted to know.

Wanda said, "Flat-out, your ass need a new car."

"Look, my shit is paid for."

"Yeah, but I mean, you need to upgrade it. Like, for real."

"I ain't into just looking rich. I want to actually be rich," Charisma asserted.

"I know that's right, but the bottom line, the Fiat just isn't cutting it, girl. Spend some money and enjoy yourself."

Maybe she would get a new car. There was this nice Lexus that she liked, but not before she really made some money first. Charisma said, "Do me a favor, Wanda? Don't tell anyone about Manny and me. Not yet."

"How can I not tell people what they can see with their own eyes? You're all over the blogs. And why hide?" Wanda replied. "I think it's great."

"Right now the blogs don't know who I am, and I like it that way. So forget what other people may think they know. I'm asking you not to confirm it with anyone who knows me. Okay?"

"My lips are tighter than fish pussy, girl."

"You crazy as hell. And how do you know how tight fish pussy is?"

Wanda laughed. "Girl, everybody knows that fish pussy is waterproof. And it don't get no tighter than that, bitch."

Charisma didn't know if that was a fact or not, but it was hard to argue with her cousin's logic. So she didn't. "I guess you may be right." Then she switched gears. "I'm going to call you back later, Wanda. I got a few things that I need to get done."

"Is everything okay?"

"Honestly, things couldn't be better. . . ."

Charisma hung up, thinking about all those flowers and the recent calls she'd received from Roc. *Well,* she silently mused, *maybe things could be a little better.*

Charisma got up off the bed, headed into the kitchen, made a stiff mimosa, and started on breakfast. She was still somewhat bothered by what the blogs were saying about her. The fact that they didn't know her didn't matter much. She knew it was only a matter of time before they uncover her identity. Halfway through breakfast her phone rang again. She didn't recognize the number and decided not to answer, but then her curiosity got the better of her.

"Hello?"

"Hey, girl. How are you?" said a female voice.

Charisma ran a quick data retrieval through her brain, trying to recall the voice. The request came up empty. She hated when that happened. Not many folks had her number, but she was about to admit that she was clueless when the caller bailed her out.

"It's me," said the voice on the other end. "Fabiola. Manny introduced us at the club." Charisma did remember the superstar R & B singer coming to their table. Fabiola was so nice that night, Charisma wondered if she and Manny had dated before.

Now Fabiola was on the other end of the

line. Instinctively, Charisma ran her fingers through her hair, straightening it out, as if Fabiola could see her. Sort of at a loss for words, she said, "Hey. Good morning . . ."

Fabiola was surprisingly pleasant. "Excuse my manners. Good morning to you also," she said. "But the reason I called is that Manny told me that you were new to South Florida and didn't have many friends or family down here."

That was true. Besides Manny, Charisma didn't have any friends in Florida.

"So I just wanted to check on you," said Fabiola. "You know, in case you needed anything or just someone to talk to. I know how it can be in a new state, away from friends and family."

"Ah, that's so sweet!"

"And those blogs can be as mean as a hungry stray dog at times. How are you holding up, by the way?" Fabiola said.

Charisma couldn't believe this was happening. A Grammy-winning, platinum-selling artist had called her to see if she was okay. She wasn't sure if she would ever get used to the fringe benefits that came with being friends with Manny. But she sure loved that someone whose music she loved was now on her telephone, asking if she was okay. Since she met Manny, life had surely been good.

"It's supersweet of you to ask," Charisma said. "But you don't have to —"

Before Charisma could get it out, Fabiola said, "Everybody needs somebody. I know how tough it is to be thrown in the spotlight. I was lucky, though. From the time I was a little girl, my mother trained me for this shit. I hated it at the time, but in the end, she knew what she was doing."

That small piece of information made Charisma feel like she knew a part of Fabiola that millions of fans didn't. Just having the privilege was an honor.

"It has been kind of wild. Like, every day they are saying something," Charisma admitted. "But I'm cool."

"I'm glad. And I may not know you that well yet, but I'm happy for you. Do you think you'll be able to have lunch with me when I get back in town next week?"

"Sure . . . ," Charisma said, sounding a little more eager than she would have like to. "Lunch sounds great."

"Cool. I'll hit you up with the details later. Until then, take care."

"You too."

CHAPTER 19
TRICKING OFF

"Nigga, how the fuck you gon' buy that basic bitch *fucking* jewelry and you won't even take care of your baby? Are you *fucking* crazy or just stupid?" Bing screamed at the top of her lungs.

Manny took the phone away from his ear and waited until Bing stopped screaming. When she was done, he said, "Just because you're in Cali and I'm in Florida doesn't mean that you have to shout for me to hear you, Bing. Believe it or not, the phone works just fine." Manny knew that to rile Bing up the most, all he had to do was remain calm. She fed off drama like a fire did gasoline. "And how come you so conveniently forget about the fifteen K a month I've been sending you since the pregnancy?" he said politely.

"Boy, please! You got me fucked up."

Manny wished he'd never fucked her selfish ass in the first place. But what was done

207

was done. Now he had to live with the consequences.

She went on. "Nor did you answer my damn question. You buying jewelry for that cheap-ass ho or what?"

Manny brought his yellow Gallardo to a squat at a red light on Biscayne. The engine sounded like a wild animal waiting to pounce. "Who told you that I bought anybody anything?" he asked, barely able to keep from laughing. The last thing he needed was for her crazy ass to think that he was laughing at her.

"No one had to tell me anything," she said, still shouting. "Yo' stupid ass let the fucking jewelry store take a picture and post it on the 'Gram, and Baller Alert reposted it."

She had him there. What was he thinking?

But he had nothing to hide. He could spend his money wherever he wanted and on whomever he damn well pleased. And right now, his focus was putting a smile on Charisma's face, to show her how much he was thinking of her. And Manny would bet a million to a Mars bar that she damn sure appreciated his efforts more than Bing ever had or would.

Manny was in such infatuated bliss, and what he wasn't going to do was let Bing fuck up his mood. So, he'd take the high road today and not give this greedy, thirsty bitch a piece of his mind.

"Okay, Bing. What is this phone call about? Because it surely isn't about me buying someone a diamond necklace."

"So you admit it." Manny imagined the steam wafting from Bing's weave. "You bought that no-class-having, basic bitch some fucking diamond necklace? Did you buy your Star one?"

Manny shook his head. "What do a one-month-old child need with a diamond necklace, Bing? That's the kind of materialistic stuff that you're into. My baby will have plenty of times to get diamonds, and whatever else she wants or needs, when she's older."

"You don't have a baby. As far as I'm concerned, you're just a fucking sperm donor with deep pockets."

That cut Manny deep, but he didn't let it show in his tone. "I'm sorry you feel that way, Bing. But I have things to do. My lawyer will be handling the suit. We may ask for full custody," he said. "Chew on that."

Click!

Manny let the finely engineered beast loose on the MacArthur Causeway, but when the speedometer of the Gallardo edged over 130 miles per hour, he eased off the gas. That was when he noticed a text from Bing. *Typical,* he thought. She always wanted to get the last word.

Motherfucker! You can bet your last bat & believe I'm going to make you wish you were in hell, wearing a gasoline jockstrap, when I'm finish with yo' sorry ass!

CHAPTER 20
CAT'S OUT OF THE BAG?

The first rays of sun shone through the glass sliding door to the balcony at 6:48 a.m. Charisma woke up immediately, welcoming nature's alarm clock. That was one of the reasons why when Charisma went to sleep at night, she never closed the blinds of her Las Olas condo. That, and the amazing view of the city from her thirty-third-floor luxury perch.

Like she did every single morning, Charisma thanked God for her being alive. She had never thought her life could be this amazing. Everybody at times dreamed of having the perfect life, but most never truly believed they would achieve it. She was now a believer.

Today she was going to have lunch with Fabiola. Not only was the singer becoming a good friend, but she was also Charisma's favorite R & B singer and had been for a few years now. How cool was that?

Charisma rolled over, picked her phone up from the night table. There were four missed calls and her usual "good morning" text from Manny, which always seemed to make her mornings so much brighter. Charisma was in the process of texting Manny back when she received an incoming call.

"Hey, girl."

Wanda said, "Rise and grind, cuzzo." Before Charisma could wish her a good morning, Wanda added, "Girl, did you see the blogs this morning?"

Charisma could tell something was wrong. She felt it in her gut. "I literally just rolled over," she said. "I was checking my text messages when you called. Why do you ask?" Charisma reached for her iPad, which rested on the other side of the bed.

Wanda got straight to the point. "Girl, you've been ID'd."

Neither the meaning nor the magnitude of Wanda's words registered with Charisma right away. She naively asked, "What do you mean?"

"Girl, you're no longer the mystery girl. They've fingered you." Wanda made it sound like Charisma had just been identified as the prime suspect of a salacious crime. Wanda went on, "They've figured out your name and where you're from . . ."

This wasn't the way Charisma had planned to start her morning. While she knew that the media would find out who she was sooner or later, she had hoped it would be later. And she had never said it out loud, but she kind of liked the mystique of it all, them not knowing. And now she would be playing on a whole other playing field. One she had to learn the rules to quickly.

"Do you know how they found out?" she asked.

Manny had spoken to her about leaking her identity to TMZ himself, to lay to rest all the speculation and innuendos. But Charisma was sure that Manny wouldn't have outed her without telling her first.

Wanda said, "You remember that girl Lisa Lewis?"

Lisa and Charisma had gone to high school together. Charisma hadn't seen her since prom. Lisa hadn't had a prom date and had worn a hideous low-cut dress to make sure she didn't leave the gymnasium dateless that night. Charisma had actually felt sorry for the girl, even after Lisa ended up sleeping with her date.

"Yeah." Charisma sucked her teeth. "I remember her. But what does Lisa Lewis have to do with this?"

"Well . . . ," said Wanda, with a dramatic pause. "She's telling any tabloid that will listen — and will give her a few bucks, I'm sure — that the two of you were the best of friends. And a whole bunch of other shit that doesn't remotely resemble the truth."

She and Lisa Lewis hadn't even been acquaintances in high school, let alone best friends.

"Are you kidding me? I couldn't stand that chick in high school, and she got the nerve to be selling my so-called story to the tabloids?" Charisma squawked.

"You have to read some of the stuff they're saying. How you're just another gold digger with a shiny pickax who hit pay dirt . . ."

Charisma powered up her iPad to see for herself. She found her way to Gossip.com. And when she did, she couldn't believe her eyes.

Mystery Girl ID'd.

Charisma Bland, a former plain Jane bartender from Baltimore, has hit the Major Leagues. . . .

And that was one of the nicer comments. Charisma got more incensed as she continued to read. They made her sound like some gold-digging whore who would do anything for a dollar. To make their point, they had done a split screen with before and after shots: a bad tenth-grade school photo and a picture of her when she was with Manny at LIV. The blog post more than insinuated that Manny's money and generosity were the only reasons that she looked the way she looked now. It was brutal the way that they were betraying her.

What was a great morning had gone to hell in a hurry. The more Charisma read, the more she began to second-guess everything. Her life. Her relationship with Manny. Even accepting the hush money for the abortion, which, to Charisma's relief, hadn't been mentioned in any of the blogs. But it probably wouldn't be long before those bones fell out of the closet too.

Tired of it all, Charisma slammed her iPad down. It bounced off the mattress and fell to the floor. She didn't bother to check and see if she'd broken it. She'd seen enough.

After biting her lip to keep from screaming, Charisma said, "Wanda, I'm going to call you back."

But Wanda wasn't having it. "No you're not," she said. "Let's talk about this. I don't like the way you sound."

Wanda was right. Charisma was vexed and wasn't in her right state of mind. If she were driving, she probably would have to pull over and get herself together before continuing. But she didn't want to talk right now.

"I have to go."

"Don't hang up this phone, Charisma," Wanda said, putting her foot down. "I mean it, girl."

Charisma didn't hang up, but she remained as silent as a church mouse.

Wanda called her name. "Charisma!"

Silence.

Charisma sat there, holding the phone, thinking that it was just a matter of time before people found out about her dirty little secret. And when that happened, what would Manny think about her?

Wanda tried to reason with her. "I know this whole thing is a lot. The move. The money. And this very public relationship. It's a lot to deal with. And you've been handling it like a champ. But you know who you are! You can't let other people's opinions stress you out. The only person whose thoughts you should care about right now is Manny. And from what you've told me, that man really cares about you."

Charisma finally broke her silence. "What if they find out about —"

Wanda cut her off. "They won't. Trust me. That's why that nondisclosure agreement was so detailed. The only people other than us who know about your secret don't want it ever to surface."

"Yeah," Charisma said, unconvinced, "but people have a way of finding out things. And if the cat does get out of the bag, what then?"

"Well, our friend has more than one hundred million reasons' worth of endorsements to make sure that cat *doesn't* get out of the bag."

Charisma wanted to believe what Wanda was saying.

"Trust me," Wanda said, "they have more to lose than you."

Charisma thought about it. "Maybe you have a point, but I just feel bad about it. It feels like I did something dirty. And given the way Manny looked at his baby's mother for using their child as a financial bargaining chip, what will he think of me?"

Wanda said, "Get that picture out of your head. Don't even think about it."

Easier said than done, thought Charisma.

Wanda changed the subject. "Aren't you supposed to go to lunch with Fabiola today? If I was you, I would go out and buy myself something fabulous to wear, and I'd forget all about this bullshit." She paused, expecting Charisma to balk. "It'll be a bigger piece of gossip to spread before the week is out, if not the day," Wanda assured her.

Charisma sucked in a long breath, trying to squelch her sense of guilt.

"Let's just pray," she said.

CHAPTER 21
CHECK PLEASE

"So you've been revealed."

Both Fabiola and Charisma cracked up at the same time. Their laughter was unforced, natural. The way it was with friends who had known each other for years. It was all love, though the two women had met only a few weeks ago. Patrons who happened to be seated near their table gazed at them with envy and wondered what the hell was so damn hilarious.

What they had originally planned to be late lunch quickly turned into an early dinner. As they conversed, the women learned that they had a host of things in common. They were both from the DMV area. Fabiola was from Virginia; Charisma from Maryland. Fabiola's all-time favorite "hood classic" movie was *The Wood,* and so was Charisma's. Their favorite musician was Diana Ross. It felt as they were long-lost sisters who had been reunited. Fabiola half jokingly suggested that they sign up on one of those popular ancestry Web sites.

"I can't believe it," Charisma said. "Not that I was exposed. But the chick that put me out there acts like we were bosom buddies or something, and the bitch barely knows me from a can of hair spray."

"Trust me," Fabiola assured her, "that wasn't anything! It's part of the game. People are going to come out of the woodwork to spread rumors. My best advice is, keep your circle tight and right. There will be only a handful of people you encounter who you can really trust."

Charisma took a bite of her grilled chicken and chewed it while digesting what Fabiola had shared with her. "It's all just so heavy," she said. "Having my entire life examined and picked apart by a pack of wolves."

"Well, the longer you and Manny are dating, the crazier it's going to get. Believe me," Fabiola told her. "And on the tenth, when you come out to my album-listening party, girl, the paparazzi are going to be out there like a swarm of nasty killer bees, with cameras instead of stingers. You are coming, aren't you?"

"Well," Charisma said, "since you've made it sound so warm and inviting, I wouldn't miss it for the world."

Fabiola made her promise. "Even if Manny can't make it, because of spring training, you still gotta come."

"You don't have to load the bases to get me up to the plate."

"On a serious note," said Fabiola, trying to stifle her bout of giggles, "it's not nearly as bad as it seems. The truth be told, I couldn't wait to become a household name. Let my mother tell it, that's the reason I was put on this earth." Fabiola then confided something she didn't talk about much. "The second my mom knew I could hold a note, she groomed me to be the star *she* always wanted to be."

Well, thought Charisma, *those are definitely two things that Fabiola and I don't have in common.* Charisma never did anything with her biological mother, and she hated being the center of attention.

Charisma had read that when Fabiola was growing up, her mother had been one of those controlling momager types, but she hadn't known if there was any truth to it. Couldn't believe everything you read. She asked, "Is that why you're such a vet when it comes to handling the paparazzi? Your mother?"

Pondering the question, Fabiola said, "It sort of comes natural to me, but now that you ask, yeah, my mother did have a lot to do with the way I handle myself *and* the press, people in general."

"Fabiola! Fabiola! Let me have your autograph!"

The fan-slash-stalker tried to rush the table where Fabiola and Charisma were sitting. Fabiola's bodyguard, Todd, who was six-six and built like a Russian tank, snatched him up before he could get close enough to smell the four-hundred-dollar-a-bottle fragrance on Fabiola's neck. The stalker was the same dude who'd been seen at more than a few of Fabiola's shows. He'd been escorted out of at least two events in the past.

"Put him down, Todd."

The fan-slash-stalker's feet were literally swinging in the air. Todd had grabbed the poor man by the neck like a farmer would a chicken at dinnertime. Todd allowed the weirdo's feet to be reacquainted with the floor. But Todd's look said, "If you do anything stupid, I'll put this size sixteen sneaker so far up your ass, you'll be able to floss with the shoelaces."

Fabiola gave the superfan a photo and sent him on his way. Todd offered his own parting gift to the fan. A piece of advice.

"Don't make the mistake of letting your

face be seen nowhere in Ms. Fabiola's vicinity again. Ever. The next ending won't be a happy one. Trust me."

Fabiola continued the conversation with Charisma as if nothing had happened and it was just another day in the business of being famous.

"It's going to become natural to you too," she said. "You'll eventually learn that you have to live your life as if someone is always watching — and waiting for that worst possible moment to pounce — so that they can use whatever info they gather to destroy you." She paused, then added, "And we all have at least one, if not more, of those moments in our lifetime."

Charisma asked, "So what do you do when that moment happens?"

"Simple," Fabiola told her. "You pray."

Charisma smiled. "I just pray that I don't disappoint Manny. I want to make him proud, and I want to be everything he wants in a woman and more."

"Well, from my vantage point, honey, you're not only everything he needs but also everything that he wants. You sitting pretty."

Charisma took a deep breath. "Yeah, but —" She stopped in mid-sentence, shaking off the second-guessing she was about to take part in.

Fabiola looked at Charisma with a sisterly compassion. "You might as well spill it. Whatever it is that's eating you. I can see it in your eyes."

"It's just that I wanna exceed his expectations, especially —" Again, Charisma swallowed her words before they could get past her lips.

"Girl, it can't be that crazy. And if it is, I won't judge you. I'm here to pick you up, not tear you down. Know that."

"I don't have low self-esteem or anything like that, but Manny's baby mama is so glamorous. That's hard to compete with."

"Bitch, please." Fabiola put her finger up. "Let me shut you down real quick. First off, did you just say *glamorous*?"

"She is," Charisma asserted for the second time. "I've never seen her in person, but she's gorgeous in the pictures I've seen."

"Charisma, you have something that ho will never have."

Charisma was curious. "What's that?" she asked.

"For starters . . . principles and morals. Not to mention that you're gorgeous on the inside and the outside."

"Thank you. But I have to give the girl props where they're due. In every shot I've seen of her, she's picture perfect."

"Girl . . . you haven't learned yet that pictures lie. There are such things as filters, Photoshop, and editing."

"Yeah, I know, but she be giving it to 'em, though." Charisma couldn't hate on Bing.

"That was when she had an unlimited access to Manny's money. Which isn't there anymore. That bitch is a wreck without the makeup, Botox, plastic surgeries, and all the designer shit and upkeep. She ain't nothing but a thirsty wannabe thot begging for a dollar."

"Tell me how you really feel."

"This has nothing to do with feelings, honey, because I have none of those to spare for the likes of her. I'm just telling you the truth. What you better do is stay on point, and don't let that shiesty ho get you caught up in her bullshit."

"Thanks for the advice. I'll remember it."

"Like I said, Manny really likes you a lot. Just focus on him and not her stupid shit. Speaking of which, oddly enough, that slick skank has been rather quiet lately," Fabiola said with a raised eyebrow. "Just know when dealing with that bitch, it's always calmest before the storm."

CHAPTER 22
$H#TT* MESS

Charisma left the girls' lunch feeling super excited. She was elated about her new friendship with Fabiola. And about her blossoming relationship with Manny. Everything was evolving so quickly. If she wasn't residing on cloud nine, she was definitely leasing a space in the same neighborhood.

As she glided to her car — high off life — the smile on her face stretched even wider when she thought about one of the many things Fabiola had shared with her. *Manny really likes you a lot.* The words spun over and over inside Charisma's head. She felt the same way, but it was cool hearing someone else say it. But when Charisma bent the corner, the track that was replaying sweet nothings in her brain abruptly stopped.

"What the fuck!" Charisma wiped her eyes with the back of her hand, as if she could brush away the vision.

Her car had been vandalized. Someone had tagged her Fiat with spray paint. It was horrible. And very, very, personal. She wondered why someone would want to desecrate her car that way.

The words *bitch!* and *whore* had been crudely sprayed with red paint on the hood and the driver's side door of her white car. And that wasn't all. A cannon had been painted on the trunk. It resembled the ones in those old war movies, the ones they used to push around on those huge wooden wagon wheels.

That, Charisma thought, *is more bizarre than the curse words.*

Hold on.

The cannon wasn't a cannon, she realized. It was a penis.

And, she would soon find out, that image of a penis and those derogatory words spray-painted on her white car weren't all that had been left for her to find.

When she opened the car door, she was met by a horrible odor. It smelled like something had died inside her car. Dog shit — at least she hoped it wasn't from a human — had been smeared all over the interior. The seats. The floors. The dashboard. Everywhere . . . About forty or fifty shitty diapers had been discarded in the

227

backseat. It was disgusting. And the diapers indicated that a baby, and not a dog, was probably the source of the feces. These days thugs were starting their life of crime at a young age. But surely a rogue toddler hadn't broken into her car and taken a dump.

Tears peeked out from behind her eyelids and charged down her face. She tried to rein them in, but the effort was useless. She couldn't stop the tears from flowing. The foul odor began to make her sick to her stomach. The combination of nauseousness and tears made her both feel and look awful. It felt as if she was free-falling through the air. She needed to pull herself together, and quickly. The last thing she needed was a picture of herself looking a shitty mess on TMZ.

Falling . . .

One had a long way to descend when one got shoved from the window of a condo perched on cloud nine.

CHAPTER 23
STALKER

"She's definitely a keeper. That, I'm sure of," Fabiola said.

Fabiola was like a sister to Manny, one his closest female friends. And Manny felt that Fabiola had an uncanny sense for reading people. That was why Manny wished he'd listened to her when she told him, after laying eyes on Bing for the first time, that Bing was going to be more trouble than she was worth. Actually, she'd said, "That one there is a piece of shit." But that was water under the bridge. And Manny would never again make the mistake of not listening to Fabiola's intuition.

Fabiola had called him as soon as she left Charisma.

"I'm glad you took the time to hook up with her," he said into the phone. "And I'm even more glad that the two of you gelled."

"Oh, it was my pleasure," Fabiola assured him. "She's a peach. You better not fuck it up with her, either."

Manny laughed. Fabiola wasn't the type to hold back on what she thought. She didn't care who you were. The truth was the truth. That was one of the reasons he liked her.

"Are you my friend or my mother?" he joked.

"Are you calling me old?" she teased. "And if I remember correctly, your mother never liked any of your girlfriends."

"Don't remind me," he said. Manny loved his mother. But he hated introducing her to his *friends.* His mother had never met a girl who she thought was good enough for her son.

Ever.

He told Fabiola, "Hopefully, you, me, and Charisma can go out one day soon."

"Definitely," she said. "Well, I gotta go."

That was how the call ended. Then Manny dialed Charisma. She answered on the second ring.

"Hey, babe."

Manny sensed from her tone that something was troubling her. "You okay?" He was concerned. "What's going on?"

Charisma didn't answer right away. Then she finally said, "Nothing."

But Manny wasn't buying it. "It's definitely something," he said.

He could hear her suck air. After exhaling — whatever she had pent up inside, he hoped — she said, "I just came out of the restaurant with Fabiola and found my car all fucked up."

"What?" Manny said. "Like a hit-and-run?" He had never heard Charisma curse before. *She must really be upset,* he thought. "I'm sure it's nothing that we can't get fixed."

"No, Manny, it's nothing like that. My car is, like, really ruined," she said. "I'm not kidding. Like, just horrible. Like, I don't want it anymore."

"I'm not sure what's going on," he said, "but I'm on my way to you right now. Exactly where are you?"

"On the corner, down the street from the restaurant." She told him which one. And read him the name of the street from the sign.

"I'm close by. I can be there in fifteen minutes. Don't move, okay?"

She said, "Hurry up."

Manny mashed the gas pedal of his Mosler MT900SP. The automobile rocketed through traffic like a heat-seeking missile in search of a hot target. He reached Charisma in twelve minutes flat. Manny jumped out of his whip and, before saying a word to her, gave Charisma a hug.

He whispered into her ear, "Baby, I'm so sorry."

Once Manny surveyed the damage done to her car, his blood rose a few degrees in temperature. Instantly, he knew that Bing was somehow behind this. It had her bullshit written all over it. Manny told Charisma about his suspicions and then took pictures of the car, in case they needed them as evidence. Then he asked Charisma to ride with him. "I'll call a tow truck for your car," he said.

Manny moved a jewelry store bag off the front seat and helped her get in. Then he placed the bag, which contained a present he'd bought for her, on her lap. "I hope this makes you feel better."

It did.

Charisma smiled. Then she said, "I would understand it if you need time away from me to sort things out with your baby mama. I don't want to be responsible for messing up your court case in any way." She didn't want to be away from Manny, but she felt that this might be best. "Don't be ridiculous," Manny quickly said. "Nothing about being with you can mess anything up with me. And I'm not going to let anything get in the way of that." A few beats went by. Then he added, "But I told you from the beginning that Bing was an impossible, selfish piece of shit, now didn't I?"

Charisma nodded her head. "But I thought you were exaggerating. I definitely didn't think that she was capable of something like this."

Well, I wasn't, and she is," Manny said after putting the car in gear. "And you got a chance to see it firsthand."

"You really think that your ex did all that to my car?" she asked. It all still seemed kind of out there, Charisma thought. Even for a crazy person. "Isn't she supposed to still be in LA?"

"As far as I know," Manny said. "But believe me, that shit that happened to your car . . . that was Bing. There's no doubt in my mind."

"How do you think she found my car?" Suddenly, Charisma started to feel afraid. "Do you think she's stalking me somehow?"

"All kinds of pictures of your car have been taken. Trust me, it wouldn't be hard for Bing to find out things." He didn't tell her that he had once suspected Bing of putting a tracker on his car. He didn't want to shake her up any more that she already was.

"She sounds psycho," Charisma said.

"She definitely makes bad decisions, does stupid shit."

"And you were in a relationship with this person?" she asked incredulously.

"Yeah, I was. But that's why I'm no longer with her. I fell for the big butt and smile," he admitted.

Charisma rolled her eyes at him. "Is that all it took?"

Manny pulled the car over, gave Charisma his undivided attention. He poured out his heart, and Charisma listened to every word he said to her. "I was young and dumb then," he confessed. "That's why I've been taking it slow with you. Thanks to Bing, I learned that everything that looks good isn't always what it's cracked up to be. I just want a real relationship with someone who has principles, morals, and respect for me and herself. In addition to that, I want her to value our friendship first and our relation-ship second. And not by the amount of money I have in my bank account, but by the quality time I invest." He paused. "I've been linked to a lot of pretty chicks . . . models, actresses. The list goes on."

"And on . . . and on," she joked. "I heard about that list, you know."

"Yeah, but that's in the past. It gets old really quick. Now I'm ready for genuine

234

companionship."

"Aren't we all?"

Manny seemed to say all the right things. When he finished playing baseball, he could take up writing Hallmark cards, she thought.

"I know you think I'm bullshitting you, but I'm not. That's why I went today and bought you this." He nodded toward the bag. It was still closed. "Open it."

Charisma did what he asked.

Manny said, "I promise I will never intentionally do anything to break your heart." Charisma couldn't take her eyes off the heart-shaped diamond necklace and the matching heart-shaped diamond ring. They were absolutely beautiful. And expensive.

Manny pulled up in front of her high-rise. "I'll call you later. And you'll have a new car in the morning."

"Manny, I don't need you to buy me a new car," she said.

"Who said anything about needs? I said I'm buying you a car. I'm doing it because I want to."

"Uh-huh." Charisma smacked her lips. "And not because you feel a little bit guilty about what happened?"

"That too," he said. "But to be honest, I didn't really care for the Fiat myself."

Charisma punched him on the arm. Hard. "You know I hate you for that, right?"

On the way home, Manny called Bing.

When she answered, he said, "Bitch, you done crossed the line. You got zero times to do it again."

She said, "Hello, darling," ignoring his threat. "I knew that you would come around."

"Take it as a joke, if you want."

"Why are you so angry?" she asked. "Is your new little friend not fucking you right? I can definitely help you with your frustration."

Manny spoke softly and clearly. "I wouldn't fuck you again with a monkey's dick."

"Whatever turns you on," she said. "You always did like it kinky."

The bitch thought that she was a comedian. But Manny knew how to get to her. And he intended to use that strategy.

"You cross the line again, and you'll never get another dime from me." That got her attention. "And there's nothing a judge or anyone else in this world will be able to do about it. I'll spend fifty million in legal fees if I have to. I don't give a fuck. As long as you suffer. If you don't believe me, try me, bitch!"

Chapter 24
Easy Money

Manny made passionate love to her on a tropical beach. Charisma couldn't get enough of him. Their bodies were in perfect harmony, as if they were made for one another. Her heart raced when he touched her. Charisma knew that it was only a dream, but it felt so real. And so good. In fact, it was the best she had ever had.

He whispered in her ear, "I can't get you out of my mind."

The voice wasn't in her dream, though. It was in her bedroom.

She smelled Tom Ford cologne. It was a scent that she would never forget. Her eyes popped open immediately.

Roc was standing over of her, smiling. He'd been watching her sleep. Her nose had not deceived her. How long had he been there? she wondered. And how the hell did he get in her house?

"The cat is out of the bag," he said.

Those were the same words she'd used with Wanda on the phone yesterday. Was he somehow listening to her calls?

Charisma said, "Get the hell out of my house, before I call the police." Roc had lost his mind, if he had ever had one in the first place.

Roc licked his lips. "I don't think you really want to do that," he said. "Besides, I'm practically your baby's daddy."

He's sick, she thought.

"What the fuck are you doing here?" She had asked what seemed like a dumb question to him.

Roc looked at her with a strange expression. "What do you mean, what the fuck am I doing here?"

"Get the fuck out of my house, Roc!" She rose up and pushed him away from her bed. "I'm not playing with you."

"Hmmm. Not a morning person, huh?" He tried to touch her face. She smacked his hand away.

"Get out!"

"You act as if I'm not welcome here. You must have forgot" — he looked around — "I'm why you got this place and everything in it. I paid for all this shit."

"You didn't pay for anything. And if you don't want to go to prison, you need to

239

leave. I'm not going to tell you again."

"I own you and everything in this mother-fucker. And I've come to collect my rent." He looked like the devil when he smiled.

Roc tried to kiss her. Charisma tried to push him away. But Roc was too strong. He forced his tongue into her mouth. She bit it, drawing blood. He backed away, but not until he was ready. Charisma tried to run away.

"Where the fuck you think you're going, bitch? Get the fuck back over here." Roc grabbed her by the hem of her flannel pajamas and pulled her back. Then he pinned her to the floor.

"Get off me!" she screamed, then kicked him in the groin, barely missing his nuts. "Get the fuck off of me!"

He tried to hold her down, but Charisma bit him on the face. This time Roc let out a howl. She had bitten through his skin, and her teeth coated with his warm blood. He slapped her.

The blow dazed her. When the stars she was seeing cleared up, she kneed him in the groin. This time she didn't miss her target. She felt his balls squish under her kneecap. And that was when Roc went berserk, rain-ing blows down on her. If he had been play-ing before, the brute force with which he pummeled her made it plain that he wasn't playing any longer.

He beat the fight out of Charisma. Then raped her.

Oddly, while Roc was inside of her, with his hand over her mouth, Charisma could hear her uncle Vess's voice in her head, as if he were speaking from the grave. *Easy money ain't never easy. It always comes with a cost.*

A moment later Roc looked intently at her and muttered, "Oh shit!" It was as if he'd just realized how badly he'd beaten her. Her face was bloody. "Baby, I'm so sorry. I didn't mean to hurt you."

Charisma couldn't move her jaw. She managed to push two words through a busted lip and a broken jaw. "Just go," she said. They were barely more than a whisper. Then she managed to say, "Please . . . just . . . go."

Roc acted as if he was shocked that this had happened. And then he insinuated that it was somehow Charisma's fault. He said, "See what you made me do?" Then he got up, wiped his semen off his dick with the bedspread, almost tripping over his Robin's jeans.

Charisma could barely see out of her left eye. And she saw nothing out of her right.

She had never wanted anything in her life as bad as she wanted to kill Roc right then and there. Roc waltzed into the kitchen and returned with a bag of frozen peas. He tossed the bag to her. Then he removed all the money he had on him and tossed it onto the bed. As if money could rectify what he'd done. He really was insane if he thought that.

"You a sick-ass motherfucker," she said.

"I'm sorry, baby. I never wanted it to be this way with you. I swear, I didn't." He started looking around the bedroom. When he spotted her cell phone, he grabbed it, went into the bathroom, and tossed it in the toilet. "I will lock the door behind me."

Once Charisma heard the door shut behind her, she exhaled. It felt like she'd been holding her breath for hours. She started to cry.

What in the world had she got herself into?

CHAPTER 25
BACKGROUND CHECK

Jacob Rothstein called Manny at the top of the morning to schedule a meeting. Two major endorsement deals were on the table, worth close to seventy million. Manny said that he could be there by 5:00 p.m., right after practice.

The moment he left the ballpark, Manny hopped in the Lambo. He let the top back and pushed the ignition button. The engine roared to life, itching to perform. Both Manny and the Lambo were antsy, wanted to be let off the leash. But as usual on I-95 at this hour, traffic was as congested as a chain-smoker's lungs. He might as well have been driving a Honda. Manny arrived at his lawyer's office at 5:07 p.m.

Seven minutes late.

Jacob, as usual, was dressed to the nines. He was wearing one of his customary Italian-cut suits, handmade loafers, a mono-grammed tailored shirt, an Indian silk tie, and a complementary pocket square. Jacob took his attire serious. Hands down, the man was the best-dressed attorney in the state of Florida, hell, maybe in the entire country. Manny, who was wearing his Marlin's sweats, took a seat.

Jacob said, "You're late." Then smiled.

Manny didn't. "Tell me something I don't know," he said.

"Powerade is offering you forty-nine million dollars. How about that?" Jacob revealed. "And we can get another twenty from a chewing gum company."

Such astronomical numbers no longer excited Manny. Once a man deposited a couple hundred million dollars in the bank, money no longer affected him the same way as before he was filthy rich. He asked, "Which company?"

Jacob used his thumb and forefinger to rub the bridge of his nose. A habit. As far as Manny knew, the only one the man had. Jacob didn't drink, smoke, or eat red meat. And he'd been married to the same woman for more than twenty years.

"Does the name of the company really matter?" Jacob asked.

Manny thought about the question a little longer than he should have. They were talking about a twenty-million-dollar deal to make a couple of commercials and maybe attend a few more functions. He finally said, "I guess not." This time Manny did smile. He and Jacob had been working together for more than a decade. And the man had never steered him wrong about anything, not once.

"I didn't think so," Jacob said. "But for accounting purposes, the name of the company is Super-Yum-Gum. They're new. But their parent company is well established. And very wealthy. But wishes to remain anonymous at the time."

"Like you said, as long as the money is good, I'm good."

They went over the particulars of the two contracts. As usual, Jacob had gone over every detail of the contracts, and Manny was satisfied that everything was in order. This part of their meeting took less than an hour.

"Anything else I need to know?" Manny said when they were done with the contracts. He stood. He was ready to hit the road. He'd take another shower and maybe get with Charisma. He hadn't heard from her or talked to her all day, which was odd, since the two of them always talked. And he hadn't seen her in a few days, a few days too many, as far as he was concerned.

Jacob took off his gold-framed Cartier glasses and placed them on the desk. "Actually," he said, "there is something else."

"Bing?"

"Heck no. I assure you Bing is nothing for you to lose one wink of sleep over. She'll get exactly what she deserves," Jacob said confidently. "I promise you won't be disappointed by the outcome."

"Okay. I'm going to hold you to it. You've always been true to your word."

"And that's never going to change, if I can help it. You can take that to the bank."

Manny took a seat on Jacob's desk. "If it isn't about Bing, then what is it?" he asked.

"It's Charisma."

At the mention of Charisma's name, Manny's brows came together like two caterpillars making out. "What about Charisma?" In the past, he and Jacob had never mixed business with pleasure. And Manny didn't want to start now.

Jacob was straight up. He always shot straight from the hip. He said, "How serious are you with her right now?" When Manny didn't answer right away, Jacob said, "If you're serious, we need to have her checked out. Thoroughly. Especially with this paternity thing going on with Bing. We don't need any more surprises stirring up

246

bad press. The maxim 'All press is good press' is bull. One bad scandal can bury you. You've had a great run, but you still have your best days ahead of you."

Manny understood exactly where Jacob was coming from. But he also trusted Charisma unconditionally. She'd told him everything there was to know about her. Where she was born. About her parents not being there for her. Where she went to school . . . everything. Hell, Manny knew the name of the guy she had lost her virginity to. If there was anything else that he needed to know, she would have told him.

Wouldn't she? he thought. *Of course she would,* he answered silently.

Then to Jacob, he said, "I'm good with that. I'll take care of my personal life. You just keep doing what you do best."

"What I do best," Jacob said, "is keeping you out of the tabloids and making lots of money."

Manny got serious. "If you think that you know something that I don't, then spill it."

Jacob said, "I've done some checking."

"I'm sure you have, and I respect that. But no one asked you to snoop around on my girl," Manny said, knowing that Jacob meant well.

"Don't get so upset. For the most part, I

didn't find much. She's lived a pretty basic life."

Cool, Manny thought. But "not much" wasn't nothing at all. What was Charisma hiding from him?

Jacob lowered his voice, as if he didn't want to be overheard, when he said, "She has more than two million dollars in her bank account. The money seemed to have materialized from out of thin air. One moment her account balance was six hundred dollars. Then, all of a sudden, it ballooned to two mill."

"Not that it's any of either of our business, but her uncle did pass a few months ago. It's probably the insurance money."

"That's what *I* thought," Jacob said. "Until I dug deeper. Her uncle's name was Sylvester Bland. He was a good dude. Not the type of dude who wouldn't have left his three natural kids a piece of that insurance also. You know what I mean?"

Manny sighed.

Jacob went on. "And I must add that about four hours ago, another five hundred thousand appeared in her account. Where did it come from? Who deposits that kind of money into an ex-bartender's account just because?"

Jacob had posed some interesting questions. And maybe there were very good answers to his questions. But Manny didn't know the answers.

Charisma, he thought, *what aren't you telling me?*

CHAPTER 26
BREATHE

Chi-Town, Illinois . . .

It was 9:05 a.m.

She was running late. It would be the third time this month that Tracy would be late for her job at Burger Chef. And if her shifty supervisor, Dexter, had his way, she wouldn't get a fourth opportunity. Ever.

Ever since Tracy declined Dexter's offer to participate in "overtime" activities outside the restaurant, he'd become a real donkey's behind. He'd done everything in his little thimble of power to make life on the job difficult for her. Actually, Dexter had always been a first-class asshole. But it was useless dwelling on this. One thing was for sure: she wasn't going to sleep with a middle-aged, George Jefferson–looking creep to keep a fast-food job. Regardless of how badly she and her daughter needed the check.

Before switching lanes, Tracy checked the

blind spot of her ten-year-old Honda. She told her daughter, Toni, to sit back down. Toni had been trying stand up in the car seat, but she listened to her mother and sat. Tracy reached back to double-check the restraints on the car seat. Toni giggled. She looked like a miniature version of her mother, right down to the hazel eyes, the button nose, and the dimpled cheeks.

"Mommy's going to get you out of that chair in a second," Tracy told her daughter.

They were about eight minutes away from the day care. And with traffic, it would take her at least another fifteen minutes to get to work after she dropped Toni off. Yep. She was going to be late.

Tracy began texting her boss. I'm going to be a few minutes lat—

The driver of the Ford F-150 was doing twenty ticks over the speed limit when he blew the red light. He was distracted, as he was trying to change the radio station. And he'd been drinking. So his reaction time was slow. This combination of factors caused the Ford truck to slam into the side of Tracy's car. The sound of the collision — metal crashing into metal — reverberated for blocks.

Tracy's Honda did three somersaults before it finally landed on its roof. The driver of the truck was uninjured, but he had passed out due to all the alcohol in his blood. Toni cried for her mother. But Tracy couldn't hear her. She'd been knocked unconscious by the air bag that had deployed from the steering wheel during impact.

The strong odor of gasoline permeated the morning air. Then the Honda burst into flames.

A lady who was standing at the bus stop screamed. "Someone do something!" She'd witnessed the whole thing. "There's a baby in the car!"

As if on cue, Toni began to bawl at the top of her lungs.

The driver of the car that had been behind Tracy before the collision took place jumped out of his Jaguar and sprinted toward the burning Honda.

Someone screamed, "Call nine-one-one!"

Another person, a woman, shouted, "I've already called them! The ambulance is on the way. They said ten minutes."

But Tracy and her daughter didn't have ten minutes to spare. The Honda was blazing like a South Carolina barbecue pit. The flames had not yet reached the interior, but it wouldn't be long. Ignoring the danger to himself, the bystander who had been driving the Jaguar reached through the flames and into the broken window on the passenger side of the burning Honda and tried to pull the child out. He pulled as hard as he could, but nothing happened.

Shit! he said to himself.

The car seat was strapped in. He had to undo the restraints first. After reaching in again and disengaging the buckles, he got the little girl out.

"Mommy!" she cried. "Mommy!"

The lady who'd called 911 was now filming the heroic rescue with her phone and was probably posting it live.

The man gave the child to the woman who had been standing at the bus stop and then ran around to the other side of the burning Honda to try to rescue the driver. If it wasn't too late. The fire was really hot and angry now. *Like a scorned woman,* the guy thought as he reached through the flames.

Tracy remained unconscious, breathing in carbon monoxide by the lungful. The fire singed the hair on the man's arm and face as he opened the driver's door. He blocked out the pain and began to struggle with woman's seat belt, which was trapping her inside the inferno. The strap was stubborn. Flames progressed from scorching the hair on his arms and face to blistering his skin.

The blackened metal of the car felt like the top of a hot stove. He wasn't sure how much longer he would be able to endure the heat. How long before the fire department got there to help? he wondered.

Then the seat belt released its hold.

Thank God.

Roc pulled Tracy's limp body from the burning car.

A siren could be heard in the distance. Roc wasn't sure if it was an ambulance, a fire truck, or the police. He hoped it was someone with medical experience. The woman wasn't moving. He felt for her pulse. Nothing.

Roc performed mouth-to-mouth resuscitation on her. He'd got first-degree burns on his arms while trying to get her out of the car, and he had no plans to let her die now that the hard part was over.

Breathe!

CHAPTER 27
WHO DA F#CK ARE U?

"I'm sorry, but that's the policy."

No one was allowed upstairs without the tenants' approval. No exceptions. The policy had been implemented to insure the safety of the residents and their property. And the security guard was only doing his job.

But that didn't mean Manny had to like it. He hadn't spoken to Charisma in three days. Her phone was going straight to voice mail. And she hadn't returned any of his messages. This wasn't like her.

Manny asked the security guard to call her intercom again. Darryl, who'd worked at the Taj for thirteen years, tried paging Charisma's intercom for the third time. He knew she was there, because she'd called him two hours ago and given him the heads-up that the delivery guy from the Chinese restaurant was on the way. She had also made it clear that she wanted Darryl to get her takeout, bring it up, and leave it by the door. The same as yesterday! And the day before that. And Darryl would know if she'd left the building. It was his job to know. Unlike the young buck who had been hired last month, Darryl took his job seriously.

Manny knew the outcome before the security guard said anything. He had that "Sorry, but I can't help you" look on his face. "Just let me go up to check on her," Manny said. If he thought it would help, he'd beg. Something he had never done.

Darryl was a fan of Manny's. Hell, his son wore Manny's shoes. But rules were rules. "I'm sorry, Mr. Manifesto, but —"

"I know," Manny said, cutting him off. "It's the policy. Cool."

Just when Manny was out of ideas, a guy walked into the lobby of the Taj, wearing a number three Marlins jersey.

"Hey, aren't you Manny Manifesto?" the guy said.

Manny felt like screaming, "Get a life," but he wasn't one of those superstar athletes who didn't know that the fans helped keep his bread buttered. "Last I checked," he said instead. "Nice jersey you got there."

"Yep." The fan's name was Tommy. "It's yours." Tommy poked his chest out, trying not to act too much like a groupie, but

Manny could tell that it was a difficult task for him to pull off. "Do you mind if I take a picture with you?" asked Tommy. Before Manny got a chance to answer, the guy drew his phone out like it was a Colt .45 and he was Billy the Kid.

"Sure," Manny said. Manny asked Darryl if he minded snapping the keepsake. Darryl was more than happy to help him out. He felt bad about not letting Manny upstairs. Afterward, Manny asked Tommy to snap one of him and Darryl. Manny posed as if he was at bat, with a big old smile plastered on his face. Then Manny said to Tommy, "How would you like for me to sign that jersey for you?"

"Would . . . I . . ." Tommy patted his pockets. "Damn," he said, thinking that he'd blown the opportunity of a lifetime. "I don't have a pen."

Darryl, magician-like, quickly made one appear. "You can use mine," he said.

Manny disregarded the offer and countered with something more suitable to his own agenda. "How about I go with you up to your apartment? You could take off the jersey, and then I could sign it properly," he said.

Tommy's eyes lit up like those of an eight-year-old who'd just hit the toy lotto on

Christmas morning. "Sure!" he said, unable to contain his excitement. "If it's not too much trouble," Tommy added.

Just for kicks, Manny thought about saying, "You're right. It's too much trouble," and walking away. But his ulterior motive for getting upstairs superseded his sense of humor.

Manny said, "No trouble at all. Lead the way."

Darryl was far from a fool; he knew what Manny was up. But he chose not to intervene. He smiled at the ballplayer's ingenuity. *The great shortstop Manny Manifesto steals another base,* thought Darryl. Nothing in the Taj's policy against that.

Tommy and Manny took the elevator up to the twenty-seventh floor, to a nice condo that smelled like fried cabbage. *And onions,* Manny thought before scribbling his John Hancock inside the top curve of the number three. "My pleasure," he said when he was done.

Tommy offered Manny a drink, as if they were besties.

Of course, Manny declined. "I wish I could," he lied, "but I have to run." Manny was out the door before the cat could say strike three.

Manny speed walked down the marble

hallway to the elevator bank. Pushed the up button. And got off on the thirty-third floor. Charisma's condo was at the end of the hallway. He rang the bell. And waited.

Nothing.

His finger jabbed the button a few more times. The light visible on the other side of the peephole momentarily vanished, then reappeared.

"Open the door, Charisma. I know you're in there."

Manny heard Charisma's voice for the first time in three days. "Go away," she said. "I don't want to be bothered."

Her voice sounded strange. At first, Manny couldn't put his finger on what it was. Something was missing, he thought. Then it dawned on him. She was normally full of life. It was infectious. Now her voice sounded lifeless.

"What's wrong, Charisma?"

She didn't say anything.

Manny put his head on the door. "Whatever it is, I just want to help you get through it," he said.

"Just go away, Manny. I don't need your help."

"Well, you don't have a choice. Because I'm giving it to you. That's what friends do for one another. We are still friends, aren't we?"

She didn't answer.

"I'm going to stand out here in this hall until you let me in and talk to me. After that I'll go away if you want me to. But not before you talk to me."

Silence.

She isn't going to open it, he thought. Maybe Jacob was right. He had said she needed to be investigated. But friends didn't hire detectives to pry into their friends' lives. If they did, they wouldn't be friends for long. But when he said he wouldn't go anywhere until he talked to her, he'd meant it. Manny took a seat on the floor, rested his back against the door. He would wait all night if he had to. She had to come out sooner or later. He'd wait until she did. Unless she or one of the neighbors called the police on him first. There were at least four tiny HD surveillance cameras silently monitoring the hallway.

Without preamble or warning, Charisma opened the door. Manny nearly fell inside her condo. He hopped up before she changed her mind.

She said, "I just want to be alone right now." She was wearing pajamas and sunglasses. And all the lights were out behind her. "I'll call you when that changes."

Manny stepped inside her condo, pushed the door closed behind him. After he flipped on a light, he noticed that the kitchen counter was covered with fast-food cartons. Pizza. Chinese. Subway. Then Manny saw the bruises. The discoloration around her eyes. The swollen lip and jaw. He gently removed the sunglasses from her face. Both of her eyes were black.

"Damn, baby." She looked as if she'd been in an MMA fight. His breathing slowed. And the temperature of his blood rose to a low boil. "Who did this to you?"

At first blush, Manny thought the culprit behind the damage to Charisma's face might be Bing. Bing was jealous of Charisma. But he didn't believe she was physically strong enough to inflict this type of damage. At least not while Charisma was awake. Not only did Charisma have a few inches on Bing, but she was also more than a few pounds heavier. And too feisty. Bing could have paid someone to do her dirty work for her, but Manny didn't think so. The bitch wasn't that stupid. She didn't like Charisma, but not nearly as much as she did *like* money. And Manny had warned her not to cross the line again.

Charisma turned away from him, hiding

261

her face. "I didn't want you to see me like this," she said.

Manny couldn't help but reflect back on his conversation with Jacob. *She has more than two million dollars. . . . The money seemed to have materialized from out of thin air. . . .*

Obviously, there was something going on that he didn't know about. Manny didn't know what to think anymore. There was only one thing that he was certain of: he loved her. And nothing else mattered to Manny. He touched one of the bruises on her face, gently.

"You never have to hide anything from me, Charisma. I love you. And whoever did this to you will pay for it. I promise."

Charisma contemplated coming clean. Revealing her dark secret and letting the chips fall where they may. She contemplated forgetting the money and the disclaimer. Forgetting it all. Just confessing it all to this man standing in front of her who had said that he loved her. But hadn't Roc said he loved her too?

Ringgg. Ringgg. Ringgg.

It was the house phone.

"Aren't you going to answer it?" Manny said.

Ringgg. Ringgg. Ringgg.

Charisma ignored the ringing, as if didn't exist. "It's no one I want to talk to."

Ringgg.

"Answer the phone, Charisma." Manny thought it might be the person who had beaten her up, and he figured that she didn't want him to know the person's identity. He put his foot down. "If you don't answer it, I will," he said.

She hurried over to the phone and grabbed the receiver. "Hello?"

"You have a prepaid collect call from . . . Chucky," said a computerized voice.

Charisma accepted the call. When Chucky got on the line, she told him that now wasn't a good time for her to talk. Manny took the phone from her.

He barked into the phone, "Who is this?"

Chucky said, "Who the fuck is this! Put Charisma back on the phone."

Manny wasn't in the mood to be taking orders. He said, "You're talking to *me* right now. How do you know Charisma?"

Chucky barked back, "How the fuck do you know her, Joe? We've been friends since third grade. Fuck is you?"

"I'm the man that's going to make the motherfucking punk that beat her up wish he wasn't born," Manny said. "That's who I am."

"Time-out." Chucky wasn't sure he'd heard that right. "Beat her up? Yo, put Charisma on the phone, Joe. What the fuck is going on?"

"She doesn't want to talk to you," Manny said calmly.

Chucky hated the fact that his hands were tied. "Okay, big man, you got the ups on me right now. But if I find out that you've laid a single finger on Charisma, I'm going to chop your hands off and shove 'em up your ass." He paused for a moment. "After I kill you," he said slowly. "And I put that on everything that I love, Joe. My name is Chucky motherfucking Johnson, nigcka." Chucky made the words sound like fire. "Remember it. And if it wasn't you, pass the fucking message on, Joe."

With good time, Chucky had six months remaining to serve before being paroled. He meant every word of what he'd said. Those six months would be the slowest 183 days of his life.

CHAPTER 28
HOMEWORK

Chucky slammed the jack down so hard, the plastic casing around the earpiece nearly cracked in two.

Fuck!

Blood rushed through his veins to his brain. He could feel his heart pumping inside his chest. And the more he chewed on the phone call, the more vexed he became. If he wasn't careful, the next decision he made could cost him years — maybe even the rest of his life — in prison. And at this very moment, he didn't give one solitary fuck! The only thing he cared about right now was the answers to the two questions ringing in his head. Who was that nigga running his mouth on the phone? And who in the hell had put their dick beaters on Charisma?

And the fact that he didn't have an answer to either question made his blood boil. The last time he was this upset, he had gone to the gym and had beaten the heavy bag until he was exhausted and drenched with perspiration. But the gym was closed now. Due to budget cuts, the powers that be had made the piss-poor decision to cut the hours back.

Which reduced his options for burning off the anger bubbling in his stomach.

He thought about teeing off on the first joker he saw, just for rec. And there was no lack of jokers to choose from in this place. He could give two fucks for a third of the clowns on the block, anyway. As long as he didn't draw blood or break any bones, he would have to lie down only for about thirty days in the SHU for fighting. Sure, he would lose a little good time, but he could use the time in isolation to get his mind right for the streets.

Still seeing red, Chucky spotted a suitable candidate on the other side of the tier. Dude was a lightweight bully who went by the name Sincere. He'd do. Chucky was making a beeline toward Sincere when a strong hand grabbed him by the shoulder. Always on point, Chucky spun around, with his left fist guarding his grill and his right ready to strike.

Blow threw his hands up, his palms showing. "Hold it, man. It's me."

Chucky dropped his guard. He and Blow

were boys. "You 'bout to get your grill busted up, sneaking up on me and shit."

Blow knew something was off. "What's going on?" he asked. "Your face is tighter than fish pussy, my nigga. Do I need to strap up?"

"I just got some fucked-up news on the jack. That's all. Nothing serious."

"I can't tell it's nothing serious. You look like you ready to murk a nigga. You want to talk about it?"

Chucky didn't want to talk; he wanted some rec. "You've been watching too much Dr. Phil, my dude. I just want to blow off a little steam. That nigga Sincere been running around selling tickets for a minute now. I'ma see if he can fight, or if he's all talk, like most of these niggas."

"Time-out, mud dude. You're a better thinker than that. I don't know what just went down on that phone, but I can't stand by and watch you mess your good time up for something that's happening in the streets. Something that you don't have control over. You can take care of the streets when you get in the streets. What if you fuck around and hurt a nigga bad? God forbid, a nigga die. You may never get out this bitch. Then how're you going to help somebody in the streets?

"Show me one of these clowns that's worth you spending one day longer than you have to in this bitch. You point him out, and I'll bust his ass for you." Blow had another ten years before he was even eligible for parole. "I don't have anything to lose. But you . . . ," he said, "you have everything to lose."

Blow made a whole lot of sense. That was why Chucky fucked with him. When he inhaled, it felt like this was the first time he'd taken a breath in about ten minutes. Like a weight had been lifted off his chest.

He and Blow slapped hands. "Say no more, Dr. Phil. You talked me off the edge," he told Blow.

"Good. If you'd jumped, I would've been the one who would've had to clean up the mess."

"So you had an agenda."

"Nigga . . ." Blow smiled. "*Everyone* has an agenda. And now that we got that out the way, you sure you don't want to talk about what got you ready to snap in this piece?"

"I just found out that a good friend of mine got hurt. I plan to return the favor to the person who did it. So until I was able to do that, I was willing to settle for one of these chumps. To get off some steam."

"I know a lot of people," Blow said. "You don't have to be up close to touch a person."

"But you do have to know who the person is that need to be touched, my dude." Chucky pondered the situation. "I got some homework to do."

CHAPTER 29
CHIRAQ

Chicago, Illinois . . .

"Jason, over the past year you've built four youth centers throughout the city for underprivileged kids. All these state-of-the-art after-school hubs are in neighborhoods that are inundated with crime and violence, where more kids go to prison than graduate from high school. This endeavor of yours has cost more than ten million dollars. I guess my question to you, Mr. Jason Albright, is, why?"

"My grandmother said to me at a young age that riches were meant to help people in need." With that giant Cam Newton smile he'd become famous for on his face, Roc looked at the interviewer for *Hollywood Digest.* The camera ate it up. "One of the reasons more of those kids are going to prison than are graduating," Roc said, "is that the state is investing more in prisons than it is in schools."

The interviewer nodded; she couldn't deny what he was saying. This was true not just in Chicago, but also in most cities throughout the country. But Chicago was a hotbed of crime. The murder rate had been compared to that in a third-world war zone.

"Speaking of schools," the interviewer said, "I hear that you intend to start a new charter school for kids in kindergarten through twelfth grade. Similar to the one Jalen Rose founded."

"Yes. Education shouldn't be based on a family's economics. Everyone should be entitled to a great education. The kids in nine-oh-two-one-oh, they can go to the public schools and get a great education, but not the kids in Chicago. So, therefore, my goal is to create opportunities for them, hire amazing teachers who take care of the students and take pride in their achievements and get the kids to the next phase. Ultimately, we want to produce highly intelligent students who can go out in the world and compete with the best of the best, as well as be productive citizens in this country."

"And speaking of children, you recently saved a woman and a child from a burning car."

"Yes. I did. It was no big deal," Roc

replied. "I only did what I felt was natural, what anyone would have done."

"You are truly an all-around hero. Investing in education and saving lives."

"Thank you."

"I'm sure your wife and children are proud of you."

Roc looked over at his wife, Jasmine. She was off camera, on the side of the stage. She stood there, fulfilling the real-life role of the supportive wife. She winked and smiled like a perfect doting wife should.

The interviewer went on. "And you two have been together for such a long time. What's the secret to staying together in such a toxic environment, one filled with so many perils?"

"Having great communication and understanding. And keeping our love alive."

"What do you say about all the groupies and all the adultery that is known to go on in the NBA? How have you managed to keep your relationship and your family so wholesome?"

"Well, first of all, I would have to give all the credit to my wife," Roc answered. "She's the glue that really holds everything together behind the scenes. Next, I'm in love, so madly in love, with my wife. I love her more and more each day, and what we stand for.

During all my free time, I focus only on my wife and making our relationship strong and happy. We keep it fresh and sexy all the time."

Roc looked over at Jasmine again. She smiled, wishing that what he'd said was true, and not bullshit lines that she had put together for him. She was a mastermind at creating the right image for him and their family. The charter school had been her idea, just like the rec centers. Jasmine was a puppet master when it came to the press and publicity. She beamed back at Roc lovingly. Black love. *Ebony* magazine had called them the "perfect couple." The "epitome of black love." Cynics said that true black love was as rare as a black Republican. If it even existed at all.

Jasmine loved Roc and the idea of being the poster family for black love. She also liked the fact that people envied them for being so in love. If only the masses knew what all went on behind closed doors.

The camera recorded a shot of Jasmine and then went back to Roc. The interview was wrapping up. Jasmine remained in her spot off to the side, watching and feeling happy that the interviewer had acknowledged them and their love for each other.

Just then her phone rang.

"Hello. This is Jasmine Albright." She felt as if she was on top of the world. Nothing could slow them down.

"Bitch, you need to control your fucking husband before you fuck around and lose everything."

Jasmine was clueless as to who was on the other end of the line. Probably just another hating ho with a dildo stuck in her ass. But it didn't matter. She had no intention of letting anyone throw shade on her moment in the sun.

She flipped on a hundred-watt smile and gave a semi-fake chuckle for anyone who was looking or listening. "That could never happen," she said, gloating. "Are you near a television? My husband and I are currently being broadcasted live on nearly every network in the world right now, honey. He's America's hero."

"Well, your husband, the American hero, fucking beat me and raped me."

The accusation came blaring through Jasmine's earpiece. Something about the woman's voice sounded familiar, but Jasmine couldn't quite put her finger on it.

"Do you find that's funny?" the woman added.

"Oh, well!" Jasmine walked away from all the people standing around — producers, production assistants, cameramen — so that she could speak a little more freely. Once out of earshot, she said, "Maybe he gets rough sometimes, but nobody will ever believe a low-life bartender who sleeps around with any athlete that will bed her. Take a long look at your résumé, honey. I do have a bit of advice for you." She paused for effect. "Suck it up, bitch. And I mean that literally. Either go find someone else's cum to drink or go spend some of that tramp money I sent you on a vibrator. But whatever you do, dear, don't ever call me again."

"Your husband is a rapist." Charisma hadn't had much respect for Jasmine to begin with, but what little she might have had was out the window now.

"My husband can be and do whatever he wants. Just suck it, little girl! You got what you deserve!" Jasmine snarled. "And one last thing. Don't fuck with me, Ms. Gold Digger. I will drop a note to Terri Manifesto, informing her of your unsavory history. And, in case you didn't know, that's Manny's mother. Yes, Manny is a mama's boy, and she is a certified piece of work. Once Terry hears how much of a gold digger you are, she will see to it that he loses all memories of you. You'll disappear from his life as quick as a groupie will shove a dick in her mouth. Believe me, I can and I will ruin what little life you may think that you have."

Click!

Jasmine was slightly more influential than Charisma had given her credit for.

Chapter 30
Maryland State Prison

Hard plastic chairs and warm, anxious bodies covered every square foot of the moss-green linoleum floor in the prison's dayroom. Every eye was glued to the forty-two-inch TV. And every person in the room shared a vested interest in the game. The Miami Heat versus the Washington Wizards.

The outcome of the matchup had play-off implications. The arithmetic was simple: if the Heat won tonight's game, they would grab the number eight seed in the play-offs. On the other hand, regardless if the Wizards won the game or not, they would be absent from play-offs yet again this year. The only way a member of the Wizards would see any postseason play was if he purchased tickets. Or watched the games on television, like the rest of the world.

But the Wizards players were hyped over playing the role of spoiler for the Heat. And they got their motivation from something other than the satisfaction of blocking the fan-favorite Miami Heat from that final play-off seed in the East. The two teams also disliked each other. In the Wizards' case, some would say that misery truly did love company.

Up until now the game had been ultracompetitive. Five minutes remained on the clock. And the score was as tight as the bootlaces on the spit-shined military combat boots of CO Rally Redneck, as the inmates called the corrections officer. Washington was ahead by a bucket, but after the time-out, Miami possessed the ball.

Everybody with a dick and a mouth was talking smack, and it was getting loud.

A guy named Swan shouted, "Miami ain't been shit since LeBron took his ball and his talents back home to Cleveland." And he'd backed up his conviction by dropping a hundred dollars of commissary on the home dog.

"You got that right!" another prisoner shouted out.

"They has-beens!" said another.

"You niggas got it fucked up," said Blow, one of the few cats with the heart to go against the grain and root for Miami. "I don't bet with my heart. I bet with my pockets, my nigga."

"Tell 'em dick-riding-ass niggas again, Blow," Chucky responded in a voice loud enough for everyone to hear. Before the game he'd announced that anybody who liked the Wizards could get a bet. It didn't matter who stepped up to the proverbial window or what they wanted to bet, he would cover the wager. And he did.

"All I know," said Swan, "is that I'm going to own somebody when this shit is over. I'ma be eating out of your box for the next two weeks, ya hear?"

"You got the game fucked up, my dude." Chucky had covered Swan's bet, so he rightfully assumed that the chump was referring to him. "All you can win is some Wing Dings and cakes. You can't win me," Chucky said, clapping back at Swan for the not so subtle shot. "But since you acting like you starving in this piece, we can double that shit up."

Swan lowered his tone. He wasn't a punk, but he didn't want to beef with Chucky over a basketball game. Chucky was strong behind those bars, and he didn't want or need him as an enemy. Cats inside there were already hating on him because he knew a lot of people in the world outside of the prison walls.

But Chucky turned up the wattage.

"That's what I figured. I knew you were scared to bet too much of that li'l change yo' mama be dropping on your books." Chucky smiled. Swan ran a pretty good parlay, so Chucky knew that he could afford money.

The hook was set.

"You got me mixed up with a nigga that give a fuck about this li'l prison shit," Swan said. "I'll bet the house."

Line and sinker.

"The house," Blow said, instigating.

Swan didn't flinch.

"Cool." That was what Chucky was waiting to hear. "Then make it two yacks," he said.

"Bet it up," Swan told him. "You ain't said nothin' but a word."

Cats were oohing and aahing. The two prisoners shook on the new bet.

After the commercial ended — a promo for a new movie based on a Nikki Turner screenplay — the noise level in the dayroom dropped a few decibels, and the focus went back to the television and the game.

Jason "Roc" Albright, the association's second leading scorer, brought the pill down the court. He was one of the faces of the NBA. Raheem, Miami's star and point guard, was assigned the job of defending him. He picked Roc up at half-court. Roc handled the pill as if it were a yo-yo. Roc's teammates loaded up the right side of the court and cleared out the paint, giving Roc the entire left side of the hardwood to operate. Raheem locked eyes with Roc, as if he was saying, *Bring it. I'm ready.* Since the opening tip-off, the two had been giving each other the business.

Roc reciprocated the stare. *Let's go, then, youngin'.*

With eight seconds on the shot clock, Roc gave Raheem a hard dribble, jab-stepped with his left foot, feigning right. But Raheem didn't bite on the fake. Instead, he stayed on Roc's dominant left hand. It was exactly what Roc had hoped and anticipated Raheem would do. Roc was crafty. He crossed Raheem over to his off hand, going right. Either the ref gave Roc the benefit of the doubt because he was a superstar and a vet, or the ref flat-out missed the hook Roc used on Raheem's waist to gain the half step advantage. That half step afforded Roc enough room to get to the rack before Raheem or the off-side help could catch up with him.

Roc reverse dunked the pill with such force, like he was angry at the world. The crowd went nuts. The dunk put Washington up by four, with 4:38 left on the clock.

Excited by the action, ESPN color commentator Doug Collins said, "No one seen this coming! Washington isn't going away! Miami is in for a fight."

Miami's shooting guard, Zoran Dragić, brought the ball down court. Dragić crossed the half-court line, surveying the opponent. The Wizards were playing a hybrid zone defense. The home crowd boos could be heard loud and clear through the television speakers. Dragić dribbled to his right and passed the ball to the forward. The small forward flicked a bullet touch pass to Raheem, who was squatting in the far left corner. Roc was supposed to be guarding Raheem, but he got caught contemplating doubling the forward. In that split second of indecision, he momentarily turned his back to Raheem. His lapse of judgment was less than a second long, but it was long enough for Raheem to get off the shot.

Water.

Raheem threw up the popular circle-and-three-fingers sign. But one of the refs ruled that Raheem had toed the three-point line. Another ref disagreed and said it was a three-pointer. After going to the monitors, the refs confirmed that Raheem's toe had been on the three-point line when the ball left his fingertips. Instead of a three-pointer, his shot was only worth two points, but that shot put Miami within a bucket of tying the game. The score was 91–89.

The dayroom went crazy. People were shouting and screaming. Talking trash. Jumping on chairs. CO Rally Redneck tried to restore some semblance of order.

"If you don't calm down," he threatened, "I'm going to shut off the TV!"

But the inmates continued to cut up, acting as if they hadn't even heard the guard. Blow slapped hands with Chucky, and then they both focused their attention back on the TV screen.

Roc came down the center of the court and drained a fifteen-foot jumper, quickly putting Washington back up by four.

Somebody in the dayroom screamed that Roc was the best playa in the league.

Swan said, "He ain't all that."

"What you mean? Roc's that nigga," the guy said.

Swan let it go. He could've told him and the others some stories that would make them think twice about the way they looked up to Roc, but he let it ride. Dudes never believed that he knew plenty of so-called celebrities, anyway.

For the rest of the game, the two teams

traded buckets. One after another. But since Miami was already down four points, trading buckets did them no good. They needed stops. When the buzzer sounded at the end of the game, the final score was 101–103, Washington.

Perspiring, Roc spoke with one of the courtside reporters right after the final buzzer.

"You had a great game," the reporter told him.

"Thank you. Hi, Mom."

"Roc, does the fact that your team isn't in the play-offs take anything away from eliminating your rival's chances of playing in the postseason?"

"I would be lying if I said I didn't enjoy it," Roc answered honestly. "But it would feel a whole lot better if the win got us in. But it is what it is."

After the on-court interview, Jasmine met Roc in the tunnel, à la Vanessa Bryant greeting Kobe, but without the adorable daughters in tow.

Somebody in the dayroom yelled, "Roc got the baddest bitch in the game!"

"That's my dude!" said another fan in the prison crowd.

Swan couldn't stop himself from spilling

the tea. "I had that bitch before him," he said.

"Get the fuck out of here, nigga! You ain't never even smelled no pussy like that before. Stop whaling," someone said.

"You a hater!" said someone else. "And a fucking liar. Lying on yo' dick and shit."

Swan said, "I ain't got no reason to lie on mine, my dude. I'm just telling you niggas the facts. I'm happy that the nigga doing good. Because his bitch still looks out for the old boy, ya hear?" He nodded, trying to get them to believe him, but nobody did. "Always has and always will."

"Stop it!" someone yelled.

Chucky wasn't tripping about losing that little bit of bread on the game. His books were stacked, and he ran a store box. But this demonstration Swan was putting on about fucking that nigga Roc's wife had his attention.

"Niggas always talking 'bout what they did before in here," Blow said. "Nigga, you ain't got to lie to kick it."

Chucky said, "Swan, you know damn well you can't say no shit like that and not be able to back it up. Not if you expect anybody to buy that shit, anyhow."

Swan swept the dayroom with his eyes. There were at least eighty-five brothers staring right back at him. Swan knew what they were thinking. Prisoners were used to other prisoners telling lies about their past lives on the streets. They called it whaling. Some niggas made shit up to make themselves look like big shots. Others did that shit just to pass the time of day. Talk about wishful thinking. There was a saying in prison. *Just like in the army, be all that you can be.*

Swan didn't mind that his fellow inmates were looking at him like he was a fraud; what made him upset was the way they spoke with reverence about Roc's bitch.

"I tell you niggas what," Swan said. "I'm willing to put my money where my mouth is."

"How you gon' do that?" someone asked.

"I want piece of that action. This nigga tripping," another inmate said.

Swan said, "I be back."

He went to his cell. While he was gone, the other prisoners joked the shit out of him. But he would have the last laugh. Swan returned with pictures of Jasmine and passed them around the room.

"Nigga, that don't mean shit. Any nigga can get a picture," someone asserted.

"I still ain't convinced," another inmate shot back.

Swan wasn't backing down. That was

286

when he flashed the envelopes with Jasmine's name on them. He let the niggas see the address on them.

"Man, that ain't shit, either," someone said.

And that was when Swan pulled out the most convincing pieces of evidence he had: money receipts in Jasmine's sister's name and love letters.

Chucky checked everything out carefully. Any nigga could Photoshop a few pictures. But no one would go to these lengths to prove a lie. He had real prison receipts and stamped envelopes to back up his claim. Swan would've had to have been setting this shit up for years in order to manufacture such a lie.

After looking at the receipts and the letters, cats glared at the nigga sitting in the dayroom with them and then at the nigga in the pictures who was hugged up with Jasmine Albright, Jason "Roc" Albright's wife. The one in the pictures was definitely Swan, and there was a whole stack of pictures. Now cats looked at Swan with admiration.

"How'd you meet that bitch, man? No disrespect. Damn," someone asked.

Swan nodded. "None taken."

"Fuck that. How's that drop?" someone else asked.

Swan was as smooth as a swan on a pond, and he was a gentleman. He wasn't about to share the low-down, dirty sex secrets that he was harboring. "That's between me and Jasmine, ya hear?"

The only thing Chucky was thinking at that moment was that he couldn't wait until the phones came on in the morning so that he could call his people and put them up on the game. Chucky was well aware that Swan wanted his blessing inside the bars and that he wanted friendship too, so that gentleman shit would go right out the window, and Chucky would get all the inside scoop he needed to make moves when he was released. Bet that.

CHAPTER 31
NEW HOME AWAY FROM HOME

Star Island, Miami, Florida . . .
Charisma drove across a white bridge from the MacArthur Causeway, the only way to access the exclusive island by land. Star Island was a private island that had been developed in 1922. Surrounded by the warm waters of Biscayne Bay, it was home to only the rich and famous.

And when it came to entering the island, there was no negotiation; all the visitors had to stop at the entrance guardhouse and show ID. Security was as tight as clam pussy. No one was allowed on the island who didn't belong on the island. No ifs, ands, or buts.

The on-duty guard checked her name off on the visitors' list, which was updated three times a day. After she checked out, he passed the ID back and allowed her to enter one of the most desirable, prestigious, and pricey places to live in South Florida.

"Thank you," she said with a smile before she pulled away from the guardhouse.

Charisma drove down one of the two streets on the island. Flowers bloomed amid the tropical vegetation, which was studded with abundant royal palms, banyan trees, and live oaks draped in Spanish moss. His modern mansion was hidden behind a high stone wall and a custom wrought-iron gate.

The gate — which bore the initials MM — slowly opened, granting her access to his premises. The driveway was lined with palm trees and sculptured fountains, and it ended with an enormous semicircle. The outside of the house was all white, and it had columns as wide as tree trunks.

Manny stood on a white marble porch, in front of two oversize French doors. He was wearing basketball shorts and shower-type sandals, no doubt made by one of the many companies he endorsed. Charisma got out of the car, smiling. It had been so long since a smile had visited her face — more than a week — and it almost hurt. Her face had to get reacquainted with the muscle motion. Manny gave her a huge hug. She almost melted in his arms. The hug lasted for a while. When Manny finally released her, he welcomed her inside his home.

Charisma just stood there.

"Are you coming in or what?" he said.

Caught up in the moment, she hadn't heard him the first time. "My bad. My mind was somewhere else."

"As long as I was there with you, I don't mind," he said.

Blushing, Charisma walked with Manny through the huge double French doors, across an open foyer, and into a humongous sitting room, which was accessorized with a grand piano and very expensive, chic, minimalist designer furniture.

Charisma had never seen anything so opulent in her life. "Your house is . . . It's amazing," she said as she continued to admire the decor. "Did you decorate it all by yourself?"

"Absolutely not," he admitted unabashedly. "I didn't pick out one solitary stitch of furniture. I just wrote the check to the interior decorator. A big one," he added casually.

"Well, it seems to be worth every penny. I've never seen a more beautiful house in my life," Charisma gushed, admiring a very large painting of a waterfall crashing down on a group of jagged rocks. The painting hung directly across from a row of oversized windows that provided a mesmerizing view of the ocean.

"Well, I did tell her what I liked, but she did it all herself."

"Gorgeous. Simply beautiful."

Up until now, Manny had taken the house for granted. To him, it was just another place to live. He glanced around at the vaulted ceiling, the crystal chandeliers, and the spiral stairway, as if admiring the place for the first time himself. He'd purchased the mansion three years ago, and given the demands of spring training, which had just ended, he had spent hardly any time there. And had never really enjoyed the place.

"Are those tourists going by?" She was gazing at the ocean through the windows and couldn't help but notice the boatloads of people sailing by and taking pictures.

"Yes." He nodded, with a smile. "There are plenty of those boats. They come by every hour or every other hour to get a look at the houses of the rich and famous."

"That often?"

"Yeah. You'll get used to it. Sometimes there are paparazzi too. You'll get used to them. I don't really pay attention to it." He pointed at the windows. "Don't worry about them seeing you. We can see out the windows, but they can't see in. Can you imagine if they could? We'd have no privacy at all." Manny took Charisma by the hand. "Let me show you around. There's a lot more to see. And then we'll have dinner."

"Is there?" she said, curious.

From the moment she arrived, she'd felt a strong sexual energy between them. Every time he touched her, the electricity got stronger. When he hugged her, she'd secretly wished that he would never let her go. And she felt the same intense energy while holding his hand now. She wondered if Manny felt the same way.

Thirty minutes, six bedrooms, eight bathrooms, and a host of other rooms later, they ended up in the kitchen. He picked up a chocolate-covered strawberry from a fruit tray that lay on the counter and put it in her mouth. It could very well have been an incredibly romantic moment; however, Chef Lester, Manny's private chef, was standing there.

Manny introduced the two of them. "This is my personal chef, Chef Lester. And, Chef Lester, this is my sweetie pie, Charisma."

"Nice to finally meet you, Ms. Charisma. Heard so many great things about you."

"Well, thanks." She didn't really know what to say, because she had never heard a word about him. So Charisma smiled and asked, with a twinkle in her eye, "Chef Lester, do you always have treats like this lying around, or is this for moi?"

"But of course," Chef Lester said, not really saying whether such lavish treats were customary at the house and also wanting her to feel like the strawberries had been made especially for her.

His duties complete, Chef Lester bid them farewell, hurried out of the kitchen, and then left the house. Manny ushered Charisma over to the kitchen table. Chef Lester had laid out fresh smoked salmon, wild rice, and grilled asparagus for them. The salmon was covered with a sweet-and-sour glaze, and it looked delicious.

As she took a seat, Charisma said to Manny, "If you're trying to spoil me, I just want to say one thing. You're doing a wonderful job at it."

After sitting across from her, Manny poured two glasses of white wine.

"You sure you ought to be drinking, now that the season has started?" Charisma quizzed.

"I've never completely stopped doing anything during the season." He looked at her suggestively, his eyes massaging her body. "But I do limit my alcohol intake to no more than one glass per night."

Charisma raised an eyebrow. "What about sex?" she asked boldly. Charisma wasn't anyone's jump off. But there was something about the marble floors and the exclusivity of the house that made her feel sexy.

"What do you mean?" he asked, wanting to be sure he had heard right.

"Do you limit how often you have sex during the season? Or are you just afraid of me?" she asked. "We've been dating for three and a half months, and we've never been intimate. And we met during the off-season." She lowered her eyes. "Aren't you attracted to me?" Acting completely out of character, Charisma had put Manny on the spot.

"Of course I'm attracted to you. I just didn't want to rush you. I wanted it to happen naturally. I can get pussy from anywhere. With us, I want a relationship."

She sipped her wine. "It's been nearly four months. Are you getting it somewhere else?" she said. Charisma figured if he wasn't doing it with her, then he must be fucking someone else.

Manny was speechless.

She wasn't letting him off the hook that easy. "Is it your baby's mother?"

"Bing?" Manny sounded incredulous. He couldn't believe that she'd asked that question. "No, I'm not fucking that bitch. Is that what you think?"

"I don't know what to think," Charisma admitted, then gulped down some of her wine. "What would *you* think? Bing is beautiful. And she has the distinct pleasure of being the mother of your child, your first child."

"That doesn't mean I'm fucking her. Well, yeah, I had sex with her to get her pregnant, but me and her are done. Finished. I wish I'd never met that conniving ho. Without question, I'm going to take care of my child to the fullest. I'll give Star the best of everything. But that's where my and Bing's relationship ends. Trust and believe, you have nothing to worry about there."

"Then who?" The wine had loosened her up. So she poured another glass.

"No one. I guess I could say that I was saving myself for you."

"Sounds good, but as handsome as you are, you have gone almost four months with nothing? You don't have to sell me the dream, baby. I still like you. You damn sure don't have to lie to kick it."

"Did I beat my meat? Yeah. And to be real, I ain't did that shit since, like, middle school. But to go up in and penetrate something? Naw." Manny looked at her and let her eyes meet his. "Could I have gotten pussy? Yup. Any and everywhere. Pussy never been a problem for me, even before baseball." He gloated. "However, it's not about who I can have but who I *want*." He pointed to himself as he looked her over, letting her know with his body language that it was she he wanted.

Charisma tried not to blush. She grabbed her purse and said, "Let me get this cash out for this dream ticket you selling me."

"Nah, baby. I'm just being real as I can right now. See, where I am in my career right now, and in my life in general, and with the BS I've been through, I'm more focused on building something with someone who is worthy and who understands my worth. Not my worth in regard to what *Forbes* says, but my worth as a human being."

"I can understand that totally."

"I just want to do this the right way, and I don't want to fuck this up."

Manny got up and kissed Charisma on the lips. The kiss went on and on and on. When the lip-lock finally ended, both of them were breathing hard and were ready for each other.

If she were asked about the details, Charisma would have drawn a blank as to the exact moment her clothes came off. Or if it was she or Manny who removed them. But she was naked now. They both were. And they were going at it on the kitchen counter. The sex was wild. Hot. Passionate. And amazing.

The made-to-order gourmet intercourse started sizzling in the kitchen, but it was ultimately consumed in the confines of the master bedroom. And the sexual smorgasbord was served all night long.

Manny woke up in the morning with Charisma cradled in his arms. He was still weak from all the energy he'd consumed while making sure Charisma's sexual needs were totally met.

"Are you awake yet?" he whispered. It was 9:39 a.m.

Charisma's eyes were closed, and she was just lying there, relaxed, desperately wanting to live in this moment of being in Manny's bed, in his arms, after the most amazing sex she'd ever had in her life. But then she tried to convince herself not to get used to this.

You know firsthand how much of a dog these ballplayers can be. If there's smoke, then there's fire. So don't get too used to this, because you're likely to mess around and get your feelings hurt.

Still, Charisma tried to keep herself together, as this was the best feeling in the world, and she wanted to be nowhere else but caught up in this dream, which was actually true.

Well, if it does end, at least it will have been magical. It will have been great while it lasted. Better to have had it and lost it than to have never had it all.

"Yes, baby. I am now," Charisma answered. Her pussy was still sore from the work Manny had put in. But he wasn't the only one who had given their all. Charisma had returned the favor with no less than equal enthusiasm, maybe more. "Please don't tell me you're ready to go at it again," she said playfully. All she wanted to do now was rest.

"Now that you mentioned it —"

Charisma didn't allow Manny to finish his statement. "You gotta let my body recuperate from last night before we can go for round four. Or is it round five? I've lost count."

"I'm just playing, baby." He squeezed her tighter in his arms. "I just want to hold you in my arms and whisper sweet nothings. Experience pillow talk and heart-to-heart talks, that's all. But you were the one talking about how you were feeling neglected sexually and shit."

"And I've learned my lesson," she joked. "I know when and how to stay in my lane." Then she got serious. "But what is it you want to talk about?"

Manny let Charisma's words marinate for a few beats. Then he said as calmly and as lovingly as he could, "About those bruises that you're still trying to cover on your face with makeup. Are you ready to tell me who did it? Or are we still keeping secrets from each other?"

Secrets? If only he knew the half of it, she thought. Some things were better left buried. People went to the graveyard either to bury the dead or talk to the dead, not to dig them up. At least sane folks didn't do that.

"Does it mean that much to you?" she asked.

"If it involves your safety and you being hurt or taken from me, then yes," Manny said. "Absolutely! It means everything to me." And he meant it. For the first time in his life, he was in love. And he wasn't about to sit back and let someone he loved get hurt by anyone. Not if he could help it.

She kissed him. "It's just a lot . . . , and I don't know how you will feel about me or what you will think of me if I tell you."

"Look, no judging, baby. None whatsoever." He turned to look at her. "Listen, my mind is running wild. This is Miami, and shit is crazy. All I'm saying is, I'm not judging, and whatever it is, we gonna get through it."

Charisma was quiet for a few minutes, trying to make sense of what she should do and at the same time not wanting to let her own mind run wild. But the reality of the situation was that by telling Manny the complete truth and nothing but the truth, she might lose him. However, if she kept everything from him and did not disclose the full story, he might find out some version of the truth, and that could guarantee that she lost him for sure.

She thought about what he had just said about Miami. "Meaning what? Crazy like what?"

"Again, this is Miami, and knowing that, I know how beautiful it is and how ugly it can be."

"But *what* are you saying?"

"What am I just saying? It's Miami, a sex industry hub. Prostitution, escorts, pimps, all that shit. I get it. I see it, and I know people in the midst of it."

"Huh? You think I'm an *escort*?" she blurted out.

"I don't know. All I'm saying is, I'm not judging. You had a life before me, and all

I'm saying is that if *that's* the case, let's figure this shit out, like who you gotta pay to get out of it."

"I'm not no damn whore, prostitute, or escort. You crazy."

"I'm just saying, I don't know if your pimp beat you up, your crazy ex-boyfriend, or what. It just seems your safety is an issue right now. And I don't want to lose you. I mean, I've been making love to your mind over the past few months, and I just made love to you for real. I don't want to lose you."

"I'm not going anywhere. And I can take care of myself."

"Don't seem like it." He looked at the white pillowcase beneath her head. "The makeup you using to cover up the last bit of the bruises is on the pillow, baby. It's there on your face, and I don't like it." Manny was trying to be as patient as he could. He wanted to tread softly so that she would confide in him, but at the same time, he didn't want to play games.

Charisma was quiet for a second. It was definitely pimp or die. Might as well bare it all, she thought. It would eventually come out in the wash. Though she had signed the nondisclosure agreement, Roc was still acting like an asshole and violating her in every way possible. So what did she have to lose? If he was going to try to take everything she had over for this, better now than years from now.

Charisma took a deep breath. "If I tell you, promise me you won't get in trouble. I'ma big girl, and I can handle myself," she said. "Although, I've been doing a pretty poor job of it lately."

Manny promised. "I won't get myself in any trouble, and I promise I won't judge, either, baby." He kissed her on the forehead to assure her. "Now I'm waiting."

Charisma took another deep breath, then began to unburden her soul. "I'm going to keep it real with you —"

"That's the only way to be," he said, cutting her off. "That goes for both of us."

"His name is Roc."

"Roc?" What was he supposed to do with that? "Who the hell is Roc? Does he have a real name?"

Charisma paused. She closed her eyes and said a quick prayer. *God, please make this man have some understanding.*

Then she said, "Jason Albright."

The words hit him like a bag of bricks. "Jason Albright . . . Roc . . . did that to you?" He sat up in the bed. The confusion on his face was unmistakable. "Why? Why would he risk his career by doing something so stupid? I didn't know you knew him. When did you meet him?" He was dumbfounded.

"One question at a time," she said. "What do you want to know first? Why? Or how do I know him?"

Manny tried hard not to think that Charisma was a professional groupie or jump-off. That was the last thing he wanted. Scratching his head, he said, "Start from the beginning."

"You sure you wanna know?" She questioned him to be sure.

He nodded. "Yes, I do."

And so she told him. She told Manny everything. About how she met Roc at the bar, about how Roc impregnated her, about the money. Everything. And whoever had coined the phrase "The truth will make you feel better" was a goddamned liar. Charisma felt horrible. Actually, she felt worse than horrible, if that was possible. She felt like a two-bit, money-chasing whore.

Manny remained quiet the entire time Charisma was unburdening her soul. When she was done, between them, you could hear a church mouse pissing on cotton. It felt like an eternity had passed them by, but in reality only a few minutes had elapsed.

Manny was the one who burst the bubble of silence when he said, "I'm going to *kill* that motherfucking nigga."

Charisma had never seen Manny this angry about anything. He was livid. "Remember," she said, "you promised me that you wouldn't do anything to get yourself in trouble. Don't throw your career away for me. I can take care of myself."

Manny shook his head. "Nah, baby. He has to pay for what he did. And I'm going to be the one doing the collecting." Manny wasn't a gangster by any stretch of the imagination, but he didn't grow up in LA by being a punk. In the hood, the minute a person showed weakness, regardless of how much or how little, the hood ate that person alive. Besides, when he made that promise, he'd had his fingers crossed.

"Manny . . ." She wanted him to look into her eyes, and she wanted to look into his. When their irises locked, she said, "Of course he must pay for this. And he will pay. But by my hands, not yours." Charisma was calm, cool, and collected. "I promise you, on my dead uncle's grave, that this sorry motherfucker will get what he has coming."

"You're right about that," said Manny. "And because your uncle is no longer with us, I'm going to handle it the way I'm sure he would if he was still around. No sweat."

"I appreciate that." She loved this man. And because she loved him so much, she said, "You've got to let me handle this on my own."

Manny said, "You're a lady. And I say that with the utmost respect. But I would feel like less than a man if you didn't allow me to act like one. Roc and I need to handle this man-to-man. You can't fight a grown-ass man." He pointed to her face. "Look what happened the last time you tried."

"Because of the delicacy of this situation, we've got to be smart about this. Calculating. And you have to let me handle it my way."

Two words. "Hell no." Manny wasn't having it.

Charisma refused to back down. "Get out of your emotions," she said. "And allow me to get into your head."

"I'm listening."

"We're a team, right? The only team that we have, yes?"

He nodded. "For sure." And he meant it.

"Then it's imperative that we look out for the team. *Our* team."

Manny said, "And that's what I'm going to do. You're making my point for me."

"You're not thinking," she said. "I'm not

one to count another person's money, but I gotta keep it real with you. I would love you if you were penniless, but I would be lying if I didn't acknowledge that I'm both happy and blessed that you are in a position to feed so many people. Employ so many people. And give back to the less fortunate in and out of the community. You've worked extremely hard all your life to achieve your status, salary, and endorsement deals. And over my dead body will I allow you to be put in a situation where you could lose it all for that sack of shit, Roc."

"It has nothing to do with how much money I have," Manny told her. "It's the principle."

"Until it isn't," she said. Charisma could tell that he was on the fence. "Just give me a few weeks," she said, "and if it isn't handled to your liking by then, we can do it your way. Trust me."

"I hear you," Manny said reluctantly.

Charisma knew it was time for her to step up to the plate and put Roc in his place.

Chapter 32
Checkmate

"Girl, I put that little bitch right in her place." Jasmine was on the phone with her sister, Katrina, telling her about how she'd checked Charisma at the door. The sisters laughed. Katrina still lived in Chicago, and today was Jasmine's last day in the city. Jasmine wanted to get with her big sister, hit up the spa, and catch up.

Katrina said, "No you didn't."

"Please. How dare that bitch call my phone, telling me some bullshit about Roc?"

"What are you going to do now?"

Katrina and Jasmine were as tight as a pair of Iceberg stretch jeans. When they were little and their mother was out tricking to support her drug habit, which seemed like all the time, they had had to fend for themselves. They'd endured a lot of fucked-up things while growing up without a real parent, but the hardship had only made them closer. Together, they had done whatever they had to do to eat and protect one another.

They had vowed always to be there for each other. Whoever made it first would take care of the other. What had seemed like a far-fetched dream was now their reality. Ever since Jasmine had ended up with Roc, their entire lives had changed for the better, and Jasmine would never allow anything to come between that. And just like in old times, Katrina always had her sister's back. By hook or by crook.

But some things got old.

Katrina said, "I know you think that you have everything that you could ever want since you married Roc." They were a real-life rags-to-riches story. "We went from being pimped out by our mama to living a life of luxury. And I'm grateful to you. But, girl, ain't you tired of that same bullshit Roc be doing, and having to always clean up his mess?"

If it were anyone else, Jasmine would've jumped down their throat. But this wasn't someone else. This was Katrina, her older sister. So she remained quiet. Jasmine genuinely cared about what her sister had to say. Katrina was the only one with whom she shared the *real* details of life. Not the fluff, which she gave everyone else. She'd never put on airs with Katrina or pretend that she and Roc lived a perfect life.

Katrina went on. "Don't you think it's time to really focus on you? Stack your paper and work on an exit plan? Before he self-destructs? It's not a matter of *if* he self-destructs. It's *when* he self-destructs."

These were very logical questions, but, of course, Jasmine had not yet accepted the person Roc really was. Jasmine was in denial.

"I think that once he gets out of the NBA, things will change," Jasmine said. "He'll calm down. Women will no longer be throwing themselves at him as much, so there won't be as much temptation. You have to understand. There are so many women who not only want Roc but also want what I got. And I be goddamned if I'm going to sit back and let it happen."

"I hear you, and you know I got your back. However, Roc is getting so sloppy that one day we are not going to be able to cover it up or intimidate these woman, and everything is going to blow up in your face. And I hate to say it, but we are going to lose everything!"

"Well, the thing with Roc is that he's totally honest with me. He tells me everything. So we can problem solve before things get gone. And thank you for always being my partner in crime."

"Well, I'm not sure no man tells any woman everything. Just keep your eyes open and protect yourself. That's all I'm saying. Don't trust that nigga as far as you can see him. And just look out for you sometimes." Katrina didn't want her sister to end up with nothing. She knew Roc wasn't going to change.

"Thank you. I know you mean well."

"I truly do. I just want the best for you, that's all," Katrina said before changing the subject. "So, you put this girl Charisma in her place?"

"Yes. That little bitch is fucking harmless. She's light work and clueless. She's probably somewhere reading a book on the *Kama Sutra* or some shit."

The sisters laughed. Then they looked at Charisma's social media and made jokes and criticized any little thing they found.

"Chile, that bitch don't wanna really fuck with us. And she knows that," Jasmine declared.

"Well, as long as you got her in check, then don't worry about her."

"Trust me, I ain't worried about the country, homey bitch!" Jasmine exclaimed. Just then there was a knock at her door.

"Trina, let me call you back. That's my room service or the contracts for that big-ass Wheaties deal I've been waiting for."

"Yes! Go get it, sis, and call me back."

"Okay. We'll talk soon. Bye."

After she hung up with her sister, Jasmine ran and opened the door.

"Mrs. Albright," the bellman said, "this was just delivered for you."

All smiles, and with thoughts of more dollar signs coming her way, she took the manila envelope out of his hands. "Thank you. These are the Wheaties contracts that I was waiting for," she said excitedly.

She placed the envelope on the desk and ran to get her purse to tip him. She pulled a few bills out of her wallet and dashed back to the door. "Thank you so much," she said as she handed the bellman the bills. Then she shut the door.

She raced back to the desk, opened the envelope, and got the shock of her life.

"What the fuck?" She sat down in the chair in front of the desk. "How could this fucking be?" she screamed. She couldn't help herself. She was hurt, pissed, and as angry as a person could be. Looking at the proof in the pudding, she sobbed. Roc had crossed her in the worst way, and there was no excuse she could find to make up for it or see it in a better light.

In her hands were copies of paternity papers and birth and christening pictures of two children who looked just like her husband but whom she had no clue about. Not one child, but two. There were also pictures of the stripper with whom she and her husband had had a threesome. How could he have kept this from her?

Beneath the pictures and the paternity papers in her hands was another paper. It was a letter. Jasmine read it silently.

You hung up before I could tell you to feel free to drop a note to Terri, but you best believe that I will sell these pictures of these illegitimate kids and his ghetto-ass baby mama — whom I'm sure he's never told you about — to the highest bidder. I never wanted any problems at all! But just so you know, I've done my homework thoroughly. I know about every affair, every rape, every trick, tramp, and tranny he ever fucked with. Yes, there's more where this came from. Just know you can't play with the devil and not get burnt by fire!

Smooches, bitch!

CHAPTER 33
LEAVING . . .

Manny got out of the shower, walked into the bedroom, and saw Charisma putting some things in a duffel bag. "Where are you going? Did I miss something?"

"Naw, you didn't. Just going to spend a few days at my house, that's all."

"Okay. A'ight. Did you put my stuff in there too, since we are both staying over there?" Manny asked, not knowing why she wanted to stay over at her house. But if that was what she wanted, it was okay with him. There was nothing wrong about spending a few days at her house. After all, it was her place. But the fact that she had been at his house for the past few weeks had made him think that he was doing a pretty good job at making her feel comfortable. He guessed a little change in routine would be good for them.

"I didn't think you would want to come," she blurted out.

314

"Why would you think that?" He didn't understand. "Did I do something?"

"No, you didn't. I'll be back in a couple of days."

Manny stood there and glared at her. "So just like that? You'll be back in a couple of days? That's all I get?" he asked, really wanting an explanation.

"Don't do that, Manny."

"It's good, baby. I'm not the one leaving."

"I'm just going home for a few days."

"It's cool. But it's funny that I thought this was now your home, your home away from home. And I thought that we stayed together, no matter where we were in the world. And I thought that we were building."

"We are, and we do."

"Then cut the bullshit," Manny said and left the room.

She plopped down in the chair as he moved around the house. They didn't talk again until he came back into the bedroom.

"Okay, listen, since we can talk about anything!" Charisma said. "I just got my period. I'm bleeding like a banshee, and I don't wanna mess up your sheets. It's just a mess. I'd rather go back home and just spend time in my own bed."

"You joking, right?"

She shook her head no.

"That's the stupidest shit I ever heard."

"No, like, seriously, this is new to me. Ever since I had that abortion almost a year ago, the cramps and bleeding have been unbearable."

"Well, that's human nature. And I could give a fuck about some got damn sheets." He looked at her as if she were crazy. "And as long as you are in the baby-rearing age range, that's going to happen."

"That's the thing. I may not be able to have children," she said.

"You can't be sure of that. Did a doctor tell you that?"

"No, a doctor didn't tell me, but I'm just saying. I went online and looked it up."

"You believe that shit?" He laughed. "That Internet doctor, MD shit will have you ready to plan your funeral if you believe all that bogusness."

"Yeah, but what if I can't have children? Don't you want more kids?"

"Then we will have Star."

"Over her mother's dead body."

"But regardless of what her mother says, if you are with me, Star is ours. And when Star gets older, she will understand."

That sounded good, but the fact of the matter was that Star wasn't yet one year old, and she had a long ways to go before she'd start to understand.

Manny went on. "Listen, before you start canceling out our kids altogether, why don't you go to the doctor and see what's going on? There could be something really going on, something big or small. Just see. Whatever it is, I'm here."

Sounded good to Charisma, but at the same time it was still scary to face whatever it was, and she didn't want any more bad news. Sometimes it was better not knowing.

"Gotta get to practice. Let me know where we are staying tonight." He kissed her on the cheek. "Make the appointment, baby!" he said right before he jetted out of the house.

CHAPTER 34
GET THIS MONEY

The sand in Chucky's proverbial prison hourglass was down to its final grains. In eighty-nine days he would be a free man. As he lay on his bunk, one single thought kept replaying in his head. It was what Charisma had asked him the last time they talked on the phone. *What are you going to do when you get home?*

It was a simple question, and he had a simple answer. *Get money.*

What else was he supposed to do? He'd been locked down for almost three long years. It wasn't as long as it could have been, but it was long enough. Time moved slowly in prison. As slowly as an old lady with arthritic joints and in the throes of the coldest winter ever. Besides, getting money was something he was good at. It was something he'd been doing since he was nine years old. That was how old he was when he was forced into making the decision to become the man of the house. When he put the burden of taking care of the family on his small shoulders.

As he lay on the bunk, he remembered that day twenty-one years ago.

Chucky got off the school bus and ran full speed. He was in a hurry to get home because he knew that his mother would be waiting for him on the front porch, like she did every day. He couldn't wait to share the good news with her. He'd got all greens on his weekly behavioral chart. Finally. It hadn't been easy, but he had learned that, like his mother told him, if he put his mind to it, he could do anything. He had also achieved a perfect score on his math test. But what his mother was going to be most proud of him for was that he hadn't had any altercations with any other kids recently.

But when he reached the steps of the apartment, his mother wasn't waiting for him.

Something isn't right, he thought.

When he walked into the small three-bedroom apartment, where he lived with his mother, Chandra, and three younger siblings, it was dark and unusually cold inside. His mother normally kept the house toasty during the winter. When he flicked the light switch up, nothing happened. He pushed it down and then back up again, but still nothing happened. He was still standing in blackness. The only light came from a few rays of sun that shone through the old blinds in the living-room window.

The house was quiet. Then he heard someone crying. But it wasn't one of his sisters or his brother. This was the crying of an adult. It was his mother's crying.

She was on the phone in her bedroom, and she hadn't heard Chucky when he came in.

"Please," she begged to the person on the other end of the line, "I just need a few more days to pay the bill." Chandra was pleading with a rep at BGE, the power company, to give her an extension on her payment deadline. "Today is Friday, and it's cold outside. I have four small children. I'm begging you. . . ." She was sobbing. "Please, just give me a little more time. Ma'am, please. I've never been late before, until this year." They had cut her hours back at the grocery store. "I'm just having a hard time," she said.

Chandra's "pleases" and pleas fell on deaf ears.

Overhearing his mother begging for a break hurt Chucky more than not having any power to play his video games. Chandra was a proud single mother who worked hard to support her children. She was old school that way. Chandra never complained, and she never held her head down. That wasn't her style.

She cooked, sewed, painted, cleaned, and worked hard. . . . There was nothing that she couldn't do. Chandra was the type of woman who could rub three nickels together and come up with a smooth dollar. Transform leftovers into a tasty full-course meal. And stitch a couple yards of material into a hot new dress. But usually she just made things for her children. The only thing she loved more than her children was God. And Chandra didn't just love her own children; she loved all children.

In Chucky's youthful eyes, his mother was a real live Superwoman and could do anything.

This was the first time he'd ever heard her cry. The pain in her voice made him sad. He was clueless as to what he should do. He wanted to rush into his mother's room, throw his arms around her, and give her a huge hug. But he didn't want his mother to know that he'd heard her crying. Unsure of what to do or how to help, Chucky peeked through the crack in Chandra's door and watched his mother sob. It made him feel worse then he'd ever felt in his entire life.

Suddenly, Chandra dropped down on her knees. She then bowed her head and called out to God. "Oh, my Heavenly Father, please help me and my family through these dark days! Please, God!"

This seemed strange to Chucky. He knew about God. He had no choice; his mother took him and his siblings to church every Sunday. But, to Chucky, calling out to an invisible entity for help didn't seem productive. He wouldn't call it a waste of time, but he could think of a few better ways to make a dollar than waiting for an invisible person to show up and pay the bill.

Hearing his mother cry and beg the lady on the phone to turn on the lights and then seeing her fall on her knees filled his young heart with unsolicited emotions. There was no one in this world whom Chucky loved more than his mother. And even at nine years old, he knew he had to do something.

But what?

His mother had always been there for other people. Once, when she and Chucky were leaving the grocery store, a woman begging for money had confronted them. "Can you spare some change?" she had asked, and then she'd explained that she was down on her luck. Chandra had asked the woman where her shoes were. Her feet were dirty, like she'd been playing kickball without socks.

"Someone stole them," the lady said. "From the shelter." Chandra gave the woman a five-dollar bill. The woman smiled. "Thank you, ma'am. I really appreciate it." The woman then explained to his mother how she had lost her job and her boyfriend in the same week. A couple of months later she'd got evicted. "Just because a person is on the street, asking for money," she said, "doesn't mean they're free-loaders."

Before they were done talking, Chandra had given the woman the shoes off her feet. When Chucky asked his mother why she had given her shoes away, Chandra said, "She needed them more than me, son."

But even Superwoman needed a superhero to lean on sometimes. So, since Chucky was the eldest child, he decided to take on the roll. He would be her Superman in her time of need.

He placed his progress report, with its all green marks, on the kitchen table, where his mother would see it when she came out of her room. Then, just as quietly as he'd come inside, he slipped out the front door. The neighborhood IGA grocery store was only a few blocks away. Chucky had made the walk many times. If he rode his bike, it took him only a couple of minutes to cover the short distance. His plan was to help the old ladies carry their grocery bags to their car for tips. It was a hustle he'd done on occasion before, but today he hoped to catch one of the women feeling extra generous.

Sometimes a person just needed to be in the right place at the right time, he thought. But he did not know if that right place and time would be the grocery store parking lot at 5:36 p.m.

Two teenage boys eyeballed Chucky as he hustled for groceries.

One of them cupped his hands over his mouth so that his voice would carry across the parking lot. "C'mere, youngin'. Let me holla at cha for a sec," he called.

Chucky pointed to himself.

"You the only li'l youngin' out here, ain't cha?" The boy looked to be around eighteen or so. "C'mere," he repeated.

Chucky thought he went to school with the dude's little brother. But he'd never seen the other teenager before.

The one unfamiliar to Chucky said, "What's your name?" He was smoking a loosely rolled Black & Mild cigar.

Chucky asked, "Who wants to know?"

The two older boys laughed. Their gold-teeth smiles sparkled under the sunlight.

The one smoking the Black & Mild said, "That right, li'l homey." He nodded. "Never give anything away for free. Not even your name. My name's Mike." Then he pointed to his partner. "And this is Buck." Buck had a cigarette tucked behind his left ear. "So," Mike asked again, "what's your name, youngin'?"

"Chucky."

Buck asked him how much money he'd made hustling for grocery bags.

Chucky didn't answer.

Buck said, "Ain't nobody fittin' to rob yo' li'l scary ass fo' no chump change."

"I'm not scared. Just don't see why it's your business, that's all." He'd made a little more than six dollars: four dollars in singles, and another two and a quarter in change.

Buck put his hands up in mock surrender. "My bad, my dude. You right. Didn't mean to get all up in yo' B.I.," he said. "I just thought you might be trying to make some real bread. But if you happy with pennies . . ."

With his hand in his pocket, Chuck fingered the $6.25 and reflected on his mother, at home, crying and begging on the phone in the dark. The reason he was outside hustling in the first place. "How much money?"

Mike said, "That depends on you."

Chucky was candid. "I need enough to get the lights turned back on," he said. He was also clueless as to how much that would take. "What will I need to do to get enough money to turn on the lights tonight?"

Buck said, "All you have to do is keep a lookout for the po-po for us."

Chucky didn't hesitate. "Okay."

They gave Chucky a burner cell phone.

"If you see the cops, just push this button," Buck instructed.

And that was how it started. After looking out for Buck and Mike that day in the grocery store parking lot, he never looked back. Over the next couple of years Buck and Mike would give Chucky an in-depth course in hustling. Cutting and packaging dope became his specialty.

CHAPTER 35
THE HUSTLE IS ON. . . .

Chucky kicked back on his bunk, that metal rack bolted to the wall of the six-by-nine-foot cage that the Department of Corrections called a room. He leafed through a Nikki Turner book as he pondered again that last conversation he'd had with Charisma. She knew him like a book.

"I already know you're going to hustle. It's ingrained in your DNA. All I'm saying is that at some point you're going to have to change it up. Just because you hustle doesn't mean that you have to continue hustling in the same way. You can hustle with anything — cars, houses, lawn care . . . anything. This may come as a surprise to you, Chucky, but drugs aren't the only way to make a dollar."

"I know, Charisma." He hated when she was right and rubbed it in.

"And you see where that violent shit will get you."

"That violent shit saved both your and my

life," he reminded her.

"And I'll never be able to thank you enough for it." And she meant it. She thought about it every night, before she went to sleep, and every morning, when she got up. If it weren't for Chucky, she would be dead as a stray dog loitering in the back of a Chinese restaurant. "I just don't ever want to see you in a place like this again."

"Me either. This shit here wasn't built for humans, girl. Not civilized humans, anyway. White folks treat their pets better than they treat us in this piece."

"That's why I want you to think of a business you can start when you get out. I'm doing well for myself, and I want to help you out."

"I'm good." He didn't want to keep taking her money. "You've done enough already," he said. "I'm just upset that I'm not there to look out for you."

"I don't need you to 'look out' for me that way. Aren't you listening to me? I'm trying to keep you away from that type of foolishness."

Chucky wasn't trying to hear it. "I'd rather be locked down for the rest of my life than let a nigga violate you physically." He was talking about the situation with Roc.

"That's going to be taken care of. Trust me. At the end of the day, karma will catch up with that nigga for what he did."

"That's some bullshit. I don't believe in leaving my beefs for nature to take care of. You remind me so much of my mother. That's probably why I fuck with you so hard. But you both believe in that supernatural shit way too hard. God helps those who help themselves, yo."

"We on a whole new playing field, right, Chucky? And we don't need to be doing anything stupid to block our blessings."

"You mean you, not we," he said, correcting her.

"If I got it, you got it," she said. "Stop being so pessimistic. Things are going to be okay. And there will be a time to pay respects to those who've wronged us. Just not right now."

Chucky said, "I hope you just blowing smoke up my ass because you're talking on these penitentiary phones."

"I'm being real," she said. "All I'm saying is that I don't want you to get out with one foot already back inside."

"I hear you."

"So, you're going to think about what I said? And let me know the next time we talk?"

Chucky knew that Charisma meant well. And most importantly, deep down inside, he knew that she was right. He definitely needed to change up his game.

His thoughts were interrupted when Pretty

Boy Rich came into his cell. "What it do, my man?" He was carrying two big commissary bags.

Chucky sat up and put his feet on the floor. "Looks like Christmas, and you Saint Nick and shit."

Pretty Boy Rich dumped out the contents of the two bags on the foot of Chucky's bunk. "I appreciate you for looking out for me the way you did."

Chucky shrugged. "Ain't nothing but the right thing to do. One hustler playing fair with another. Ya feel me?"

Chucky didn't know much about Pretty Boy Rich except that he was a pimp on the land and he'd got hit with an asshole full of time for human trafficking. When he got to the compound, he'd been broke because he couldn't reach his folks and it took a couple of weeks for your money to catch up with you from another camp. Chucky had stepped in and had helped him out by paying for some stuff he needed.

"That's what makes it a big deal. There's not that many real niggas left. You didn't know me from a hole in the wall, but you looked out for me. That's why I'm paying you back double. Just to let you know that I appreciate it. My main bitch just got back to rolling, and my money just caught up

330

with me. My books stacked like Nicki Minaj's ass in a string bikini in this bitch. If you need anything, let me know."

Chucky gave Pretty Boy Rich a mock salute. "Respect."

Then Chucky began to look through the stuff on his bunk. As he combed through everything, he ran across a commissary receipt. It belonged to Pretty Boy Rich. The balance on the bottom of the receipt was seventy-nine hundred dollars. That was official baller bread inside the walls. Chucky wasn't impressed. And if Pretty Boy Rich had left it there intentionally, that was some cornball shit to do. Chucky hoped that wasn't the case, because he liked dude. But he wouldn't let that stand in the way of him peeping game when game presented itself.

"Here you go. This yours," he said and held out the receipt.

Pretty Boy Rich took it and then asked, "You from out here? You don't really flow like a Maryland cat."

"Baltimore born and bred," Chucky said. "What about you? Hold on. Let me guess. Cleveland?"

"Memphis."

Chucky nodded. "How'd you get caught up in this part of the world?"

"The same way any hustler gets caught

331

up. Chasing," said Pretty Boy Rich.

Chucky nodded. "And the chase always involves one of two things."

They both said it at the same time. "Money or bitches."

"If not both," Pretty Boy Rich added.

They laughed and talked some more.

"Nigga, you short, huh?" Pretty Boy Rich asked later in their conversation.

"Yeah, I'm short." Chucky smiled. He would never let another inmate know how short he actually was.

"Nigga, I'ma have to give you a course on breaking these bitches. That violence shit will get you caught up with football numbers. You smooth enough to get these bitches to pay you."

Chucky laughed. "That ain't really my thing, bro."

"Well, it sure don't hurt to listen."

"You're right about that."

Chucky wanted this last little bit of time in prison to pass by quickly, so he listened to the pimp talk the whole time. He knew that good behavior time was a motherfucker, and all he could do was listen so he didn't caught up. Who knew? He might be able to use what he learned when he tried to turn over a new leaf down the road.

CHAPTER 36
THE JAM

After three hours of grueling practice, Manny was back in the locker room. He had just come out of the shower and was getting dressed when his cell phone rang.

He put his earpiece in and pushed talk. "Hello?"

"Hey, Manny. It's Fab. Quick question. You got a minute?"

Tying the laces on his sneakers, Manny said, "Sure. What's up?"

"Just working hard, that's all. I performed to a sellout crowd at the Garden last night."

"And I wouldn't expect anything else."

Fabiola let out a chuckle. "But I called to find out what you guys are going to do for Charisma's birthday. Something private, or are you throwing a party? Because I'm in town tomorrow, and if it's going to be a party, I'll stay an extra day, as I wouldn't want to miss it."

Manny was flummoxed. Charisma had

been practically living full-time in his house for the past three months, and she hadn't whispered a peep about a birthday coming up. And Manny was clueless. What kind of man didn't know his girl's birth date?

Damn. He was slipping!

"I didn't think she told anyone," Manny said. "She certainly hasn't told me. How did you find out?"

"Well, you know how she is. She never wants anyone to make a big deal out of anything as far as she's concerned. But I know the date because she mentioned it when we had lunch that first time. I asked what her zodiac sign was, because we act so much alike. Come to find out are both Taurus. Her birthday is on the tenth, seven days before mine. I think that's one of the reasons we hit it off so well. So what do you have planned? Anything?"

Nada. Zilch. Not a thing was what he had planned. But there was no way on God's green earth that Manny was going to admit that he did not know Charisma's b-day. Not a chance.

"Shit!" Thinking on his feet, Manny said, "I'm throwing her a surprise party at Club Shine. Nothing big. Just a few of her closest friends and family from back home."

"I know I don't have to tell you, but make it really nice for her."

"I will. I'm going to call Jacob, 'cause he's part owner, to make sure I can get the club and the party planner chick he uses."

"A'ight. I will be over early tomorrow. Catching the red-eye, so as soon as I land, I will come straight there, and she and I can go shopping. Girl stuff."

"She'll be thrilled to see you, and don't tell her about the party."

"A surprise, huh?"

"Yep. She has no idea."

And just a few minutes ago, neither had he. Luckily, Manny didn't have a game tomorrow.

"I'm there," said Fabiola. "You can count me in."

"Cool. And remember. Don't spill the beans. If you tell her, I'm going to be mad."

"The secret is safe with me. I'll see you later," she said before they ended the call.

The first thing he had to do was get Jacob to book the party at the club. Then he had to locate Charisma's closest friends and family from Baltimore, fly them to Miami, and put them up in a hotel — without Charisma getting a whiff of his plan. And he had about forty-eight hours to whip it all together. No problem. He'd make it happen.

Anything for the love of his life!

Chapter 37
The Birthday Girl . . .

"Happy birthday to ya! Happy birthday to ya! Happy birthday!"

Charisma eyes popped open to the soulful voice of Fabiola. When she realized that God had given her another day, and that her great friend and favorite singer was serenading her in her handsome, rich boyfriend's house, which she now shared with him, a joyous smile immediately covered her face.

"Happy birthday to our dear friend Charisma! Happy birthday to you!" Fabiola sang, hitting a high note.

Charisma sat up in the bed and smiled when Chef Lester held a beautiful heart-shaped birthday cake in front of her so that she could blow out the candle. "Oh, my goodness. Aw."

"Make a wish, baby!" Manny said.

Charisma closed her eyes and blew out the candle, and everyone else in the room started clapping.

"Happy birthday, baby." Manny kissed her. "And I want this to be the absolutely most special day ever!"

"Aw!" everyone else in the room said in unison, taken by how sweet the moment was.

After that Fabiola's assistant stopped recording the scene on a phone and then handed the phone to her boss. Fabiola played back the video and exclaimed, "Oh, my God! This is so amazing!"

"Girl, let me see that." Charisma took the phone out of her hand and played the video. "I can't believe you were recording me while I was sleeping."

"This is amazing. Just look at it," Fabiola told her.

"I look crazy," Charisma said.

"No you don't!" Fabiola looked over her shoulder and examined the video a little closer. "You look like Sleeping Beauty."

Charisma looked closer too. "This hair, though?" Still, she couldn't deny that her long, wavy weave had just somehow fallen into place, even though she had slept on it.

"That's the good hair. That's expensive, high-quality stuff," Fabiola quipped.

Everyone laughed.

"I wasn't even expecting anything at all.

How did you know it was my birthday?" Charisma said.

"We never forget the important days of the people we love," Manny said.

"Ms. Charisma," Chef Lester said, "in honor of your birthday, I'm making all your favorite things for your birthday breakfast."

Charisma smiled. "Aw, thank you so much! It means a lot to me," she said to Chef Lester. She was always so nice not only to him but also to the rest of the staff. Though they were the hired help, she realized that they were humans, and she treated them as such. That was her demeanor; she was always so humble and gracious with anyone who did anything for her.

"Of course, we really like having you around here. You've really brightened the place up. And we all want you to have a wonderful day," the chef said.

"Is that so?" Manny said to Chef Lester. He hadn't known that was how Chef Lester felt about Charisma, as the man usually didn't say much.

"Yes. All the staff thinks so," Chef Lester admitted. "It was always a house, but she makes it feel more like a home."

Manny smiled and had to agree that having Charisma at the house was definitely a treat.

"Would you like me to leave the cake here or take it into the kitchen for later?" the chef asked.

"Kitchen for later, please. It's going to ruin my appetite for this amazing birthday breakfast you're cooking up."

"Yes. You are very right." Chef Lester left the room and took the cake with him.

Fabiola plopped down on the bed, beside Charisma. "So your big spender here" — she motioned with her head to Manny — "is taking us to dinner tonight, so we gotta go get you something fierce to wear. I have a guy coming over with some things, but I think we should hit the streets and go shopping."

"Aw, Fab. You don't have to. I can wear something in my closet. I have some new things."

"Girl, no!" Fabiola wouldn't have it. "You already know that I'm going to be posting them pics of your birthday all day, making these chicks jealous."

Charisma shook her head. "No, don't do that."

"Yes, do it," Manny urged, adding fuel to the fire. Then he said, "A'ight, ladies. I'm thinking breakfast will be ready in about thirty minutes, and then you can go to do y'all girl things." He put one of his credit cards on the night table. "Get whatever nice things you want."

"Oh my!" Charisma said. "You don't have to do that."

"It's the least I can I do. It's my pleasure, baby."

While Manny and Charisma bantered back and forth, Fabiola laughed as she looked at the likes and the responses she was getting from the video she'd posted. It wasn't even 9:00 a.m. yet, and the video had already gone viral. It was everywhere, and everybody was talking about how sweet it was, how elaborate the bed and the other furnishings were in the room in which Charisma slept, and how beautiful the blue water that surrounded the huge, lavish house was.

Most of the comments were very kind, but with every positive, there was always a negative. The president of their Hater Aid Club was Bing. And best believe, she was going to make sure that it wasn't a happy fucking birthday, but a birthday to remember!

CHAPTER 38
CLUB SHINE

"Surprise!" everybody said in unison when Charisma entered Club Shine.

Charisma had the surprise of her life when she looked around and saw her cousins from Baltimore and a couple of her high school friends, ones Wanda knew she would be happy to see again. Not to mention the beautiful decor, the flowers, the ice sculptures, the chandelier that hung from the ceiling. The place was stunningly gorgeous!

Club Shine had a private restaurant on one side and a club on the other, and it was one of the most elite private venues in Miami, available only to the very rich and famous who were close friends and favored clients of Jacob and his partner.

"Oh, my goodness," Charisma whispered. Her smile lit up all of South Beach as she gave hugs and kisses to her family and friends and to Manny's closest friends and family.

Manny really wanted Charisma's birthday party to be special. And not only did he want to show Charisma how special she was to him and how blessed they all were to know her, but he also wanted his family and his friends to meet her and see firsthand how special she truly was.

Manny's mother, Terri, who was extremely overprotective of her only son, had put it in her mind a couple of months ago that she wasn't going to like Charisma. In fact, nobody was going to be good enough for her son. So she had been side-eyeing and watching Charisma, and studying her body language and her interactions with her family and friends, since the party began, wanting more than anything to find something, any little thing, to validate her a priori negative opinion of Charisma. But all she had seen so far was a wholesome, genuine lady who wasn't into her son's glitz and glam and who had even been catering to Manny on her own birthday. Looks could be very deceiving, but Charisma's doting on her son did something to her. As much as Terri didn't want to like Charisma, the young woman had won her over.

"If this girl is a fraud, she's good," she said to Manny's aunt.

"Well, I guess after all that mess he went

through with that Bing character, anybody is better than that thing," Manny's aunt replied.

"I like her," Terri said to her son after he walked up to her, bringing her a glass of champagne.

That made him smile. That was something he had never heard from his mother.

Just then Charisma appeared. "How are you enjoying yourself? Is there anything I can get you?" she asked Terri.

"Baby, it's your birthday. We are all here to cater to you," Terri assured her.

"Yes, but you are my guest. And you are my man's mother, and you are special, so I have no choice but to cater to you."

Terri gleamed. She was about to choke, because in her eyes this girl had the potential to be everything that she wanted for her son, if indeed she had to come to terms with the fact that her son would one day get married and settle down. Charisma wasn't as flashy and flamboyant as Bing was, and she was truly what Manny needed.

"You are such a sweet girl," Terri said.

"Thank you so much! I'm happy to meet you, and I just wanted to say thank you for raising such a wonderful man, one with manners and principles and morals. Those are the things that only a mother can instill in a son."

Terri nodded, which took her off her square. "I like you for my son. I hope you two really work out. And I hope I don't have to whip your ass, like I had to do to that goddamned Bing."

"No', ma'am. That won't be necessary," Charisma said, not knowing what else to say.

Manny stared at his mother. "Mama, stop."

"Forgive me, honey. I had to be real with you. But please forgive me. My son won't tolerate that. And I don't want him to be mad at me."

"No problem." Charisma smiled. She couldn't help but think that Manny's mother was off the hook and that his baby mama was insane. Manny for sure had to find solace in her.

Once they met her, everyone loved Charisma, and if they had any kind of reservations about her not being the one for Manny, they abandoned them at that party and realized that she was definitely what he needed and wanted in his life.

The vibe in the room was so electric, and the champagne bottles and pictures were popping. Fabiola had her assistant with her, and the assistant seemed to be acting as

Fabiola's personal photographer and videographer. Fabiola sorted through the photos and posted the best ones, along with the hash tag that the publicist for the event had created. Other celebrity guests did the same. As a result, things were going viral again, and folks were heading down to Club Shine, wanting to get in on the party and the fun.

Charisma posted a message on her own social media. Today is the best day of my life.

She was always amazed at how when she moved to Miami, she'd had only twelve hundred friends, but ever since her and Manny's first date at that basketball game, she had had over half a million followers.

And you haven't even seen your gifts yet! Manny responded to her post.

The blogs ate up everything about this day, and every single thing they posted about her birthday created a buzz. All their lovers and haters were watching.

By then the party had moved into the club area, and that was when it had gone from being a private affair to being off the chain. Three superstar DJs spun the hottest, most intoxicating beats and melodies, giving folks no choice but to hit the dance floor. Every ten minutes someone said happy birthday to Charisma.

While folks danced, confetti fell from the ceiling. Manny had pulled out all the stops. Then Cirque du Soleil dancers and trapeze artists appeared above and performed over the dancers' heads. Lots of Manny's athletic and celebrity friends were there, and when the Cirque du Soleil act was over, his friends who were singers and rappers serenaded Charisma. It seemed like there was a concert going on, and there was one performance after another. Given the way the pictures orbited on social media, those who hadn't been invited to the party felt jealous, as it was the best party of the night.

While his friends performed, Manny and Charisma mingled, hand in hand, entertaining their guests and enjoying her birthday and this celebration of her life.

Mission accomplished! Manny thought as he stood at Charisma's side. Now he could finally relax.

He leaned over and whispered in her ear. "Babe, I'll be back. Going to have a cigar with my peoples to celebrate your life," he said as he let her hand go.

She nodded, smiled. "Thank you, baby! For all of this! This is way more than I could have ever asked for!"

"You deserve it," he told her before she sent him on his way with a long, passionate tongue kiss. And he meant it. In fact, it was the best money he'd spent in a while. Making her happy made him feel good.

He slipped away and headed to the back of the VIP suite, where he finally got a chance to kick it with his boys, Raheem and Jamar.

Raheem couldn't help but give his boy his props. "Man, you outdid yourself. I ain't never seen you go this hard for a broad."

"That's 'cause he ain't never had no bitch worth shit. And deep throating don't count," Jamar joked, but he was serious as a heart attack.

The three fellas laughed as they lit expensive Cuban cigars and smoked them with a certain swagger, as if they were in a Mafia movie.

"She's a good chick," Jamar mused while they puffed away. "I met her, and I think she brings out the best in him."

"Yeah, she do," Raheem agreed. "Don't fuck this up!"

"Never thought I'd see my man fuck with a chick this hard, though," Jamar added before pulling on his cigar.

"Definitely, she worth it." Manny nodded.

The three old friends were laughing and kicking it when Manny looked up and couldn't believe his eyes. His smile turned into a frown. Manny watched the unwanted guest walk through the place like he owned it. The man drank the champagne like it was Kool-Aid, one glass after another, as he made his rounds around the place, looking, it appeared, for Charisma.

Across the room, Roc approached Wanda and pulled a small wrapped box out of his pocket and proffered it to her, but Wanda refused to accept it from him. He said something to Wanda, and she gave him a dirty look. It looked as if she wanted to hit him, but she didn't want to make a scene. It was the wrong place, wrong time.

Manny felt disrespected. How dare this motherfucker show up uninvited at a party he had bankrolled for his woman's birthday?

"Who the fuck invited that nigga Roc?" Manny snarled. "I can't stand that nigga. On the court, all he does is whine to the referee. Fucking dick. His old ass need to retire."

The trio watched Roc take pictures with the waitstaff and several other people and then boldly walked around the place, as if he was the nigga who had sponsored the event. Then he even had the nerve to post a picture on his social media, saying Happy born day to such an amazing lady. Oh, what a night, my great friend!

Manny's blood pressure rose. He felt like he had egg on his face the way Roc walked around the place and continued to act like he was having a ball, disregarding what the hell he had done to Charisma. Roc was carrying on conversations, laughing, giving people five. The more Roc worked the room, the angrier Manny got.

Manny's veins looked like they were about to pop out of his head as he watched Roc approach, and Big Dre could see it. That was how it was between Big Dre and his boss. He had been working for Manny for years. And Manny never had to say anything to Big Dre; the trusted bodyguard could read the expressions on Manny's face and figure out what was going on. That was how Big Dre knew now that Roc's ass had to go, before there were some serious problems.

Someone directed Roc to the VIP suite, which was where Roc assumed Charisma was most likely to be. He walked into the VIP.

"You gone have to leave up outta here, my man," Big Dre said to him.

"A'ight. No problem." Roc put his hand on his stomach. "I just gotta shit so bad, so I'm going to use the restroom and go. Too much liquor too quick." Roc moved past Big Dre quickly, before Big Dre could even stop him. Roc's moves were smooth, almost like they were with the guys on the court, and a minute later he was in the VIP restroom.

Big Dre was perplexed that this nigga had skated past him so quick.

"Yo, man, you need to leave. Some shit 'bout to go down, and I don't want you in it," Manny said through his teeth, almost spitting venom. "This nigga just disrespectful, showing up."

"Nigga, I got you."

"Aye, yo, Big Dre. Secure the door. Don't let a motherfucker in this bitch! Ya hear me?"

Dre nodded, thinking Manny was going to go in the restroom and have a talk with Roc. But with every step he took, Manny resembled the Incredible Hulk more and more. He looked like he was about to bust out of his shirt. He got to the restroom door, with his two homeboys in tow.

"Don't let a motherfucker in here, and don't fucking stop me," Manny said to Jamar.

Roc was sitting on the toilet, taking a dump, with his phone in his hand. "Yeah, Jasmine. I'ma be home in a few. Just out at a friend's birthday party."

Just then Manny kicked the door in, like

he was the motherfucking police or an MMA fighter. The door hit Roc so hard, it knocked him off the toilet. Sent him to the concrete floor. Roc had kicked the door straight off the hinges.

Roc had no clue as to what had hit him. All he knew was that he had indeed been caught with his pants down.

"You wanna be disrespectful!" Manny yelled. Then he gave Roc a hard blow to the head, which left him facedown on the concrete floor.

Manny grabbed him around the neck and put his head in the toilet with the bowel movement he had just made and flushed it a few times, making Roc almost choke to death. Roc was trying to catch his breath, and then he stopped trying.

"Motherfucker, breathe!" Manny screamed at him, letting him up from the toilet for a few seconds. "I'm going to kill you, but you don't get to die that quick."

Once Manny knew he hadn't killed Roc, he wanted Roc to know just what the fuck had hit him. He started wringing his neck again. With shit all over Roc's face, Manny dragged him out of the stall and proceeded to beat his head against the urinal. Manny was in a rage, and blood was everywhere. Manny wanted to kill him. Every time he thought about what Roc had done to Charisma's face, and about the makeup she'd had to wear for weeks to cover the bruises on her face, the makeup that had ended up on his expensive white pillowcases, he punched Roc and stomped on his balls.

Blood was everywhere, as if someone had given Roc a blood bath. Horror movies didn't have that much blood.

Raheem stopped him, grabbed his arm. "Man, you can't kill him."

"Oh, the fuck I can't!" Manny yanked his arm away.

"You got too much to lose."

"I'm sorry . . . ," Roc cried out, barely getting it out.

"Man, you kill him, you go to prison, and you can't be with your woman," Raheem said calmly.

Manny hit Roc again, imagining Roc's face was a wall and his own hand was a bat.

Just then Jacob entered the restroom. "Oh shit!"

Jacob began to access the situation. Then he walked over and looked at Roc, who was barely breathing. He looked him in the eye and said, "Listen, you absolutely brought this on yourself. You know this. If you press charges, we will release the video of you raping Charisma at her house."

"Video?" Roc looked surprised.

"That's right. We secretly installed cameras in her house, just to make sure we could trust her," Jacob said, bluffing, but Roc didn't know that. "Press charges, and you will lose every single endorsement deal and contract. I will personally see to it. So just . . . let the shit go."

Roc was crying like a baby; his lip was quivering.

"Hello! Roc! Hello!" A voice was coming from Roc's cell phone, which was lying on the floor, with a cracked screen.

Raheem picked it up. "Yeah? Hello."

"Where is Roc?" Jasmine yelled.

"Um . . . he's not available right now. He just got his disrespectful ass mopped across the floor. You might wanna pick his ass up from the alley of Club Shine!"

"Do you know who you are fucking with?" Jasmine screamed into the phone.

"Bitch, karma just caught up with this nigga," Raheem said and then disconnected the call.

"I need to see a doctor, please," Roc barely managed to say.

"Should've thought about that before you came in here," Manny shouted.

Jacob walked over to Manny. "Listen, you've made your point here. Being that I'm part owner of this place, we will get it cleaned up and you cleaned up. Put out that Roc was drunk and had an accident. You will pull it together and take your family home and carry the party to your house. Take pics and have everyone continue to post, as if everything is fine, fun, and it never happened."

"I need you to get to Charisma," Manny said to Jamar.

"No, I will go," Jacob said just as Big Dre entered the restroom and surveyed the scene. "Big Dre, I'm going to need you to get this motherfucker outta here. Wrap him in this and put that motherfucker in the alley. Meanwhile, Manny, I'm going to get you moved to the back office and get you cleaned up. Guys will be in here to bleach this place down."

Jacob tiptoed across the blood, fixed his suit, and headed out the double doors of the suite's restroom while everyone fell into place to clean up the scene of this gruesome ass whipping that Manny had given Roc.

Thank God there was a private entrance to get in and out of the VIP suite. Otherwise, they would have been fucked.

Big Dre picked up Roc like he was a feather.

"Oh shit! My ribs are broke," Roc screeched.

"Shut the fuck up. Better be happy your legs ain't broke," Big Dre growled.

"Oh, don't forget that nigga's teeth on the floor, Dre," Jamar said, but Dre kept it moving.

Outside the double doors of the VIP, the party was still going on. Everybody was lit and was dancing and drinking.

As soon as Jacob walked out the door, he spotted Charisma, who looked as if she was looking for Manny.

"Hey, Jacob, have you seen Manny?" she called.

"Yes! I have." He smiled, then leaned in to whisper in her ear. "Don't look surprised when I tell you what you have to do," he said. "Keep smiling. Don't let your face crack."

She nodded.

"Manny just beat the living shit out of Jason Albright in the bathroom."

Charisma's heart dropped, but she kept a poker face on and kept her mouth from dropping. "Is he okay?" she asked in a worried tone. "I need to see him."

"Yes. We are cleaning it up now. Gather your family and closest friends together and head outside. Manny will be out shortly and will get them all in the Sprinter, and he'll move the party to the house."

"Should I wait on him?"

"Yes!" He nodded.

"Okay." She smiled, relieved, and then she took a deep breath. "Are you sure he's okay?"

"Yes. I'm positive." Jacob nodded.

"Okay. Thank you so much, Jacob, for helping out with this. I truly appreciate you having his back," she said with a slight smile as she grabbed his hand. "Thank you again."

There was something about the concern and the warmth in her voice at that moment that made Jacob change his opinion about Charisma.

Charisma did exactly as she was told, and rounded up her family and friends and headed out the front door. Her phone went off. It was a text message. She hoped that it was Manny . . . but it wasn't.

Burn . . . baby! Burn!

And someone said, "Oh shit!"

High-pitched screams and chatter pierced the air.

"Somebody call nine-one-one!" a man shouted.

The sounds of the panicked crowd redirected Charisma's attention from her phone to what was going on. Just then

357

Fabiola's security guard grabbed her hand, and in turn she took Wanda's hand. The guard whisked Charisma back into the club, with Wanda in tow. Charisma looked out the window and saw a Bentley with brand-new paper tags on it in flames! The flames were high and red hot.

"What in the hell?" she murmured.

"Someone set the car on fire!" Wanda exclaimed.

"*Damn!* Whose is it?" Charisma said.

"Talk about burning to a damn crisp! That shit is done!" said Fabiola's security guard.

The mayor, a friend of theirs, came over and was in tears. "My car. I just got it today."

The ladies were shaking their heads in disbelief, trying to figure out how a wonderful night could turn into something so crazy. They were thankful that they were nowhere near the flames.

Some of Jacob's staff went to work on the fire. Once it was out, and the coast was clear, Charisma and her friends and family headed outside again. They started walking toward the Sprinter, a large van, intent on heading to Manny's house to finish out the night.

As Charisma headed in the direction of the Sprinter, she couldn't believe her eyes.

Just when she had thought the night couldn't get any crazier, in front of her stood none other than Chucky!

Happy motherfucking birthday . . . Damn right.

This had turned into a birthday to remember.

CHAPTER 39
IN THE WEE HOURS

Miami-Dade Police swarmed down Ocean Drive like a mass of angry bees. Red and blue flashing lights reflected off the buildings and cars. And no one was allowed to leave Club Shine without first being interviewed by the cops. Money and fame meant nothing at that moment. No one was going anywhere anytime soon.

The new Bentley Mulsanne that had been torched in the parking lot was now at full-blown barn fire status. Trucks from two separate stations were on deck to extinguish the flames before the $350,000 automobile exploded.

And just like the Bentley, social media was on fire with the news.

Posts of Roc wearing ripped clothes and looking disheveled were all over the Internet. He was also stumbling in some of the photos that appeared. People were posting that the famous basketball player Roc was as drunk as an inebriated fish. His publicist tried to spin the story by saying that he'd got trampled by hordes of frightened club goers. But pictures later revealed that Roc had been caught the bad end of a vicious beat down and had not been trampled on.

News and tabloid vans squatted behind the yellow police tape like hungry vultures in search of a piece of decaying meat. And they acted as if they would kill one another for an exclusive.

From the Mercedes Sprinter, which remained parked in the parking lot, under police supervision, Charisma and her gang watched it all unfold live and in living color, all the while recording everything on their smartphones.

Under her breath, so that no one could hear, Charisma asked Wanda if she'd seen Chucky.

Wanda said, "He's locked up, isn't he? Unless you know something I don't know."

"Not really," she said. "It's kinda weird."

"How so?"

"Before we got in the van, I locked eyes with him. He was just standing there, watching."

Wanda asked, "Are you sure it was him?"

"We were no more than twenty feet apart from each other. But there were at least a hundred people between us. I turned away for a split second to tell Big Dre to give me a minute. And by the time I turned back around, he was gone."

"Don't he have another year to do?" Wanda was skeptical. "Did you know he was home?"

"Not a clue. But that good behavior shit is a bitch. Maybe I should've been paying attention to what was going on since his time was a little closer. And why wouldn't he tell me he was home?"

"If it was him," Wanda said, "maybe he wanted to surprise you."

"I've known Chucky all my life. I know what he looks like. It was Chucky, all right."

Wanda was momentarily speechless. She didn't want to alarm her cousin, but the shit seemed hella sketchy to her. "I'm sure he has a good reason for not telling you, girl."

To be honest, neither cousin knew what to think.

Charisma's cell rang. She thought it was a text message from Manny. But she was only half right. It was a text message. But the message was not from Manny. It was Chucky.

Hey, baby girl. It's me. Chucky. I'm going to call you in the morning. I saw someone I need to address! Whatever you do, be careful and stay put!

Charisma examined every word of the text for a secret meaning. If he was trying to tell her something, she had no clue as to what it was. Her mind ran wild with no explanations. Who in the hell did Chucky know in Miami? Was he planning to do something? Was Chucky going to do something to Manny?

Melvin, Charisma's cousin, overheard the entire conversation between Wanda and Charisma. He told Charisma, "You already know that nigga Chucky got some shit up his sleeve." Then he added, "But it's all good."

Charisma spotted a friend of Manny's trying to ear hustle her conversation. Melvin noticed it also and killed the conversation.

Charisma texted Chucky back.

Please! Please! Whatever you do, be careful. And don't do anything crazy! Please! I'm begging you!

Then she inhaled a deep breath of air and tried to relax. But it didn't work. She couldn't stop thinking about Chucky and wondering what he was planning to do. Charisma kept trying to tell herself to think positive thoughts. But it proved to be more difficult to do than it sounded in her head.

For one, Charisma knew that Chucky didn't play games. And he had no problem doing what most people only thought about doing. So that she wouldn't go crazy, she reminded herself that they were in Miami. It was possible to run into anybody on South Beach. After all, it was one of the hippest tourist spots in the United States.

"Oh shit!" said Fabiola's assistant.

Her outburst caught the attention of most of the people on the van. Charisma sat up straight in her seat, now more in tune to what was going on outside the van.

"How in the hell did she get in here?" the assistant asked.

Charisma was curious. "Who?"

"That bitch Lisa Sanchez." Fabiola shook her head in disbelief. "She stays in the trenches."

"With the rest of the snakes," said the assistant. "But the bitch can smell a story like a shark smells blood in an ocean of salt water."

Right then the light on the camera of Lisa's cameraman lit up, turning red. Lisa got her microphone ready, someone touched up her makeup, and then she posed for the camera. She was about to go live.

Charisma immediately searched her phone

for a stream of the live broadcast. She found it.

"Breaking news . . . This is Lisa Sanchez from WYGH Action News, Miami, reporting live from Club Shine on South Beach. We are the first station that was able to get past the yellow tape to report this exclusive. It's five in the morning, but as always, we bring you the news where it happens, when it happens. . . ." Lisa smiled for the camera.

"We are still gathering information by the minute to uncover what *really* happened here tonight. But the facts are sketchy. However, what we do know is that this story promises to be filled with plenty of intoxication, extravagant gifts, all-stars, and superstars. Can anyone say scandal? Here's what else we do know."

Lisa looked into the camera as if she were talking to a good friend. "The exclusive Club Shine was filled to capacity, with everybody from socialites to runway models, drug lords, and heavy-hitting and big-balling athletes. They all came out tonight, dressed to impress, in honor of baseball superstar Manny Manifesto's girlfriend, an aspiring author, Charisma Bland." Lisa's face lit up with pleasure as she delivered hearsay news to her legion of fans.

"Manifesto spared no expense on the

shindig. I was told that he wanted not only to celebrate his new lady's birthday but also to confess his love to her." Behind Lisa Sanchez were some photos showing the club's decor and some of Manny and Charisma arm in arm. The couple looked to be happy and in love.

"Evidently, Bing Foo, the ex-girlfriend and the mother of Manifesto's only child, who is not a stranger to the media, did not take too kindly to this lavish shindig. And from what I'm being told, Ms. Foo traveled all the way from California to crash the party. When she got a glimpse of the brand-new Bentley Mulsanne, which she was sure Manifesto had purchased for Charisma, Ms. Foo snapped."

Lisa pointed to the torched Bentley. "This is the outcome of her anger. The only problem is, the car doesn't belong to Manny's girlfriend. Ms. Foo torched the wrong automobile. What a colossal mistake! We have concrete proof that the arson was committed by Manny's baby's mother. We have a video. And before anyone asks, this video is authentic."

This time when Lisa looked into the camera, her expression was much more serious. "The video we are about to play is extremely graphic, so please remove young children from the room."

The station rolled the video footage. It revealed a woman dressed in red-bottomed, spiked Christian Louboutin sneakers, a jumper, and bright red lipstick. It was definitely Bing.

"As you can see, this video clearly reveals that the arsonist is no other than Ms. Foo." The video showed Bing holding a five-gallon gas can. It was followed by footage of Bing being handcuffed and placed in the back of a police cruiser. The camera faded back to Lisa Sanchez.

"Too bad that Ms. Foo didn't check the car's registration, because, I repeat, the car was in no way, shape, or form connected to Manifesto or Ms. Bland."

Charisma sat in stunned silence. She thought she would feel good after seeing Bing arrested. Bing hated her. But Charisma didn't want to see a mother separated from her child just because she was a selfish, jealous bitch. The news made Charisma sad.

Charisma was confused about whether Bing had actually torched the Bentley. None of Lisa's footage had actually shown her doing it. But then Fabiola's assistant found the Bing video herself on social media and handed her phone to Charisma and Fabiola.

"Bing must have thought that Bentley was

yours, because look," she said.

They all watched the Bing video on social media. The video had already gone viral. On the little screen they saw Bing torch the car.

"Didn't I tell you that's the dumbest bitch I know?" Fabiola said to Charisma.

Charisma shook her head. "Damn. She burned up the wrong car."

"She just assumed that Manny had gotten you that Bentley for your birthday," his mother interjected. "See what I'm talking about?"

"Well, she's going to be out of my hair once and for all!" Charisma exclaimed.

So I win, dumb bitch!

Lisa wasn't finished. "To make things more intense," she reported, "I have a source to confirm that Jason 'Roc' Albright wasn't in a stampede or trampled as people were making a mass exit from the club. He was beat down to a pulp. The sixty-four-million-dollar question is, by whom? I don't know the answer to that question right now. But I promise you, I will get to the bottom of it soon. But right now, I have a person that was in the parking lot. Let's see what he has to say."

"Hi, sir."

A man in a blue sweatshirt and a baseball

cap flashed a toothless smile. He appeared to be high on something.

"Can you tell us what you saw?"

"You gon' buy me something to eat?"

Lisa nodded. "Sure. The station will make sure you eat a nice meal. Now, what all did you see?"

"It was, like, an hour ago," the man said. Then he put his hand up to his mouth, as if he was thinking, and nodded. "Yeah, like, an hour."

"Before or after the car burned?" asked Lisa.

"I was in the back alley of Club Shine. See, I ain't want Johnny to get first dibs on the leftover food they throw out. 'Cause we saw the food being delivered. I knew I was going to eat good this here night. So I was hiding behind the Dumpster all night, waiting."

"Okay," Lisa said, prodding. "And what did you see?"

"Well, you see" — the homeless guy put his hands on his hips — "the door came open, and when it did, I thought they were bringing the food out."

Lisa smiled, egging him on. That was when the homeless guy took the mic out of her hand. Lisa tried to get it back, but the man was quicker than he looked.

"Don't get yo' panties in a bunch," he said. "Now, listen here. I seen this man crying like a little girl. He could barely stand up. He was tall. Real tall. A couple of other guys had to help him along. I thought he was drunk, but he wasn't. Trust me." He nodded. "I know a drunk person when I see one. Yep. He'd had his ass whipped. His eyes were black and some mo' shit."

Lisa asked, "Is that all?" But her question was barely audible, because she didn't have the mic, and the homeless guy wasn't trying to share his fifteen minutes of fame.

"A black car pulled up. And that's when I heard somebody say, 'That's Roc Albright.' " The homeless man frowned, scratched his head, and continued. "I said, 'Roc Albright?' And took a closer gander. And I'd be damn. It was dat nigga. I was like, 'Oh shit!' It was him. Roc was the man I saw that had been beat up like he'd stole something."

"Thank you," Lisa said. "Thank you for that info." Lisa knew she had to get her story back under control.

"You welcome, Lisa. Anytime. Just want people to know that when you see a homeless person, know we ain't all bad and we all don't stink." Then he put his arms up in Lisa's face so she could take a whiff. Just in case she thought he was lying.

Lisa was mortified. She motioned for her security personnel to get the man away from her. Once the homeless man was gone, Lisa regained her composure.

"I've just received a text message from Jasmine Albright. She says she wants to meet with me shortly. She wants to give her version of what's going on." Lisa beamed from ear to ear. "As promised, I will get to the bottom of this scandal."

Charisma's phone chirped again. Another text.

Bitch, your nigga done fucked up! I'm about to expose your ass to the world. I'm going to tell the world how you extorted us for more than two million dollars!

Charisma's heart dropped.

In the blink of an eye, her birthday had gone from the best day of her life to the worst day of her life. She tried to conceal the tears that escaped from her eyes when she caught a glance of Jasmine standing off to the side, waiting for Lisa Sanchez to sign off and come and talk to her.

Charisma thought, *I have to do something. I have to get off this van.*

CHAPTER 40
NOW SCRAM. . . .

Jasmine waited in the shadows, not wanting to be seen. She was so focused on Lisa that she didn't notice when Chucky approached.

He was in her personal space, mugging. He also had a concealed weapon in his jacket pocket, pointed directly at Jasmine.

"Bitch, you need to think hard about your next move, because it may just be your final move. If you think I'm going to stand by and watch your trick ass try to hurt somebody that I love, you mistaken. If you ain't mo' careful, you gon' be the one to get exposed, sugar mama. Thanks to my man Swan, I know all I need to know about yo' trick ass. And I got pics and letters to prove it. I also know where you and your sister live. And you know what? I love fucking and getting my dick licked by sisters. Don't make me be the animal that prison turned me into."

Jasmine looked into his eyes and believed

everything he had said to her. She was scared shitless. She nodded. "Please . . . ," she said, with a knot in her throat. "Please don't do anything with the pictures. I will pay you."

"Oh, you gon' pay for sure. Now scram."

Chucky watched Jasmine speed walk to her car, get in, and burn rubber trying to get off South Beach as quickly as she could.

Meanwhile on the van, the driver made an announcement. "The police said we are going to be able to move in the next few minutes."

Charisma got two texts back-to-back: one from Chucky, letting her know that everything was going to be okay; and the other from Manny, saying that they were going to have to get his daughter, Star, since Bing was in jail.

The last text melted her heart. Having an opportunity to spend time with Manny's child and take care of her like she was her own might fill the void she felt.

Charisma started thinking about how things were finally falling into place for her. Things weren't perfect, but she had got her man, and now she had a child to share her world with. However, she hated having to carry a secret around and have it held over her head. She felt that there was only one thing left to do to free herself: write that book she had been planning to do for so long! And she was going to tell the whole truth. She'd have it done by her next birthday.

As the van pulled off, she thought to herself that this was one of the best days of her life. But somehow she was sure that there would be more happy days . . . and more drama to come.

ABOUT THE AUTHOR

Nikki Turner is the author of the *New York Times* bestseller *Black Widow,* the #1 *Essence*® bestseller *Forever a Hustler's Wife,* and the *Essence*® bestsellers *A Hustler's Wife, The Glamorous Life,* and *Riding Dirty on I-95.* She lives in Richmond, Virginia.

1·30·18